Someone to Love Me

Someone to Love Me

Nicole S. Rouse

URBAN
CHRISTIAN

www.urbanchristianonline.net

Urban Books
1199 Straight Path
West Babylon, NY 11704

ISBN- 13: 978-1-60162-992-0
ISBN- 10: 1-60162-992-3

First Printing June 2009
Printed in the United States of America

10   9   8   7   6   5   4   3   2   1

This is a work of fiction. Any references or similarities to actual events, real people, living, or dead, or to real locales are intended to give the novel a sense of reality. Any similarity in other names, characters, places, and incidents is entirely coincidental.

Distributed by Kensington Corp.
Submit Wholesale Orders to:
Kensington Publishing Corp.
C/O Penguin Group (USA) Inc.
Attention: Order Processing
405 Murray Hill Parkway
East Rutherford, NJ 07073-2316
Phone: 1-800-526-0275
Fax: 1-800-227-9604

"For I know the plans I have for you," says the Lord. *"They are plans for good and not for disaster, to give you a future and a hope."*
Jeremiah 29:11

For my nephews and niece:
Bernard, Rayven, and Russell
Continue to trust in God. I'm expecting great things from you!

Acknowledgments

To God be the glory! For loving me, and for continuing to bless me when things seem so far out of my reach. For strengthening my faith and encouraging me to reach higher.

I thank God for blessing me with the support of family and friends throughout the last few years of my life. Through all of my triumphs and trials, you have continued to encourage my visions. I truly appreciate your love and patience. Thank you for investing in my dream.

I'd especially like to thank: My mother, whose love and support over the years have blessed my life tremendously. What would I do without you? I love you! My father, for being a part of my literary journey. Your computer skills are definitely appreciated (smile). I love you! My editors, Joylynn, Linda, and Heather, thanks for keeping me focused. My best friend, Chairese Smith, for nineteen years of friendship. The beautiful women of Zeta Phi Beta Sorority, Inc, especially my Philly sorors and the men of Phi Beta Sigma Fraternity, Inc. To Sorors Dannette Hargraves and Donna Clark, you are the best promoters ever! I thank God for your sisterly love. My friends at Willow Creek Community and New Faith Baptist Church. My friend and writing partner, Sheila P. Miller, for her endless words of encouragement. My longtime friends from the HSES Class of '89, especially Kymyetta Oglesby and the Pearson Scott Foresman family. To all of the readers that supported my first novel, thank you and may God bless you!

I'd also like to thank the Urban Christian family for their support and words of encouragement. Let's continue to bless the world with our gifts!

Prologue

~ *Jerome* ~

Coatless and shivering, Jerome stood in his backyard facing the underdeveloped garden Renee had started last summer. His thick, wool sweater shielded his upper body from the bitter wind, but every now and then, a cool rush seeped through. In the distance, the sound of cars and buses traveling along Lake Avenue seemed closer than the three blocks that actually separated them. Normally, he'd be among the commuters heading home, but he had taken the day off. A snowstorm was headed west, and Jerome wanted to prepare himself for his first winter in Chicago. Born and raised in Philadelphia, he was used to the cold, but needed new equipment—a sturdy shovel, ice scrapers, window washer fluid, and snow boots to make the bitter Chicago winter more bearable.

Jerome rubbed his hands together until the heat from the friction warmed them. Before they started to tingle, he pulled out the letter folded in his pocket. He'd already read it several times, but its contents were still hard to digest. Taylor, the woman with whom he'd had a long-term affair, had tracked him down. Slowly, he unfolded the letter as he looked over his shoulder. Through the patio doors, he could see his children playing a video game in the living room. Renee was fast asleep in her favorite section of the chaise lounge, her delicate frame filling out from the unborn child she was carrying.

A strong wind raced through the backyard, and Jerome held the letter tight. It was difficult to read the one-page note again outside, but it didn't matter. The letter had arrived two weeks ago, and he'd practically memorized the words.

Dear Jerome,

I pray this letter finds you in the best of health and spirits. It has taken a lot for me to put my thoughts into words, but I can no longer keep my feelings bottled up inside. Every day, I pretend that you were never a part of my life, but my heart won't let go of the memories. I've tried to move on. Even started dating again, but it's not the same. I know that you and Renee are trying to make things work. For that reason, it pains me to have to share this news. But from the first time I saw you, I knew we were meant to be together. I guess God thought we'd make a perfect match, too.

Jerome, there's no easy way to say this, but I'm pregnant and you're the father. Please call me. My number is still the same.

All my love,
Taylor

Jerome reached into a different pocket and pulled out the book of matches he had grabbed from a kitchen drawer. Before permanently destroying the evidence in his hand, he looked back at his wife. As much as he wanted to be honest with her, he knew Renee would never forgive him for having a child outside of their marriage, especially in her current condition. How could he have been so foolish and irresponsible?

He moved closer to the garden and out of his family's view. Then without hesitation, he ripped a match from the book. In one smooth motion, Jerome struck the match and set the letter on fire. When half of the letter was consumed with flames, he let it drop. Tapping it quickly on the cold ground with his new pair of Timberland boots, he didn't stop until there was nothing but scattered ashes on the ground. "This can't be real," he said to himself. "This has to be some kind of trick." But deep inside he knew Taylor was telling the truth. She wasn't a devious woman.

It would've been easy to walk away, pretend that he never received Taylor's letter, but Jerome knew better. If he didn't respond, Taylor would use her last dime to fly out to Chicago from Philadelphia.

He kicked at the ground, hoping the dry, grainy soil would camouflage the ashes completely. Once he was satisfied, he took out his Blackberry. His fingers, stiff but not yet numb, automatically dialed Taylor's number. The phone rang twice before she answered.

"Hi, Taylor. This is Jerome."

"I knew you'd call," she said, a hint of pleasure in her voice. "I knew you wouldn't let me do this alone."

"Hold on, Tay. I'm not calling for the reason you think I am," Jerome began. He then cut straight to the point. "Are you sure you're pregnant?"

Taylor's attitude turned sour. "Of course I am. Why would I lie?"

"It just seems . . . well . . . it's ironic," Jerome stated. "You get pregnant when I tell you my wife and I are getting back together? Doesn't that sound funny to you?"

"What are you saying, Jerome?"

"I'm not accusing you of anything. I'm saying it's strange; that's all."

"It wasn't strange when we were together four months ago, was it?"

Jerome could tell he was upsetting her. "Let's not argue. I need to think about this some more."

A heavy wind chilled Jerome's cheek bones, and he rubbed them with his free hand. Taylor was quiet; they both were for at least a minute.

"I'm not going to leave Renee. She's having a baby, too," Jerome said, breaking the deafening silence. "If your baby is mine—"

"If?" Taylor repeated, her shrill voice breaking his heart.

Jerome heard the patio door slide open and he jumped.

"Aren't you cold, Daddy?" Jerome's youngest son, Jerome Jr. asked, standing on the low, wooden deck in his house shoes.

Jerome lowered his cell phone and covered it with his hand. "Close the door, Junior. You don't want to let cold air in the house." He hoped his response was sufficient. The last thing he needed was for his inquisitive son to ask uncomfortable questions. "Go on now, Junior. I don't want you to wake your mother. I'll be inside in a minute."

Oscar, the family dog, ran up to Jerome Jr.'s legs and distracted him. This was one of the few times Jerome was happy he'd bought the dog.

As soon as the patio door closed, he lifted the phone to his ear and sighed. "Okay, Taylor. If the baby is mine, I'll send you money every month. I promise. Just please, please don't say anything to Renee. Okay?"

The line went silent again, neither of them sure what to say next. The numbness in Jerome's hands returned, and he blew hot air on them. In the background, he could hear Taylor sniffling, and his heart ached. He opened his mouth, ready to apologize, but the words wouldn't escape. He wished there was something else he could do, but he'd made a promise to Renee. Under no circumstances was he to contact Taylor again. And that was one promise he wanted to keep for the sake of his marriage.

"How can you live with yourself?" cried Taylor between bouts of tears. "Don't you worry about me or this baby. I am confident God will take care of us."

Drenched in sweat and gasping for air, Jerome popped straight up in bed. Darkness filled the bedroom, and for a moment, he was unsure of his surroundings. He closed his eyes as he wiped his face with the edge of his damp T-shirt. When he reopened them, he turned to face the bright red lights and flashing dots on the alarm clock next to his bed. His wife's touch was the only confirmation that the dream had ended.

"Another bad dream?" Renee asked, rubbing her husband's arm to comfort him.

"I'm fine," he answered, then cleared some of the grogginess from his throat. "Go back to sleep, babe."

Since Reverend Hampton's sermon last month, the same scene had replayed itself in Jerome's dreams. "What's done in the dark comes to light eventually," Reverend Hampton had said, igniting memories from a troubling and wayward time in Jerome's life.

Many years had passed since the guilt of his affair had affected him. And now, like a broken record, the harshness of Taylor's voice resounded inside his head stronger than ever. *How can you live with yourself?* Taylor's words jolted Jerome out of his sleep every morning, interfered with business meetings, and hovered over him when he made love to his wife.

Jerome swung his legs off the bed, and his feet landed on the freshly laid plush carpet. Renee stirred, kicking the cotton sheet completely off her body, then rolled onto her flat stomach.

"Where are you going, honey?" she asked.

"I need some water."

With one eye open, Renee faced the clock. "We only have an hour left to sleep. Can't you wait?"

"I'll only be a minute," Jerome promised as he pushed himself off the bed.

Renee let her head sink deeper into her goose-down pillow. "Suit yourself."

All the way to the kitchen, Taylor's chilling voice echoed in Jerome's head. *"How can you live with yourself?"* He leaned against the sink and shook his head frenetically. A steady drip from the faucet intermingled with Taylor's question and eventually drowned out her daunting words. Jerome turned the water on and let it sift through his fingers. Cupping his hands midstream, he lowered his face into his palms. Soon, his tears blended in with the flow of the water, allowing him to release the pain of his past. When the tears ceased, Jerome pushed down the faucet handle and fell to his knees and prayed.

For the last sixteen years, he had faithfully sent Taylor money to help raise the child they'd conceived together. But now God was calling him to do more. He needed to meet his daughter, and he needed to tell his wife about her.

Chapter One

~ *Joi* ~

Joi studied the multi-colored sketches along the wall of Harry's Tattoo Parlor. She'd been in the shop with her teammates for the last twenty minutes trying to agree on one design. There were so many to choose from. They had narrowed their choices down to ten different types of basketball images, but couldn't decide which would look the best at the base of their backs.

In a nearby room, what sounded like the drill dentists use to fill cavities could be heard, causing a few of the girls to have second thoughts.

"Are you sure this isn't gonna hurt?" one of the younger players asked.

Sensing the player's fear, the captain of the team said, "It's too late to turn back now. We made a pact."

"And we'll look good at the step show Friday night," the showboat of the team added. She loved extra attention. It was her idea to get the tattoos in the first place, recommending Harry's from personal experience.

Joi didn't want to admit it, but she was nervous, too. The thought of a tiny needle puncturing her skin several times was unnerving, yet she wanted to show her commitment to the team.

Rayven, Joi's best friend, pulled her away from the others. "I don't think this is a good idea," she hummed in Joi's ear.

"We promised," Joi reminded her. "If we don't go through with it now, we could ruin our winning streak."

"I don't believe in jinxes, and you shouldn't either." Rayven glanced around the dimly lit parlor. It looked more like a poorly renovated basement than a professional establishment. Apart from the bright lights in the two rooms reserved for the artists to create their masterpieces, there were only two lamps, one with a green bulb, the other white, but with a low wattage. The waiting and receptionist area was no bigger than a cheap studio apartment. A lounge sofa bursting at the seams and a couple of beanbags were the only places for customers to sit. "Is this place even certified?" queried Rayven.

The receptionist came out of the corner room with several boxes of latex gloves in her hand. "There's no need to be afraid," she said as she put the boxes in a cabinet by her desk. Tattoos covered almost every inch of her body. "My brother's been doing this for five years. Our tools are clean and sterile, and we keep them in a safe place." She smacked hard on a stick of gum while she spoke. "We've only had one complaint, and that was from my mom." She twisted her ponytail into a bun on top of her head then pointed to the long, winding, colorful snake that stretched the entire length of her arm. "I got this when I was sixteen. It's exactly like the one on my mom's arm. She wanted her snake to be one of a kind." The twenty-something receptionist cracked a smile and walked into a vacant room. "So," she said with a smirk, "who wants to go first? My brother will be down in a minute."

The team captain stepped forward. "I think we should go with something simple. How about the flaming basketball?"

"Ahh, good choice," the receptionist replied.

Most of the girls agreed. Rayven, however, stared at the chosen image tight-lipped. The drill in the other room shrieked louder than before, and someone yelped in pain.

Rayven shook her head and plunged on the worn sofa, crossing both her hands and feet. "Uh-uh. Nope, I can't do this."

"You know if we lose our winning streak, we're gonna blame you," another teammate said, but Rayven didn't budge. She wasn't moved by her teammate's threat.

"Well, whoever is going first needs to come on. We have quite a few appointments today. You all need to be done before five," the receptionist told them.

Everyone looked at Rayven. The agreement was for the entire team to get tattoos. Most of the team gave Rayven an evil glare; she pretended not to notice. As her best friend, it was Joi's place to smooth the situation so Rayven wouldn't later be the object of ridicule.

"Why are you changing your mind?" Joi asked, not the least bit as angry as the team.

"I'm not going to do it." Rayven walked to the waiting area and sat on the long sofa.

"I'm with Ray," the younger player stated and sat in one of the beanbags. "I'm not ready to get something so permanent. Maybe if we win the championship, I'll reconsider."

"See what you've done?" the showboat yelled, but Rayven was not fazed by the teammate's irritation. Her mind was made up.

Gripes and moans filled the small shop, and the receptionist grew impatient.

The co-captain rolled her eyes. "Well, I'm not changing my mind. I guess I'll go first," she said and followed the receptionist into a back room to get prepped.

The remaining players stared at Joi, and Joi, in turn, stared at Rayven.

"I'm not changing my mind," Rayven stressed. "My mother will kill me . . . if that needle doesn't." She picked up a battered copy of *Essence* magazine. "You go ahead without me. I won't be mad."

Although the two friends were different in many ways, their love for basketball had bonded them as freshmen. Joi sat behind her during tryouts, secretly admiring the natural crinkles and waves in her hair.

Taylor, Joi's mother and self-proclaimed fashion diva, would never let her get away with hair so wild and carefree. Joi and her younger sister, Leah, had regular appointments at their cousin's beauty parlor. Maintaining fresh perms was a must. But last summer, Joi convinced Taylor that the mixture of sweat and a chemical relaxer would eventually damage her hair. She'd been wearing various braiding styles ever since.

Joi looked at Rayven, fiddling with the twists she'd finished two nights ago. "But we agreed to do this together," Joi reminded her.

With one hand in her hair and the other flipping the pages of the magazine, Rayven responded, "Not this time, boss. I'm sorry."

Joi leaned on Rayven's shoulder, pouting in an effort to sway her decision one last time.

Sometimes Joi's persuasive tactics worked. For several months, Rayven covered for Joi when she was with Markus and fibbed about the parties they went to. But this time Joi had gone too far. A tattoo would be a permanent reminder of her disobedience.

Rayven closed the magazine. "This doesn't feel right. You and I both know we'll get grounded, and I don't know about you, but I like my freedom."

Remembering the punishment she recently received for an unacceptable progress report, Joi thought little about how her mother would react. *It's not the worst that could happen*, she reasoned. "It's just a tattoo, Ray. Please . . ."

"I don't think any of our parents would agree. We'll be the only team that can't play because we're all grounded. And I doubt this is what our parents pictured us doing on an early dismissal day." Rayven shook her head and re-opened the magazine. "No, I won't do it, and please don't keep pressuring me."

Respecting Rayven's position, Joi eased up. "Okay, I won't push. But Mother can't punish me forever. I'll take my chances."

Chapter Two

~ *Taylor* ~

After a long day of running around with the kids and managing Second Chance, her own consignment boutique, Taylor found comfort in the arms of Lance, her husband. At fifty years old, raising four children and managing a business was beginning to take its toll, especially now that her oldest daughter's teenage hormones were in full blast.

Joi had been an eleventh grader for less than two months, and already she was having problems. Not to mention, she challenged Taylor's every word and action. When Joi's progress report came in the mail, what should've been a notice to confirm A's and B's in all subjects was instead a warning. Joi's grades bordered C's in most subjects, and she received one D in computer class.

Most days Taylor didn't recognize her daughter. The sweet and innocent child she'd given birth to no longer existed. Joi had turned into a full-fledged teenager whose attitude on any given day could be intolerable.

Taylor's own adolescence wasn't perfect. She had been labeled "too sassy" on numerous occasions, but she grew up caring for a broken-hearted mother and defending her sporadic episodes. More often than not, her mother was in a depressive slump, leaving Taylor to be the adult of the house. Joi didn't have the same issues. So what was her problem?

Despite Joi's progress report, Taylor gave her permission to attend a college step show at the University of Pennsylvania. She was only allowed to go because Rayven, Joi's best friend, had a sister who attended the school. Taylor knew the family and trusted that her daughter would be in good hands. Even still, she wouldn't have normally made this kind of provision.

Lance had convinced her to come up with a long-term incentive plan that would reward Joi for her progress each week, in hopes that it would motivate her to do better. As Lance suggested, Taylor decided that Joi would work at her boutique after school on Friday and Saturday afternoons. If Joi's teachers confirmed that she was doing better each week, she would be allowed to spend some Friday and Saturday evenings with friends. It was an amiable situation for both of them. Joi could use any free time to study, and Taylor could use the extra help in the store.

Taylor and Lance had been married fourteen years, and although their marriage wasn't perfect, she could honestly say that they loved one another. Taylor couldn't have said the same for her parents when she was Joi's age.

Taylor eased into the small space left on the bed, careful not to interrupt her husband's sleep too suddenly. She tried to get under the sheets without much movement.

Lance sensed her presence and pulled her close. "What took you so long?" he asked, half-asleep.

Lance and Taylor repositioned themselves, she resting in the crook of his left arm, he lying flat on his back.

"The girls weren't waiting at the McDonald's like I had asked them to," she said.

Lance stretched and accidentally hit his knuckles on the headboard. "Where'd you find them?" he asked, returning his arm under Taylor's head.

"There was no place to park, but I saw a bunch of kids headed to the dorms, so I double-parked and followed the crowd. The look on Ray's face when she saw me was priceless." Taylor giggled at the image. "She looked like a deer in headlights. Of course I had to follow her."

"What were they doing?"

"Your daughter *claimed* she was watching some sorority girls." Taylor lowered her head and nestled against Lance's chest. "Rayven said the girls were stepping or singing or something. But I'm not buying it." Taylor would've believed Rayven under different circumstances, but something inside of her didn't feel right about that moment. Taylor didn't mention it to Lance, but she saw the way the boys ogled Joi in her hip huggers and cropped denim jacket. She also noticed how much Joi appreciated the attention. At least she wasn't showing any skin, like some of the other girls parading around campus.

"Don't assume they were up to anything, Tay." Lance yawned. "For a girl in high school, that kind of stuff is exciting. I'm sure that's what they were doing."

"You always take up for her." Taylor turned away from him and lay on her own pillow, snickering to herself. "You should have seen them when I showed up."

Lance grinned. "They were probably scared of what you might do. Your track record *does* precede you."

Taylor lifted her head and uttered, "Raising kids isn't exactly an easy job. I'm doing the best I can."

"And you're doing a wonderful job," Lance responded, gently rubbing the tiny hairs on Taylor's arm. "But I need you to relax just a little more. Our daughter is a good kid. She's just being a typical teen."

Lance's touch soothed her. "You're such a softie," Taylor replied.

She closed her eyes and recited her bedtime prayers silently. Memories of her life as a sixteen-year-old weren't so complicated. Taylor's mother had been too busy chasing after her father to keep up with her child's whereabouts. As a result, Taylor lost her virginity sooner than she was ready to, to a neighbor whose intimacy lasted longer than their romantic relationship. She prayed every day that God would shield her daughters from that kind of life. She hoped that Joi wouldn't develop an itch for boys anytime soon.

"I'm gonna keep a close eye on that girl," she blurted aloud. "And she'd better get up for work tomorrow."

Lance kissed the back of Taylor's head, and she placed her hand over his.

Lance was a good man and father. It was hard to believe that she had almost let him get away. When they were both drivers for SEPTA, Philadelphia's public transportation system, Taylor had broken up with him because her heart belonged to another man. Months later, when that man walked out on her and the child she was carrying, Lance re-entered her life. They'd dated steadily for two years before Lance proposed. Although it was clear that Taylor loved Lance and that he would be a good husband and father to her infant daughter, she feared she wouldn't be the kind of wife he deserved. It had taken her months to accept Lance's marriage proposal.

"Before I forget," Lance said, "Gram wants to have Thanksgiving at her house this year."

Taylor's eyes popped open. "But we've always had dinner here. What's going on?"

Lance rubbed her arm again. "Nothing. She knows you've been busy with the store and—"

"Since when have I let my job interfere with the holidays?"

"You have work *and* the women's conference to plan for church. When are you gonna have time to organize a large dinner?"

"I've been managing my time for over sixteen years. Have you forgotten that I have *four* children? If I don't know anything else, I know how to manage my time," Taylor argued.

Lance's held his wife tighter, his tone still steady and smooth. "I really think she wants to treasure her last moments in the house."

Taylor tried her best not to show her disapproval. Gram, Lance's mother, was moving into a retirement community in Maryland after the New Year to be closer to her oldest daughter. Before the house could be put up for sale, Lance willingly volunteered to modernize her home by himself. There's nothing a son won't do for his mother.

Taylor didn't mind Lance's generosity. It was one of the many traits she loved about him. But she wondered how long she could let her mother-in-law borrow her husband before she started to complain. Lance spent every free moment at his mother's house, cleaning, repairing, and remodeling, while she and Lance had been walking around misplaced furniture in their bedroom, and staring at paint swatches on the walls since June.

Taylor didn't want to give in to her mother-in-law's request. She'd been living by her rules since Leah was born twelve years ago. But over the years, she'd learned to choose her battles wisely. This was not a battle she wanted to try and defend.

"I'll call her in the morning to see if there's anything I can help with," she simply said, avoiding a heated discussion.

Lance kissed the back of her head. "Thanks for understanding."

Taylor stared at the Basket Beige swatch on the wall. She wasn't sure she liked the reflection of the color at night. "Sherry saw Jerome at the SEPTA depot the other day." Her words seemed to echo off the walls. She pinched Lance to make sure he was still awake. "Did you hear me?"

"I heard you," he answered. "Is that why you've been so jumpy?"

"I'm just nervous," she said, and her leg twitched.

Lance sat up and reached over his wife to turn off the lamp. "Jerome comes to Philly all the time. This is his hometown. He still has family here, remember?"

"I know. But what if—"

"*If* he chooses to contact you . . . us, then we'll deal with it *together*. Now get some sleep." Lance lay down and wrapped Taylor in his arms again. "You have nothing to worry about."

Taylor knew he was right. "I make you crazy, don't I?" she responded.

"I plead the fifth."

Taylor pinched him hard. "I love you, too."

A few minutes later, Lance's snores filled the room. Taylor, on the other hand, was still awake. Bringing up Jerome made her restless. She stared at the professional 16 x 20 photograph hanging on the wall by the door. It was taken at a Sears studio many years ago. Tonight, the moonlight shining through the half-closed shades illuminated Joi's face, and although Taylor had seen that picture every day, Joi looked different.

Taylor silently wept, filling her pillow with salty tears. She couldn't explain it, but the anxious sensation that swirled around in her stomach had always been God's way of telling her that something big was about happen.

Chapter Three

~ *Jerome* ~

By 5:30 P.M. Jerome still hadn't heard from Renee. She had been on the West Coast attending a leadership conference for the last three days. The hotel she worked for had recently merged with another large chain, and as one of the executive managers and a valued employee for many years, she had been doing a lot of traveling. Jerome often joked that she was only a step away from becoming president.

Renee's flight landed at 9:30 A.M., but she had little time to talk. From the airport, she rushed off to a meeting in Schaumburg and then to another in the Downtown hotel. If it had been Jerome, he would have cancelled the meetings and gone straight home from the airport. But not Renee. That woman would work twenty-four hours a day if she could.

Jerome didn't know how Renee could sit in meetings every day. Meetings bored him. He preferred hands-on projects and interacting with several people throughout the day. As a supervisor of four employees in the community relations division of a professional basketball team, he did just that. An athlete by nature, Jerome's dreams of playing basketball were shattered when he damaged his knee in high school. Not interested in much else, after he and Renee married, Jerome toyed with many temporary jobs to help take care of his family. It wasn't until he ended an extramarital affair and surrendered to God that he was offered a job compatible with his talents. Jerome believed the job was God's gift for making amends with his wife.

Jerome responded to his last email for the day and logged off the computer. From the corner of his eye, he noticed a pair of long, slender legs in the doorway, legs that undeniably belonged to Melanie, his boss's twenty-nine-year-old assistant. She'd been making frequent trips to his office in the past month, and quite frankly, it made him nervous.

"Hey, Thomas." Melanie always addressed Jerome by his last name. "Renee back in town?" she asked and leaned against the door, the split in her mid-length skirt showing even more of her skin.

Jerome's eyes shifted from her legs to her finely sculpted face. "What's up, Mel?" he replied. "Yes, my baby is back. New hairdo?"

Melanie invited herself inside the office. "It is." She rubbed the tiny curls on both sides of her head. "You're very observant. My boyfriend thinks I'm crazy for cutting it so short, but I wanted a change. You like it?"

Melanie turned around slowly, so Jerome could get a better look. Cut low and tapered in the back, it reminded him of an old Toni Braxton style. This was a big change from the long, bouncy curls she'd previously had. The new trimmed hairdo gave her a more mature and sexier appeal. Jerome wanted to compliment her, but feared she'd place a deeper meaning to his polite gesture.

Last month she came into the office wearing a tailored, bright pink jacket. It was hard for anyone not to notice. Several people made comments, so he figured it was safe to add his own. "Pink looks good on you," he had said. That simple statement encouraged Melanie to invite him to lunch the next day. Jerome felt bad, but he had to decline. A single lunch could send mixed messages her way, and he didn't want to risk the drama that might occur as a result.

"It's nice," he said after a five-second observation. Jerome quickly opened his day planner and pretended to update his schedule. Maybe Melanie would see he was busy and leave.

"Thanks," she said and moved closer to his desk. "Mr. Usiskin wants to see you before you go home." Melanie leaned down and picked up a framed photograph by his computer, exposing the tattooed rose above her right breast.

Jerome turned his chair to avoid staring too hard. "Should I go now, or can I go up in a few minutes? I need to call my wife," he said, making it clear once again that he was a married man. He didn't like the vibe Melanie was giving off. At any other time, he'd think his 53-year-old mind was overreacting. But Melanie was an attractive woman, and the proximity in which she stood made him nervous. She could've easily called or sent an email to deliver Mr. Usiskin's message.

Melanie sensed his uneasiness and smiled, backing away slightly. "I don't think you need to hurry," she remarked slyly. "He wants to touch bases about your *Future Ballers* idea. I think he really likes it."

Jerome looked up from his planner. *Future Ballers* was a mentoring program he'd come up with that would target high school athletes interested in pursuing careers in sports. He had learned from experience that no matter how great a player a kid was, longevity in the field was not guaranteed. Nor was there room for every gifted player in the league. Jerome had many regrets in life, one being his lack of preparation for life beyond basketball. He had seen so many young kids in that position, their lives lost because of a broken dream. It was Jerome's mission to help children avoid the slump he had experienced when his basketball career suddenly ended. *Future Ballers* would not only help aspiring athletes tighten their skills, but it would also educate them on various sports-related careers off the court. As a bonus, the participants would receive instructions from some of the local professional athletes.

Had it not been for Renee's expertise with drafting an effective proposal, Jerome's vision would have stayed in his head.

"Great news!" he exclaimed. "I'll be up in about ten minutes."

Melanie put down the picture she was holding. "Your wife's pretty. How long have you two been married?"

"We got married right out of high school. So"—Jerome hesitated to mentally compute the years; then finished his sentence—"thirty-four years."

"Awww," she cooed. "That's a long time. I don't know if I can stand to be with one person *that* long."

"You're still young," Jerome added and shuffled some papers on his desk. "When you meet the right person, there won't be a question about being with him for the rest of your life."

"We'll see about that. My boyfriend and I have been together for two months, and I already want to kick him to the curb." Melanie ran her index finger along the top of the picture frame. "You two look like you're still newlyweds."

"We are," he answered and stood up.

Melanie walked to the east corner of the office where Jerome kept a collage of old family photos: a Father's Day gift from his daughter-in-law. "All boys, huh?" she said. "Any grandbabies yet?"

"Actually, I have two grandsons, and one very precocious and beautiful granddaughter. She's two," he said, beaming with pride as he took out a picture from the wallet in his back pocket. "She's the princess of the family."

Melanie moved back to Jerome's side of the office and took the picture from his hand. "Isn't she precious? I bet you spoil her rotten."

Her chestnut-colored eyes were like a magnet, making it hard for Jerome to avoid them. "That's why I've been working so hard. She takes all of my extra cash."

She returned the picture, and her hand gently rubbed against Jerome's. "I'm sure you're a great grandfather. She's lucky to have you."

Widening the space between them, Jerome put the picture and his wallet back in place then lightly tapped the side of his leg with his forefinger. "Okay, I'll be up after I talk to my wife. I want to catch her before she leaves her office."

"I'll let you go," she replied. Melanie smoothed the hair at the nape of her neck with her palm as she headed to the door, which she closed gently behind her.

Jerome's eyes couldn't help but follow her body as she left. He inwardly prayed that God would forgive him as he picked up some folders from his desk and yawned. He walked to the metal file cabinet, pausing at the square mirror hanging on the side.

He was not a vain man, but he'd been told by many that he'd aged well. Thanks to his twelve-year sobriety run and Bally's membership, he had a body many men his age envied. He rubbed his chin and nodded in approval. He had expected to be bald by fifty, like his younger brother and father, but the strands of silver mixed throughout his hair and beard showed no signs of thinning. In fact, the fullness of his hair gave him a distinguished appearance. Many women Melanie's age were looking for a man like him: confident, mature, and stable. And as much as he didn't want to disappoint her, she didn't stand a chance. She was a very attractive and tempting young lady, but Jerome knew to keep his distance. He'd be a fool to cheat on his wife again. And he feared God might not be as forgiving the second time around.

Jerome yawned again. He found it hard to fall back asleep this morning after his recurring dream. As snippets from his past replayed themselves in his head, his heart saddened. Dwelling on his life in Philadelphia did that to him every time. He rubbed his tired eyes and focused on the present. He would soon see Renee, and everything would be all right again.

Back at his desk, Jerome dialed Renee's direct work number and was relieved when she answered.

"Hello, this is Mrs. Thomas."

"Hey, sexy," he replied.

"Hi, babe." Renee's professional tone changed into the sweet voice he loved to hear. "Are you home or at the office?"

Jerome filled his briefcase with documents he needed to review. "I'm still in the office. I'm heading out soon though. I just need to see the boss, and then I'm out the door."

"Everything okay?" she asked.

"Everything's fine. He wants to talk about the proposal I submitted last month."

"I can't wait to hear his response," Renee replied excitedly. "I'm sure he's going to love your brilliant idea."

Jerome blushed. There was a time when he wouldn't have accepted Renee's help with anything. His pride was strong in the early years of their marriage. That's what made this project so special. "How do you feel about Mac Arthur's for dinner?" he asked. He knew Renee was too tired to cook after traveling across the country and working a long and busy day.

"Sounds like a plan," she stated then pulled away from the receiver to talk to someone in her office. When she came back, she said, "All right, honey, I need to go. I can't wait to see you."

Renee's words made him tingle inside. "Same here." He closed his briefcase. "Hurry home."

When the garage door opened, Jerome was pleased to see Renee's ruby-colored Infiniti. He parked his Yukon next to it, leaving enough room to open his door without making a small ding on hers. Leaving his briefcase and other work documents on the backseat, he slid his body out of the truck and grabbed the two large plastic bags of food.

His hands had barely touched the knob of the door leading inside the house when it opened. Standing in the entryway was Renee dressed in a long khaki skirt and striped tank top. Even in casual clothes she exuded sophistication and sensuality. Jerome's hormones raged at the sight of her.

"Hey, handsome." She greeted her husband with a warm, passionate kiss.

Dinner in hand, Jerome matched her intensity as they eased into the house. Her lips still intertwined with his, he pushed the door closed behind them.

"How was the conference?" he asked when they paused for air.

"As good as conferences can be. Everett did ask if I'd be interested in playing a more active role in this merger," Renee responded.

Jerome's face went blank. Renee currently managed

three hotels: one in Schaumburg, another in Northbrook, and a third in downtown Chicago. What more did the top players at Luxury Inn want from his wife?

"I know what you're thinking, Jay, but Everett said everyone was impressed with my presentation."

"Of course they're impressed. You're wonderful at your job." Jerome handed Renee the bags and took off his coat.

"How exactly would you help from Illinois?"

"I'd need to visit all the sites, old and new."

"And let me guess—you're the only candidate up for consideration." Jerome hung his coat in the closet and then relieved Renee of one of the bags.

"Who else knows Luxury Inn better than me?"

"This merger is taking up too much extra time. How long would you be on the road?" he asked, clearly disapproving of her increased travel.

Renee pulled him close and planted a kiss on his lips. "I'm an important woman. You know I wouldn't go if I didn't think it was worth it."

"You've been away three times already this month," Jerome whined, unashamed that he sounded childish.

Renee stood behind her husband and massaged his temples. "This won't be too bad. Everett and I estimated that I would be on the road off and on between six and eight months."

"And then what?" he asked, still a bit tense.

"And then I'm back to my Illinois offices." Renee grabbed Jerome's arm and escorted him through the house, past the dining room and into the kitchen.

"I don't think I like you spending so much time away from me." Jerome placed the bags of food in the refrigerator, complaining with every movement.

Renee's tall, dark, and handsome boss, Everett Coleman, had been training Renee for an upper management position since they moved to Illinois sixteen years ago. Everett and Renee were a magnificent team. It took years for Jerome to accept that a man and woman could work so closely and not develop deep feelings for one another. He had brought it up a few times, but because of his infidelity, it was a subject he had to tread very lightly.

Renee nibbled on Jerome's earlobe until his frown disappeared, and he surrendered.

"But I guess I have to be supportive." The thought of sleeping alone bothered him. It wasn't something he wanted to become a habit. The last two nights she was away, the bedroom seemed so cold and lonely.

Renee took his hand again, and they continued through the house, pausing at the winding stairs.

Jerome kicked off his shoes, one of the many new rules he had to get used to. For over ten years, he had grown accustomed to hardwood floors. Since Renee had the upstairs carpeted, no one was allowed to set foot upstairs in outdoor shoes. The house looked fine to him the way it was, but Renee was the lady of the house, and whatever she wanted, she got.

"How was your meeting with Mr. Usiskin?"

"He loved the proposal. It looks like *Future Ballers* will be in schools next fall."

"Praise God!" Renee slowly backed up the stairs, her hand still touching his arm. "So you're the man, huh?"

Following her lead willingly, Jerome replied, "I couldn't have done it without you."

"It was your idea, honey. I only helped put it on paper," she said, making Jerome blush like a teenager in love. "I'm very proud of you."

Although Renee had always been attractive in his eyes, her beauty had become even more refined over the years. Whenever he looked at her, she made his heart leap. "We make a good team," he said.

Renee cocked her head to the side and grinned. "Just the way God intended."

"Do you know how much I missed you?" he asked as they entered the bedroom.

"I missed you, too," she whispered then freed her hands from his and worked her way under the Egyptian cotton sheets she'd purchased on sale at Nordstrom.

"I'm glad you're home," Jerome replied. And for what felt like an eternity, he made love to his wife.

Completely satisfied and sleeping soundly, Jerome rested in Renee's arms. He'd been in this position for an hour before his temperature rose and his body jerked. Renee stroked his arm softly, and his head twitched back and forth a few times. She rubbed the side of his face and whispered soothing words in his ear, but that only caused his heart to race faster. His moans frightened Renee, and she called his name aloud as she kneaded his back gently with her fingertips.

Jerome jumped up, heavily breathing as if he had just finished a marathon.

"Relax, honey. I'm here," she said, but Jerome didn't speak. "You can't let the job stress you, Jerome," Renee said, assuming Jerome's new responsibility at work was the root of his panic attacks. "God wouldn't have given you this vision if He didn't think you could carry it out. Don't let the devil get the best of you. *Future Ballers* will be a success."

Jerome cracked a smile as Renee wiped the sweat from his forehead.

"Hungry?" she asked. When Jerome nodded, Renee rolled out of bed. "I'll go heat up the food."

Jerome watched the love of his life slide into her silk robe and leave the bedroom. Still sitting straight up, he waited until he heard Renee set the timer on the microwave. He rubbed his face with his hand several times and lowered himself to the side of the bed. "Lord, show me what I have to do to make this stop. I can't go on like this much longer."

In nothing but a ragged pair of shorts and bedroom slippers, Jerome strolled into the kitchen. The smell of fried catfish and collard greens permeated the air, and his stomach grumbled.

"I tried to wait for you," Renee said, her mouth full of cornbread. She turned the volume down a notch on the small flat-screen television hanging from the corner of the kitchen. "But you took too long. It seems I've worked up an appetite." She chuckled and continued to eat as she listened to the news on CNN. "Your plate is in the microwave. Just hit the start button."

As Jerome waited for his food to warm, he gazed out the window. Thanksgiving was only a month away. Soon the city would transform from its comfortable autumn weather to a brisk and windy winter. He wasn't looking forward to snow-covered streets and icy roads. He especially wasn't excited about shoveling his driveway and sidewalk. It was great exercise, but not the kind he liked, especially since he and Renee had moved into a bigger home.

About six years ago, Renee had convinced Jerome to leave their cozy Oak Park townhouse and move to River Forest, a neighboring suburb. There was nothing wrong with their townhouse in Oak Park; Renee just wanted something larger, a place for the grandchildren to enjoy. Thanks to their middle son and Jerome's namesake, they had three grandchildren, including a six-month-old baby.

When Jerome Jr. was in high school, Renee was constantly on his case about the number of girls he dated. Every time he brought home a new female, she hinted that he'd inherited his love for women from his father. There was little surprise when Jerome Jr. announced that his "friend," Grace, was pregnant during his third year of college.

The grandchildren came by frequently, but not enough to justify the larger rooms in the house, the extra bedrooms, or the miniature playground installed in the backyard. It also didn't justify the need for all the extra closets to store things they should have sold or given to charity. In Jerome's opinion, they were content in the smaller home.

A cool draft chilled Jerome's leg, and he shivered. He looked around for the source and noticed that the patio door was slightly ajar. Before he could ask why, Renee said, "I'm having a private summer."

Jerome knew not to respond. Renee recently entered menopause, and even though he was hardly dressed and cold, he was sensitive to his wife's changing hormones.

The microwave timer beeped, and Jerome removed his steaming food. He sat at the table and blessed his food quickly, concentrating on his dinner and not the cold coming through the door. But five minutes into the meal, Jerome put his fork down and rubbed his hands together vigorously.

Renee looked at him and chuckled. "I know you're cold, Jay," she said apologetically, finishing the last of her candied yams, "but I'm burning up!"

"It's okay, babe. I'll go put more clothes on." Jerome excused himself from the table and walked to a rarely used closet by the stairs in the hallway. There were years of clothes inside, but he searched the back and came across an old, long wool coat. It was silly wearing a coat inside the house, but Renee's comfort was his priority tonight.

Renee was pouring another glass of homemade iced tea when she noticed her husband's new outfit and almost dropped the pitcher. "You look like a flasher," she joked.

And in typical flasher character, Jerome snatched the coat open and wiggled his middle.

Renee shook her head and laughed out loud. "The doctor says it'll take some time for me to adjust. In the meantime, I hope I can handle this without making you too miserable."

The front door opened, and Jerome tried to button his coat quickly in case Joshua, their youngest son, brought home a friend. "No worries. I can handle a little cold. We do live in Chicago," he said, reclaiming his seat.

Joshua entered the kitchen alone and dropped his bag by the kitchen table. "What's good?" he asked, more in reference to the food. "I hope you saved a little something for me. All I see are empty containers." He kissed his mother on the cheek and gave Jerome the "one" head nod. "I won't even ask," he said, referring to his father's attire.

"You're on your own, working man," Jerome replied. "You should've stopped at Wendy's before you came home."

"You can have what's left of mine," Renee offered. "The leftovers are in the fridge." Out of all her children, Joshua was the unspoken favorite. Unlike the older boys, he was easier to raise, a testament to the maturity and happiness in their marriage at that time.

"Thanks, Mom," Joshua said and headed directly to the refrigerator.

Tall and muscular like Jerome had been at that age, Joshua acted more like his mother. He was interested in business and had dreams of becoming a CPA for one of the top five firms in the country. He was on his way, too. Joshua was the youngest student selected from his high school to participate in an internship at ComEd, an electric company that serviced most of Illinois.

Joshua piled the leftover food onto a paper plate and put it in the microwave. "It's like an Arctic blast in here," he commented then looked at his father. "Mom hot again?"

Both he and Jerome tried to contain their laughter.

"If you were a woman, you'd understand. This is no joking matter." Renee sat her glass on the counter then closed the patio door. She changed the thermometer on the wall and popped Jerome on the back of his head. "Sometimes I wish God would've blessed me with a daughter."

"It's not too late to try," Joshua joked.

Renee cut her eyes his way. "Again, if you were a woman, you'd understand why that isn't funny."

Joshua leaned against the counter with his hot plate in hand and started to eat. "You know I'm just kidding."

"You're not funny." Renee took her plate from the table and dumped it inside the trashcan. "And take a seat. It's not good for you to stand up and eat."

Normally, Jerome would join in by adding a few comedic lines, but this time, he couldn't. Thoughts of Taylor and their love child crossed his mind. To avoid eye contact, he pretended to be more interested in the developing news story on the television.

Joshua's cell phone rang before he sat down next to his father. "I gotta get this," he said after checking the screen, then rushed into the family room.

"You need to get more sleep. Have you seen the dark circles beneath your eyes?" Renee said as she walked to a section of the kitchen she used as her office. This was one of three spaces in the house she designated as her business space.

Jerome feared that she'd soon convert a portion of every room in the house to accommodate her business needs. He considered telling Renee the truth behind his restlessness, but decided against it almost as quickly as the thought entered his mind.

Renee hit a button on her laptop, and the black screen was replaced with a Hawaiian screensaver. "Reggie called me at work today," she said, using the wireless mouse to navigate through electronic files.

Jerome scratched the back of his leg. The wool was beginning to irritate his skin. "Oh yeah? What's new with him?"

"He was offered a job in New York," she said, displeasure in her voice.

Jerome removed his coat and put it on the back of his chair. "Is that a bad thing? We knew he'd be looking around after he graduated from med school."

"Of course it is. New York is big and busy, and a little too aggressive for my taste. It's not a place to raise my future grandbabies."

"You don't want your son to leave the nest," Jerome said. "Reggie will be fine. In case you haven't noticed, he isn't a little boy anymore. He's a grown, married man."

Renee pulled her personal mini fan from one of the drawers in her desk. "I'm proud of him." She flipped on the power switch. "I just don't want him to live in New York."

Reggie, their oldest son, was a doctor, specializing in sports medicine. His career choice came as a shock to everyone. In high school, his grades were average and his effort mediocre. Renee and Jerome doubted he'd ever go to college, much less graduate with a medical degree.

Jerome believed Zora, Reggie's wife, had played a major role in his shift in attitude. Career-focused, Zora received her doctorate by the age of twenty-five, and was currently an English professor at DePaul University. Reggie and Zora had met in junior high school, much like Jerome and Renee, and had struggled through some similar challenges. It's funny how children sometimes follow in their parents' footsteps without even trying.

"What's wrong with the job he has?" Renee got out of her chair and moved closer to Jerome, the wind from her fan chilling his neck. "Can't you pull some strings? Maybe he could be a doctor for the Bulls or even the Bears. You have football connections, don't you?"

Jerome splashed hot sauce on his greens. "Renee, if Reggie wants to work for the Bulls, he knows all he has to do is ask. We can always fly to New York. This is a good thing, babe. Be happy for him," he said as he gulped down the mushy vegetables.

"I told Zora they shouldn't go. It's time for them to think about having kids," she said and paused. "She might be a tad upset about my comment."

"I told you to stop meddling." Jerome devoured another mouthful of greens. Juice dripped from the side of his mouth, and he used the back of his hand to wipe it away. "Zora is in her early thirties. I don't know why you keep pressuring her. She has plenty of time to have children."

"I know. It was probably her idea they move, anyway."

"You didn't say that to her, did you?" Jerome asked.

Renee looked away.

"I thought you liked Zora."

"You know I love her. She's like a real daughter to me, but . . ." Renee's voice trailed as she turned off the fan and put it back. "All of Reggie's family is here. Why can't she be more like Junior's wife?"

Jerome scraped his plate clean then got up from his seat to stand next to his better half. "I thought Grace wasn't good enough for Junior."

Jerome believed his middle son married Grace because of Renee. Although Renee was not in favor of Jerome Jr. marrying so young, she refused to have her grandchild born out of wedlock. Never wanting to disappoint his mother, Jerome Jr. agreed to marry Grace before she started to show. Renee meant well, but at times she came off too strong. She was used to being in control at work and, from time to time, had to be reminded that she couldn't control her family the same way.

Renee looked at Jerome sideways. "That's not the point. Whose side are you on?"

"Then what is the point?" he asked, all the while thinking that Renee was cute and sexy when she "played" mad.

"Grace is from Chicago. Of course she wants to stay here. You forget that Zora moved to Chicago for Reggie. She's been away from her family for a long time. I'm sure she's eager to get back East."

"Well, I may have overreacted *slightly*," Renee huffed.

Jerome said nothing. He kissed her forehead instead, and her light perspiration moistened his lips.

"I know you don't want Zora to take Reggie to Philly for Thanksgiving this year, do you? If you keep pushing, they'll be there with her family."

Renee thought about her options. "I'll try to behave." She sighed. "I'll apologize in the morning."

Jerome made himself a glass of lemon water. "Ready for dessert?"

"You still have room?" Renee questioned. Jerome had eaten every bit of his catfish platter, his plate practically licked clean.

He opened the refrigerator and pulled out a small Styrofoam cup. Mac Arthur's had the best banana pudding on the west side of town. He took a clean spoon from the silverware tray and offered a scoopful to his wife.

"No, thanks. Dinner put enough pounds on me."

"You don't hear me complaining."

Renee pinched Jerome's arm playfully and then licked half of the pudding off the spoon.

Jerome tried to give her more.

"That's enough, Jay," she said and backed away. "I'm going to burst if I eat one more bite."

"Had enough of me, too?" Jerome mischievously asked, and Renee batted her eyes at him. *God, I love this woman.* "Meet me upstairs in five minutes."

Chapter Four

~ *Taylor* ~

Uncomfortably seated in a hard, plastic chair, Taylor stared at Joi's report card. Not knowing whether to shout or cry, she put her elbow on the teacher's wooden desk and sighed. Her daughter had never brought home more than one C at a time. Even though Joi's progress report had forewarned her, Taylor expected her to do better.

Taylor placed her hand on the side of her face and looked at her tall, five-eleven daughter slouched in her seat. If Joi's body language were a book, it clearly read that she wasn't concerned about her future.

For a brief moment, Taylor wanted to take off her belt and whip her firstborn into caring, but feared Joi would go into shock. None of Taylor's children was familiar with spankings. Taylor and Lance—mostly Lance—had agreed to use alternative forms of punishment a method new to Taylor. She grew up in a household where the mere mention of her great-grandfather's legendary leather belt made her burst into tears. That belt; old, thick, and worn, had straightened out many generations.

Staring at the multiple C's, Taylor knew it was time to

change the current method of correcting bad behavior. But how? Lately, the more Taylor reprimanded Joi, the more defiant she became.

Taylor let her hand fall on the desk and slid the report card closer to the edge. "Care to explain this?" she asked.

Her pride as thick as a mule's, Joi avoided looking at the document in question. Taylor waited for her to admit fault or, at the very least, say she was sorry, but Joi sat in her chair staring at the silver ring on her finger.

"Would you please explain why your grades have dropped?" Taylor asked with an ounce more bass.

Still Joi said nothing.

Taylor's leg twitched, and she had to pray to keep from popping her daughter. "You did bring up the computer grade, but what is this D in math about?"

"Mrs. Belle," the teacher, Ms. Harris, cut in, "I can speak for her math grade. Joi missed a few assignments because of her basketball games."

The inflection in the teacher's voice insinuated that Joi's education may not have been Taylor's priority. Or maybe it was guilt that made her feel that way. Taylor's focus had been on keeping her store on track and helping the twins with their homework. She just assumed Joi was old enough to be a responsible student. How did things get this far out of hand?

A flashback of one childhood parent-teacher conference surfaced, and Taylor shifted in her seat. Her mother had come to the school early one afternoon, excited because Taylor's father was in town for a few hours. The teacher explained that Taylor's grades were slipping and that sometimes she was uncooperative. Her mother's burly and strong hand came into contact with Taylor's mouth so fast, she hadn't seen it coming.

"You know better than to disrespect an adult. If I hear

of this again, I'm gonna light your tail up. Do we understand each other?"

Frightened, Taylor nodded and massaged her lip until the stinging sensation disappeared. Her mother never mentioned the declining grades, and the look on the teacher's face scarred Taylor from that day forward.

Mrs. Harris had that same disconcerting look on her face; a look that questioned good manners and extra-curricular activities being given higher priority than academics.

It wasn't until Taylor became an adult and had children of her own that she understood her mother's behavior. She had done the best she could with a tenth-grade education. Although Taylor had forgiven her, it would've been nice to have a mother who read bedtime stories, helped with homework, accompanied her on field trips, or signed her up for ballet classes. Taylor loved her mother, but she refused to follow in her footsteps when it came to her own children's education. She wanted them to go to college and obtain jobs that exceeded their expectations. Options for Joi would be limited if she continued to perform on a C level.

"Is that why she's not doing well?" she asked Ms. Harris.

"Basketball has never interfered with her work before."

"No, ma'am," Ms. Harris replied.

Taylor ground her teeth together. The word *ma'am* bothered her ears.

"I give Joi assignments to take home on the days she has to miss my class. She's supposed to turn them in with her homework the next day." Ms. Harris opened her grade book and counted aloud. "She missed five assignments, and two so far this marking period. I don't accept late work." Ms. Harris looked at Joi and then back at Taylor. "My guess is that she is doing the same thing in her other classes."

Taylor turned her head to face her daughter. "What's going on that you can't finish your work at home?"

Joi sucked her teeth and crossed her arms. Her nonchalant attitude was beginning to annoy Taylor. Without realizing it, she hit Joi's leg with her signature Coach bag. "Watch yourself! And answer me before I *really* embarrass you."

Joi unfolded her arms and sat up straight. "I can't do all the class work *and* homework in one night," she murmured.

"Your life is not hard or complicated, young lady," Taylor announced. "This is the only job you have. If basketball is making life too hard, then we can solve that easily today."

Joi's eyes widened. The threat of being off the basketball team hurt her more than Taylor's disappointment.

"Basketball isn't the problem," she declared.

"Then what is?" Taylor questioned sharply.

Joi bit her bottom lip, just as she always did when she was angry or upset. She looked around the classroom and eyed the few students waiting for their turn to be seen, some just as apprehensive as Joi had been. She played with the silver hoop in her ear and looked at the floor. "Algebra is hard," she whispered nervously.

"Then you ask for help. We could get a tutor if you need it," Taylor replied with little regard for who was in the room. "What about science and history? Are those classes hard, too?"

Joi pressed her teeth deep into her bottom lip.

"This is unacceptable, Joi." Taylor touched the report card, pointing to each C as she spoke. "You can't get into college with these grades. You have a chance to be the first in our family to go. An opportunity many people wish they had. Don't you *want* to go to college?"

Taylor's emotions were running high, and she paused mid-speech. At Joi's age, the only goal Taylor had was to receive a high school diploma.

"I'll be happy to help Joi after school or during her

lunch," Ms. Harris said, picking up on Taylor's concern. "Also, I help a few other students after school, and a few during their lunch period, if I'm free. Joi is welcome to join either group."

For the next five minutes, Ms. Harris discussed how challenging algebra was for several students in the school. She told Taylor that with a little more effort and perhaps close supervision at home, Joi could possibly earn a B by the end of the year.

Frequently using words and phrases Taylor would have to google later on the Internet, Ms. Harris questioned Joi's ability to grasp the more difficult concepts. "Perhaps that's why she doesn't do her work," Mrs. Harris said, now perky and optimistic, certain that she had figured out Joi's problem. "Either way, I believe we all can help to turn this grade around."   ·

Taylor didn't say a word as the teacher spoke; her silence might have been mistaken for agreement and approval. But Taylor didn't agree with the educational terms Ms. Harris spewed at her. Nor did she approve of the comparisons made between Joi and some of her classmates. Joi was not a special case. In Taylor's opinion, her daughter was just lazy when it came to school. Basketball was all Joi was really passionate about.

Taylor grabbed the report card, stuffed it inside her Coach, and stood up. "Thanks for your help. I'll see that Joi does better," she said, forcing a smile. "Let's go," she barked at Joi. Then with her head held high, Taylor walked out of the classroom, Joi trailing listlessly behind her.

The ride home was quiet. Parent conferences had never been so exhausting. All of Joi's teachers basically recited the same line. "She would have done better if she turned in all her work on time."

Taylor squeezed into a parking space near the corner

and turned off the engine. It was 8:42 P.M. She hoped Leah and the twins were in the bed, so that her full attention could be given to Joi tonight.

Joi, who had been listening to her personal iPod the entire ride home, got out of the car before Taylor could lecture her. Although Joi had a head start, she hadn't made it inside by the time Taylor caught up with her.

Watching Joi struggle with her key in the lock, Taylor trudged up the steps and relieved some of her frustration. "Let me give it a try," she said. The old lock had been bad for almost a year. It was the first thing Lance promised to fix when he was done renovating his mother's home. Taylor took the key out and reinserted it slowly, wiggled it, then applied the right amount of pressure. As if she had just performed a magic trick, the lock released.

Once inside, Joi immediately charged up the steps to the second floor.

"One second, young lady." Taylor tugged the back of Joi's jacket, jerking her backward. "I think you need to take a break from the team until I see an improvement."

Joi snatched the earphones from her ears. "You can't do that, Mother. The team needs me."

"I can," Taylor responded as she walked into the next room. "And, you'll thank me later."

Joi followed her. "You're gonna mess up the team's balance," she cried. "We have an undefeated record."

Taylor hung her coat in the closet then took the report card out of her purse. "Spare me the drama, Joi. We wouldn't be having this conversation if you were doing the work your teachers gave you."

"I didn't fail anything, Mother," Joi whined. "Last time you said if I *failed* anything I was off the team."

Taylor waved the report card in the air. "This D you earned is failing, in my eyes. Am I supposed to wait until it drops to an F?"

"The coach accepts C's. And I promise I won't get an F," Joi pleaded.

"You're off the team." Taylor dropped the report card on the dining room table. "And I promise *you* there won't be another bad grade coming in this house."

"I can't wait to leave this place!" Joi yelled and walked away. "I feel like I'm in prison!"

"I can arrange a real prison in here, if you're not careful, sweetheart," Taylor snapped.

Lance emerged from the kitchen, still dressed in his bus driver's uniform. "What's going on?"

"Mother said I can't play ball anymore, Daddy," she whined from the center of the next room. "We're undefeated!"

"That's not what I said," Taylor corrected. "I said you are *temporarily* off the team. Your grades are more important than dribbling some ball up and down a court."

"We can't have her benched, baby," Lance affirmed, seemingly just as upset as Joi.

The smirk on Joi's face angered Taylor, but she kept her cool. Pitting her against her husband tonight wasn't going to work. Taylor thrust Joi's report card into his free hand, convinced Lance would have a change of heart once he actually saw her grades. "You need to look at this."

Lance brushed his hands on his jeans and examined the card. "Okay, so this isn't great," he replied and placed it on the table, "but we can come up with something more appropriate, Tay."

Stunned by her husband's words, Taylor frowned. Lance had never disagreed with her in front of Joi before. "Then what is more appropriate, Lance?"

Joi rolled her eyes so hard, Taylor thought they were going to get stuck.

"Basketball is my ticket into college. I could get a full scholarship and go to a school far away from here."

Taylor moved closer to Joi, and Joi took a few quick steps back. "Keep talking. You're not too old to get whipped for the first time," Taylor assured her child.

"Okay, okay, you two," Lance said, trying to bring a halt to the situation before things got out of hand. "Go on up to your room, Boss. Your mother and I will come up with something by tomorrow."

Joi shoved her earplugs back in her ears then moaned and grunted up the stairs, heavily stomping on each step.

When her door slammed shut, Taylor faced her husband. "Why do you always take her side?"

"I'm not taking sides, babe," Lance said. "We should just be certain her punishment is fair."

"The punishment she got for that progress report was *fair*, and look how that turned out."

"Then we need to come up with something different."

"Why?" Taylor couldn't believe her ears. What had gotten into her husband? If they didn't exert authority over Joi now, they would be tortured later. Why couldn't he see that? "You know, it doesn't help my relationship with her when you go against me."

"I know, and I really do apologize. I just feel strongly against removing her from the team. That will only make her attitude worse. You don't want that to deal with, do you?" Lance said. "And her grades will only be fit for community college, *if* we're lucky. Basketball is her outlet. Maybe the coach can talk to her or help us come up with something that will make a difference."

Taylor twisted her lips. Lance had a point, but she was not in the mood to tell him he was right. The bottom line was that Joi was actually an excellent athlete. Lance had coined the name *Boss* for Joi when she broke a scoring record in the ninth grade. The name was quickly adopted by her coaches, basketball fans, and friends. But no matter how great an athlete Joi was, Taylor wanted her to command academics the same way she commanded the ball on the court.

The room grew quiet. Taylor and Lance stood in the dining room at opposite ends of the table, as if they were adversaries.

"Despite what you think, we are in this together," Lance said. "We have to trust that we instilled the right things in Joi. She's a good kid. We need to try communicating with her a lot more than we have."

"Talking doesn't always work with teenage girls," Taylor stated and threw her Coach on her shoulder. She loved her husband, but sometimes felt he criticized her parenting skills. Sure, he'd been raised by both parents and had the childhood Taylor wished she'd had, but that didn't mean she didn't know how to rear children.

She wanted to say more, but held her tongue. She didn't want Lance to indiscriminately mention what had happened today to his mother and later deal with a sermon on how to be a better, and in so many words, submissive wife. "But I'll try it your way."

"That's all I'm asking you to do," Lance said warmly. "I left you some chicken and mashed potatoes. Hungry?"

"Maybe later. I want to check on the kids," Taylor said. She headed for the stairs, and Lance disappeared in the kitchen.

Upstairs, she stopped by the twins' room first. Tyrell, the younger of the two, was already asleep and hidden under his Batman sheets. Long and stocky like his father, Tyrell would soon outgrow his twin bed. Taylor gently put his dangling feet on the bed and covered them with a blanket, and he shifted his weight toward the wall. She rubbed the place where she believed his head to be and whispered, "Sleep tight, sweetheart."

On the other end of the room was Dennis, alert and watching an old rerun of *The Fresh Prince*. Although he was older, he was much shorter than his brother. Somewhere down the line, Taylor believed they would be true identical twins because they favored one another in every other aspect. Tyrell's growth spurt just came sooner.

"Set the timer for one hour," she said softly, blocking his view of the television. "It's getting late."

"Uh-huh," he answered in a comatose state. "Excuse me, Mother, but I can't see," he said, moving his head from side to side. "I'm missing the funny part."

"I'll be back to check on you in—"

"One hour," Dennis said, finishing her sentence. He grabbed the remote from under his Spiderman pillowcase and fiddled with the buttons.

When the television was on, nothing else in the universe mattered to Dennis. Although the mindless hobby was a great way to keep him silent, if Taylor wasn't careful, her son was sure to turn into a couch potato before he hit puberty.

"Thank you," she said and waited for him to set the timer. She hoped their teen years would be a lot easier to handle. Bright and full of energy, both twins were typical ten-year-old boys. Often the culprits of silly pranks and antics, their teachers never complained of their academic progress, and Taylor prayed it would stay that way. "Good night," she whispered and proceeded to Leah's room.

Sitting at her desk surrounded by library and textbooks, Leah rapidly typed on her keyboard. Crumpled sheets of paper, note cards, and highlighters were scattered across the floor. Had it not been for the princess décor, someone could have mistaken Leah's room for a college dorm. Leah had established a stringent work ethic early on. Having been on the honor roll since the second grade, Taylor's 12-year-old daughter was also well-rounded and gifted.

Focused on the report she'd been working on all week, Leah hadn't heard Taylor enter the room. She watched Leah work, flipping through her books, jotting down notes, and typing, all the while mumbling to herself. Leah brought a smile to Taylor's face. She always did. Observing her, Taylor had an idea. *Quality time in the library might do Joi some good.*

"Almost finished?"

"Hi, Mother," Leah said, typing without looking at the keyboard. "I'm having a hard time coming up with a conclusion."

Procrastination was a trait Taylor was glad Leah learned to avoid early in life. "It'll come to you. But don't stay up too late, okay? You have the weekend to work on it."

"I won't," Leah said and picked up one of the crumpled papers from the floor.

Taylor left Leah's room and stood at the top stair. Too tired to walk back down the long flight of stairs, she projected her voice and called her husband. "Lance!" She waited for what she deemed a reasonable amount of time then called him again. "Lance!" This time, she heard his heavy work boots trudging across the tiled kitchen floor.

"Did you call me?" he asked, a fresh chicken leg in one hand. When Taylor confirmed she had, he wiped his mouth with the back of his free hand as he approached the stairs.

"I'm still working on the details, but what if Joi goes to the library after school every day for a couple hours. Well . . . maybe not on days she has a game or practice, but I figure it's quiet there. She'll have no choice but to study."

Lance smiled in approval. "I like your thinking. I can even meet her at the bus stop if it gets too dark."

"Fair enough," she replied and moved slowly down the hall. She walked into her bedroom and paused at the family picture by the door. A chill ran through her body.

"It's time," a small voice whispered in her ear.

Taylor turned around. There was no one else in the room. The voice she heard must have been God speaking to her spirit, but what was He saying it was time to do?

Chapter Five

~ *Jerome* ~

After a summer hiatus, Calvary Baptist church opened its gym for a new season of basketball. This was the second year that Jerome served as the league organizer. He had played on a team when the league started many years ago, but the pressure on his troubled knees became too much to bear. Not wanting to give up on the ministry completely, he received, with open arms, the invitation to be a leader.

The ministry was about more than just basketball. From late October to mid-March, men from all walks of life came together every Tuesday and Thursday for a night of fun and fellowship. There was no pressure to convert unbelievers, but it was the ministry's prayer that all the men would develop a deeper relationship with God by the end of the season. Jerome knew this ministry was his calling. He loved basketball, but most of all he loved being a witness and helping men cope with their problems.

Jerome stepped out of the office he shared with two other leaders and watched the men warm up. His middle son, Jerome Jr., was among them. He watched as his son attempted lay up after lay up without making one basket. Jerome Jr. wasn't much for being coached, especially by his father.

Jerome wanted to tell his son that he was applying too much pressure on the ball upon release. As his current skills displayed, Jerome Jr. wasn't the best athlete, but he was persistent, something many aspiring athletes lacked, including Jerome's oldest son, Reggie. Reggie easily excelled in every sport he played, but he didn't have the passion or determination it took to last as a professional. The scoreboard buzzed, letting everyone know that the warm-up period was over. Bouncing balls stopped, side conversations ceased, and the players made their way to center court. Because it was the first meeting of the season, Jerome was in charge of delivering announcements and sharing a scripture for the week. He stood tall, Bible in hand, in the middle of about three dozen men and a small mass of spectators. He had no fears or jitters. Speaking in front of a group in casual settings was his forte.

"Good evening, men. It's so good to see new and returning faces in the crowd tonight. Thanks to all of you, we have added five more teams to the roster. And we want to keep it at five," he said, "so please see me before November eleventh if you haven't paid your dues or picked up your jersey." Jerome opened his Bible to the page he had studied all morning. "As some of you know, before tip-off we like to give you a message of encouragement. This week, I'd like you to meditate on Judges, chapter seven."

Jerome read the scripture then roughly explained that Gideon was told by God to go into battle with a limited number of men. "When faced with a challenge," Jerome continued, "Gideon was afraid. God understood Gideon's fear, but didn't excuse him from the task he had to do. If you're facing an overwhelming situation today, know that God can give you the strength you need to handle it." Jerome paused as the words pricked at his heart. "But, my brothers," he continued, "you must listen to God and obey Him. Know that you are never alone. No matter what it feels or looks like, God will provide courage the very moment you start to feel weak." Jerome stared at the Bible verse, momentarily forgetting that all eyes were on him. He placed a bookmark between the pages and asked, "Are there any prayer requests?"

For the next five minutes, several men shared testimonies and gave God praise for what had taken place in their lives. This was an important part of the night.

Many men didn't have outlets to pour out their true emotions. Besides Jesus, Jerome only had Brandon, his brother in Philadelphia, with whom he could share his innermost feelings. Jerome needed this time just as much as the other men. He waited patiently for the last man to speak then called Pastor Hampton to the floor to pray.

Jerome Jr. slapped his father's back when Pastor Hampton was done with his prayer. "What's up, old man? You're about ready for the pulpit," he teased and tossed him a basketball.

Jerome caught it with one hand and dribbled the ball to the basket, taking a shot about a foot away from the hoop, and it glided through the net. "If you make shots like that, you'll win tonight," Jerome bragged.

Jerome Jr. chased after the loose ball and attempted to repeat his father's moves. He was unsuccessful. The ball bounced off the rim and landed in Jerome's hands. "I didn't have much time to practice over the summer with the new baby and all. I'm a little rusty," Jerome Jr. said.

Rather than agree with his son about his skills, Jerome encouraged him. "It'll come back to you in no time," he said and ran to the basket again, this time trying to score from a different angle, but Jerome Jr. blocked the shot with force, bruising his father's left arm.

"Slow down, Pop," Jerome Jr. said. "I still got a little game left in me."

The buzzer sounded again, indicating that it was time for the games to officially begin.

"You're lucky," Jerome said, massaging the pain in his arm. "Rematch on Sunday after dinner?"

Jerome Jr. nodded then joined his teammates.

Jerome stood on the sideline, ready to enjoy his son's game when a pain shot down his arm. He couldn't believe how out of shape he was. He held on to his arm until tip-off then headed to the office in search of Tylenol.

Dressed in an old Adidas sweat suit and a pair of 90's Jordans, Reverend Hampton stood in front of the Xerox machine making copies of release forms. "You have a good bunch of men this year," he said.

Jerome placed his Bible on the desk and thought about the message he'd delivered, the message God had placed into his spirit seconds before he spoke it aloud. "Yeah. I think going into the other neighborhoods helped." Jerome riffled through his desk drawers for a pain reliever. Unable to find what he needed, he sat down. Maybe the pain would go away on its own.

Pastor Hampton closed the cover of the copy machine and prepared to leave. "I'm going to hang around a bit, but it's my turn to cook tonight, so I can't stay long."

"Say," Jerome said before the pastor had reached the door, "do you have a minute to talk?"

Pastor Hampton put the copies he made on top of a file cabinet and closed the door before sitting in an adjoining chair.

Years ago, the last place Jerome would've been was in an informal counseling session with the pastor of a church. But as Jerome bared his soul, he was surprised at the level of comfort he felt. Maybe it was the fact that Pastor Hampton didn't have on his formal clergy attire. Or that he was only two years older than Jerome. Whatever it was, Jerome could be himself without sugar coating certain details.

Not once wearing the face of judgment or shame, Pastor Hampton silently waited for Jerome to finish talking. "I have to be honest," he began when Jerome concluded. "I believe you and I both know your dreams may be God's way of telling you to reach out to your daughter and her mother. It might hurt, but you have to decide what matters most to you." He uncrossed his legs and relaxed his hands on each of his knees, and his tone became even more serious. "If you don't tell Renee and this got out—"

"I know where you're going, Pastor. I just wish there was a way to handle this without hurting so many people." Jerome lowered his head. "I almost lost Renee once, and I'm afraid she'll leave me for good this time."

"I can't deny that you have a challenge ahead of you," Pastor Hampton said, "but like the passage you read tonight, you must do what God tells you to. Things could get worse if you don't obey Him."

Tiny beads of sweat formed on Jerome's nose, and he frowned. "God spared my marriage when I had the affair. He might not give me a second chance."

"God does not operate the way man does. He wants to bless you. I can't say what the outcome will be in this situation, but I will say that secrets do expose themselves in time. I've lived long enough to know that to be true." Pastor Hampton unzipped his sweat suit jacket. The small office overheated when the door was closed longer than ten minutes. "Protect your family, Jerome. Trust that God will lead you in the right direction."

Jerome stood to his feet and sighed. He wanted to get back to the games and the fresh air. "Your sermon on what's done in the dark spoke to me. It's what started the dreams."

Pastor Hampton nodded his head. "Continue to pray. Remember there's not one problem too hard for God."

There was nothing more for Jerome to say. He knew what he had to do. "Thanks, Pastor Hampton. I think I needed to hear that."

"That's what I'm here for," Pastor Hampton replied. "Before I go, shall we pray?"

Jerome sat atop his desk. He closed his eyes when Pastor Hampton was ready and let the preacher's words into his spirit. He didn't know where to begin, but believed that God would help him.

Jerome walked into the house prepared to release the burden he'd been carrying about Taylor and their daughter. It was almost ten, but he knew Renee was upstairs in her home office. Joshua was also awake and in the kitchen perched in front of the flat-screen television doing three things at the same time: eating ice cream from a huge bowl, talking on the phone, and watching the game.

"'S up, Pop?" Joshua said, his mouth full of Chunky Monkey ice cream.

"Shouldn't you be in bed?" Jerome laid his briefcase on the table. Joshua was a responsible eleventh grader, but it was still too late for him to be on the phone on a Tuesday night.

"The game is in overtime," Joshua replied. He then whispered something into the receiver.

Jerome took off his coat and threw it over the back of a kitchen chair before sitting. "Who's winning?"

"The Sixers are up by three. It's only a minute left."

Not a sports fanatic like his father and big brothers, Joshua was a fan of only the Philadelphia teams: the Phillies, the Eagles, and the Sixers. Being the only one in the immediate family born in Illinois, he adopted the Philly teams as his favorites as a way of bonding with his relatives.

Jerome focused on the game and listened to Joshua smooth talk the girl on the line. He smiled at his son's "game." Far from the player Jerome had been at his age, Joshua was more like his oldest brother. He remained in relationships for long stretches of time. In Jerome's opinion, it was better to date several girls in high school, but Renee didn't agree, and she was the queen of the house.

The Sixers' head coach called a time-out, and the station cut to an M&M Halloween commercial, reminding Jerome that the end of the month was near, and it was time to send Taylor a check. In sixteen years, he had not missed a payment. It was the least he could do.

He opened his briefcase and took out a pre-stamped envelope and checkbook, both of which he kept inside a side compartment specifically for this purpose. The game came back on, and in between basketball plays, he filled out the check, adding in the memo line: Have a blessed Thanksgiving! That was the first time he'd written anything personal. In his mind, it was the first step in reestablishing contact with Taylor.

The Sixers' star player made a three-point play, placing them in the lead, and Joshua jumped out his chair.

Jerome tried to lift his arm, but the pain from earlier returned. He jumped up, instead, anticipating victory as the seconds on the clock wound down.

"I thought I heard you come in," Renee said.

At the sound of her voice, Jerome quickly stuffed the check in the envelope then shoved it inside his coat pocket. He prayed Renee hadn't seen him. "Hey, babe."

"I should've known you'd get sidetracked," Renee said, plucking her son on his temple as she passed him to get to the fridge. "You two shouldn't have anything left to say. You've been on the phone since I got home."

Joshua winked and smiled then turned away from his mother to get a little privacy.

"That girl should be in bed," Renee said as she took a pear from the fridge.

"They won!" Joshua shouted. "Now I can go to bed." Before leaving the kitchen, Joshua turned to Fox News.

Since Renee befriended a popular news anchor at that station, besides CNN, it was the only news segment the family was allowed to watch.

Joshua put his empty bowl in the sink, and Renee popped his hand. "Dishwasher, please. You don't have a maid in this house." She sat in the empty chair next to her husband and put one arm around him.

Joshua put the dirty bowl in the dishwasher, said good-bye to his girlfriend, then kissed his mother good night.

"Don't forget you're meeting me downtown tomorrow."

"I'll be there by five," he said and went upstairs to prepare for bed.

Jerome looked at his wife, her cotton shorts showcasing her healthy thighs. He rubbed her legs, slowly building up the nerve to speak. *God will provide courage the very moment you feel weak,* he repeated to himself.

"Everett and I are flying to Texas on Thursday," Renee said and crossed her legs.

Jerome's hands trembled, and sweat rolled down his back. "How long will you be there?"

"Just two days." Renee noticed the change in Jerome's demeanor. "You okay?"

"I'm fine," he uttered, trying to relax.

"You sure, honey? I thought I was the one going through the change, but you're the one sweating."

He wiped his hands on his sleeve. "Maybe I'm coming down with a cold."

Renee touched his head, and he smelled traces of *Ro-*

mance cologne by Ralph Lauren on her skin. The scent made him dizzy. That had never happened before.

Renee took a bite of her pear. "Or maybe you're letting the job get to you."

"Just a lot on my mind, I guess. The fundraiser is tomorrow."

"Things are going to be fine. You always do well at those events."

Glassy-eyed, Jerome gazed at his wife. "You're a good woman, Renee. I'm blessed to have you in my life."

"You sure you're okay, honey?" Renee asked, more worried than before.

Jerome stared at his wedding ring and took a deep breath. "I need to tell you—"

Ring. Ring. Ring.

"Hold on, Jay. I'd better get that. It might be one of the kids." Renee leaped out of her seat and grabbed the cordless phone on her small desk. "Hello." She looked at the clock on the microwave. "No problem, Melanie. He's still awake." Renee handed Jerome the phone and took another bite of her pear.

Curious, Jerome put the phone to his ear. In the three months that they had been working on the project, this was the first time Melanie had called his home. "Hey, Mel. What's up?"

"I'm so sorry, Mr. Thomas, but I thought you should know. Our most valuable player was in a car accident a few hours ago."

"Is he all right?"

"He's fine. Only a few bruises and a dislocated arm. But I'm calling because he was supposed to be the host for tomorrow's event."

Jerome ran his fingers through Renee's silky, long hair. "Thank God he's all right. Make sure you send flowers and a card from our department."

"What about tomorrow? We didn't have a backup," Melanie noted.

"Contact one of the other players, but if no one wants to, I'll host."

"Okay. I'm sorry for calling so late—"

"Not a problem. Glad you did."

"Should we go over details tonight? I'll be up for another hour or—"

Jerome cut her off again. He didn't want to stay on the line any longer than was needed. Renee was not a jealous woman, and he didn't want to give her a reason to be. "Why don't I meet you at the office around seven? That should be enough time."

"Oh, right. I forget not everyone is a night owl like me." Melanie giggled softly. "I'll be there at six forty-five."

"See you then," he replied and disconnected the call.

"How's the player?" Renee asked and leaned on Jerome's slightly sore shoulder.

"He's got a dislocated arm. He'll more than likely be benched for some time, but he's alive."

Renee took another bite of her pear. "We should probably head up to bed."

Jerome agreed. The nerve he had when he first arrived home had been lost. He would have to have the talk with Renee a different day. He used the remote to turn off the television.

As Renee got up, she knocked Jerome's coat on the floor. "I guess you missed the closet," she said and picked up his coat.

The envelope Jerome had placed in his pocket fell out, and both he and Renee reached for it. Jerome's heart felt like it was about to burst through his chest.

"I was looking for this," he said, practically snatching the letter from the floor. "I need to mail it tomorrow."

"You need me to mail that?" Renee offered.

Jerome had to think quickly without appearing suspicious. "I need to print something from work before it gets mailed. But thank you." He put the letter in his briefcase and secured the lock. "Ready for bed?"

Renee took one last bite of her pear then tossed it in the garbage can. Together, they headed to their bedroom hand in hand like true lovebirds. He prayed Renee hadn't noticed the small tremors of fear traveling through his body.

"I better hit the shower tonight," he said as soon as he entered the room.

"Good thinking." Renee hopped under the covers and grabbed a book from the nightstand that she'd been reading all week.

Jerome undressed, putting his clothes in the hamper right away. Renee had trained him and their sons well. He darted into their private bathroom and leaned against the door as soon as it closed. That was close. He thought about what could happen if he didn't obey God.

Tap. Tap. Tap.

Jerome opened the door wide enough to get a full view of his wife. "Yes," he said, controlling his angst.

"What did you want to tell me earlier?" Renee asked.

"Oh, it's nothing, baby. Go back to bed. We can talk about it later." Jerome had missed his window of opportunity.

Renee walked away coolly, but after thirty-four years of marriage, she knew he was hiding something.

Jerome closed the door and started his shower. Before the water could reach a comfortable temperature, he stepped into the shower stall. As the water touched his back, he covered his face with his palm and prayed that God would spare him until the next opportunity presented itself.

Chapter Six

~ *Joi* ~

Mother's always late when she knows I have some-thing to do. Joi paced the floor of her mother's up-scale consignment shop in downtown Chestnut Hill. Taylor had left over an hour ago to pick up Leah from dance class. The studio was less than ten minutes away. Unless her mother had been involved in a serious fender bender, she should've been back by now.

For nearly six long hours, Joi had listened to customers whine about their weight fluctuations, helped others make decisions about clothes, and answered a bundle of questions. She was now hungry, tired, and bordering on crankiness. While her friends roamed around South Street in downtown Philadelphia, enjoying the last days of the beautiful fall weather, she was confined inside. Joi had no one but herself to blame. The D she received in math didn't go over too well with her mother. Still, working all day in a resale store was no way for a high school junior to spend a weekend. Saturday was now the only day of the week she had time to spend with friends *and* with her boyfriend, Markus.

Markus, a sophomore at Saint Joseph's University, had been Joi's summer college tour guide. He escorted Joi and a few other classmates around the campus, explaining the history of each building they passed. Although he was attractive, it wasn't Markus's looks that summoned attention. It was his deep, baritone voice that drew people to him. He was articulate and confident.

Attentive to his every word, Joi often giggled at humor no one else found funny. The only time her friends had seen her that happy and alert was on a basketball court.

To say the chemistry between them was one-sided would be an untruth. Within thirty minutes of the tour, he subconsciously talked directly to Joi as if the other members of the group were invisible.

Joi had no business showing interest in a college man, but reasoned that her flirtations were harmless. Markus would never want to deal with an eleventh grader, no matter how mature she appeared to be. At least that's what Joi tried to convince herself. But in Markus's farewell speech, he extended his contact information, and Joi didn't hesitate to jot it down. Although her parents would never approve of the relationship, calling Markus two days later was one decision she didn't regret.

Thanks to Taylor and the revised "remediation plan" she had come up with, Joi got to see Markus more often. Rather than ask Joi's coach to bench her for a few games, it was decided she would go to the library three days a week for a couple hours. Most of the time Joi did go to the library, but not just to study. Some days she met Markus there, and then they went to his dorm room. Other days they'd ride the El to Penn's Landing and walk along the boardwalk, dreaming about the places they would one day travel together. The times she treasured most were the days they played one on one at the recreation center.

To make up for the study hours she missed, Joi stayed

up late, sometimes after midnight completing her school assignments so she wouldn't fall behind. It was exhausting at times, but her mother had made it painfully clear that Joi needed to improve her grades if she wanted to remain on the basketball team. So Joi did what she felt she had to do.

It didn't seem fair that a parent could threaten to spoil a child's basketball career. Joi didn't think her grades were *that* bad. Juggling athletics, academics, and the special man in her life was difficult, but Joi was confident she'd get back on track soon.

Joi ran her fingers through her strands of tiny braids and fixated on a clock on the wall. Her eyes followed the second hand as it rotated, each ticking sound seemingly louder than the last. She took a deep breath. If Linda, Taylor's prized employee, hadn't stepped out for her daily Starbucks Java Chip Frappuccino, Joi would've left. When she agreed to work at the store, it was with the understanding that it wouldn't be an all-day commitment.

Work hours were supposed to be between 9 A.M. and 4 P.M. every Saturday, unless Joi had a special basketball practice or game. It was now 3:57. Taylor was dangerously close to violating their verbal agreement. If Joi didn't leave within the next ten minutes, she and Markus would be late for the movie.

She stared at the clock once again, her lips twisted in anger. Taylor would regret her tardiness if Joi had to miss her date with Markus. Often referred to as the problem child, with her "teenage hormones and bad attitude," Taylor would be in for a rude awakening if she didn't come back to the store soon.

Joi tried to occupy her time by changing the clothes on a mannequin. That quickly got boring. Joi had little interest in fashion. Taylor was the undiscovered fashion model. She knew how to coordinate and make a plain pair of shorts look like they belonged in *Vogue* magazine. More often than not, Joi preferred casual outfits like the one she had on: a deep red Apple Bottom hooded sweat suit. Other days, jeans and a simple Old Navy printed top worked just fine.

Taller and a touch more muscular than most girls her age, it was hard for Joi to find clothes that complimented her frame. That was one of the reasons she wore jeans and sweat suits all the time. Although Joi made sure she always looked neat, she knew her mother prayed she'd wear more skirts and cutesy shoes or boots with a matching purse.

Joi leaned against the counter, and her cell phone buzzed, alerting her that she had received a message. She flipped open her phone and read the screen: *I'm outside.*

Joi was tempted to run around the corner and tell Markus she was going to be late, but that would be risky. If Taylor spotted her talking to Markus, she would interrogate him and discover that he was in college. Then after Taylor yelled at her for leaving the store unattended, she'd be grounded until her twenty-first birthday. The best thing to do was to hit reply and text back: *W8ting 4 mom 2 get here.*

With both arms crossed, Joi surveyed the store for something to do, to kill even more time. When nothing came to mind, she did what she knew best—played ball. She dribbled an imaginary basketball in place for ten seconds, then bobbed and weaved up and down an empty aisle as if she were on a real court. Shuffling her legs rapidly, Joi tried to outsmart her invisible opponents. In her mind, they were trying to double-team her, but she twisted to the left and right in quick, short movements and advanced to the next aisle.

Joi lifted the imaginary basketball in the air, preparing to make a shot from half court, but changed her mind.

The few customers in the store watched, and Joi imagined they were sitting in bleachers surrounded by friends, cheering her to victory. To give them even more of a show, Joi dribbled forward a couple of yards then pushed herself up on the tips of her toes. Careful of her poise, she raised the ball high above her head. With moderate force, she let the ball roll off her fingertips. "All net," she said aloud.

Joi's hands fell to her sides. The performance was over, and the customers resumed their shopping.

Waltzing into the store with a half-empty drink, Linda greeted each customer personally. As she glided around the store, her sun-dried and feathered hair bounced with every step. It reminded Joi of Farrah Fawcett's hair in the role she played as Jill Munroe in *Charlie's Angels*. Standing five feet eight inches tall, Linda was skinny, not bone thin, but lean. If she wore more than a women's size ten, Joi would be surprised. Although she was slender, Linda had a mean sweet tooth.

"It has to be hereditary," Taylor would say sometimes as she watched Linda eat an entire box of cookies or pack of candy bars. "Nobody can eat so much junk and still look that good."

Linda chuckled every time. "I have a *very* healthy metabolism," she'd say.

Linda, or Ms. Linda, as Taylor insisted Joi call her, even though she was only four years her senior, grabbed a handful of Skittles out of a candy dish on the counter. "You've been awfully quiet today."

"I'm always quiet," Joi answered, staring at her cell in hopes that Markus would text back.

"Yeah, but this is different. What's up?"

Joi knew better than to mention anything to Linda. Although she was cool, Joi knew her loyalty was to Taylor. She put her cell in her pocket. "It's been a long day."

"If you say so," Linda replied and looked at her watch. "After four already? Your mom should be here soon."

She should've been here fifteen minutes ago. Joi walked to the back to get a broom. She'd sweep around the store one more time, and if Taylor hadn't returned by the time she finished, she'd leave for sure.

"I saw you and your friends at Penn's step show," Linda said.

Joi jerked around.

"You were at the quad, too, weren't you?"

Joi remained still and silent.

"Don't worry," Linda laughed. "I won't say anything to your mother. Just make sure you leave that college boy alone."

Unintentionally, Joi's jaw dropped.

"Yeah, I saw you in that guy's face."

"He . . . uh . . . ," Joi couldn't think of anything to say to redeem herself. She didn't want Linda to know that she had a boyfriend. "He just wanted—"

"I *know* what he wanted," she bounced back. "College boys are different from your little high school classmates. They expect more from their women. Trust me on this."

"He's not like that," Joi tried to convince Linda. "He was just flirting. It was innocent."

Linda gave Joi the eye.

"For real. I'm serious, Linda. He was just talking stuff."

Linda laid her drink on the countertop and grabbed another handful of candy. She popped them in her mouth, staring at Joi as she ate every fruity morsel. Joi wasn't sure what else to say, afraid anything more would reveal a lie. She couldn't afford to have Linda mention this to Taylor.

With all the candy in her hand gone, Linda grabbed a tissue from the box next to the candy dish and wiped her hands. She strolled to the trashcan next to the counter and dropped the tissue inside. "Just don't compromise yourself in any way."

"Excuse me," a customer said. "Are these the only jeans you have in petite sizes?"

Linda excused herself, and Joi exhaled. If Linda questioned her any further, she might have unintentionally told on herself.

Joi checked the clock again and rolled her eyes. Taylor had never been this late before. She dragged her feet across the coarse carpet, with hunched shoulders, and stopped in front of the display window. Without touching the glass, she stretched her neck as far as it would go. Looking both ways, she prayed her mother and Leah would bounce down the street any minute. No such luck. The big clock on the building across the street reminded her that she was going to miss part of the movie. And as each second passed, she became more and more aggravated.

Joi turned around abruptly and strolled to the main counter. In Taylor's rush to leave, she forgot to put her personal laptop in the office. Joi sat in front of the outdated computer and pressed the power button. Maybe a game of Solitaire would calm her nerves.

Linda was still busy with the customer, convincing her to buy a pair of snazzy corduroy pants. As Joi waited for the computer to fully load, she mouthed the lyrics of "Melodies from Heaven," softly playing in the background. The CD was one of Taylor's favorites, and it stayed in rotation during business hours. Joi tapped the side of the computer to the beat of the music until it booted. The time at the top of the monitor flashed in bright red lights, and she mumbled words she'd have to repent for on Sunday. Gently, Joi bit her bottom lip. Where was her mother?

"What time do you close?" an unfamiliar customer asked.

Joi was so focused on her situation that she didn't realize someone new had walked into the store. "Six o'clock," she said, clicking the attached mouse rhythmically.

Unaffected by Joi's cold response, the customer dumped a handful of clothes on the countertop. "Could I ask you to hold these items until I come back? I need to run to the cash machine."

Joi stopped playing and grabbed a pen from the side of the register. "What's your name?"

"Chairese. Chairese Gunter. That's *C-h-a-i-r-e-s-e*. I promise I'll be back before five. I just need to find a bank that won't charge me a high fee. These banks are getting ridiculous," she uttered.

Joi scribbled her name on the back of a business envelope. "Is there a Chase nearby?"

"I'm not sure," Joi said. "I think there's a Sovereign Bank at the corner."

"Okay, I'll be back soon." The customer threw her weathered leather bag on her shoulder and left the store.

Joi played one game of Solitaire, finishing with a low score. Though she'd lost more than triple the games she'd ever won, Joi blamed her mother for the defeat this time. Instead of trying for a better score, she decided to fold the clothes left by the customer. To kill even more time, she put the clothes neatly inside a plastic bag. Taylor was still a no-show. *She has ten more minutes before I walk out.*

Just as Joi hung the plastic bag on the rack behind her, she saw Leah running to the front door. *It's about time.*

"Joi!" Leah called through the store and ran behind the counter. She took off her coat then threw her arms around Joi's waist and squeezed her tight. Unlike her sister, Leah was an outwardly affectionate child, freely showing signs of love.

"What's up, Leah? How was dance today?" Joi tickled her round belly. Not built much like a typical ballerina, Leah looked the part in her pink leotard, tights and miniskirt.

"I got a part in the Christmas recital." She gleamed and

handed Joi a wrinkled Auntie Anne's bag. "I saved a cinnamon pretzel for you."

Joi noticed a navy Gap bag hanging from Leah's shoulder and frowned. She couldn't believe they had gone shopping. "What'd you get?" Joi asked curiously. Whatever was inside that bag had to be important.

"I needed new pajamas and slippers to match my sleeping bag," Leah gloated. "I'm going to camp with my Girl Scout troop in January."

"That's over a month away," Joi sharply replied. "You had to go shopping *today*?"

Sensing her sister's annoyance, Leah shrugged her shoulders. Any response would've made matters worse, so she kept quiet. Leah had learned to keep her distance when Joi was upset with their mother.

Joi was angry, but also a little surprised. Just last week she'd asked for a new pair of Nike Air Max shoes. She wanted them to play in an upcoming tournament, but was told to wait until after the New Year. "You can still get a few good uses out of the many pairs you own," Taylor said that day.

Leah was clearly the favorite daughter. She was mild-mannered and compassionate like their father and shared their mother's looks, build, and interests. By the time she was five, Leah could coordinate the color of her sheets with the paint on her bedroom walls. She could also verbally express which outfit to match with her growing collection of shoes and jewelry.

At five, Joi was more into playing street games with the neighborhood kids and getting dirty in the backyard. Joi didn't mind that Leah received most of Taylor's attention. She was a great kid and an even better little sister. Joi only wished Taylor would be less obvious.

Joi watched Leah play with the brass bracelets on display. It wasn't fair to take out her frustration on her sister.

This wasn't her fault. Taylor knew Joi wanted to leave the store on time. "Thanks for the pretzel," Joi said to make Leah feel better. "Where's Mother?"

"Outside talking to some lady," she replied, piling the bracelets onto her arm one by one.

Joi walked to the front of the store. From the window, she witnessed her mother laughing with two women, like she was at a comedy show. Tapping lightly on the glass, Joi motioned for Taylor to come inside.

Leah stood close to her older sister, her hands and nose pressed firmly against the window, sprinkles of cinnamon and sugar smearing the glass.

Joi put her hand on her left hip and waited for Taylor to reprimand Leah or, at the very least, give her "the stare." Instead, Taylor laughed and resumed her conversation. Had it been Joi's face smashed against the glass, she would have scolded her for the smudges she'd made.

Joi urgently tapped the window, this time capturing Taylor's full attention. Using both hands, she waved for Taylor to come inside again. From the look on Taylor's face, Joi knew her gestures weren't appreciated, but at least her mother got the hint.

After saying goodbye to her friends, Taylor marched inside. "That was rude," she said and wiped her feet on the rug. She moved around the store, straightening clothes and other merchandise. "Leah, take that jewelry off your wrist."

Leah shook her arm a few times, smiling at the rattling sound before doing as she was told.

Ignoring her mother, Joi put on her winter jacket. "Okay, Mother, it's quarter to five. Time for me to go. Rayven and I are going to the movies," she lied. "Her sister will bring me home by curfew."

"We're going to Bible study tonight," Taylor said. "You can go to Rayven's after church tomorrow." Taylor circled the store, briefly greeting Linda and the few customers.

Bible study? Joi had never agreed to go to Bible study. Joi secured her knapsack on her back and followed her mother. "Can't I go with you next week?"

"We're all going. It's family night, and your father's ushering," Taylor announced as if Joi should've remembered. She picked up a belt that had fallen on the floor. "Did you tidy up like I asked?"

"Yes, I did," Joi mumbled. "But what about my work hours? You promised me that I could have some time on my own." Joi's cell phone vibrated against her leg, and she jumped. As suspected, it was Markus. She hit the IGNORE option and turned to Taylor.

One of the customers headed out of the store, and Taylor flashed a smile. "Hope you come again soon." Taylor looked back at Joi and eyed her suspiciously. "What movie is so important that you can't spend time with your family?"

"Nothing, Mother. Just yesterday you said I could go," Joi huffed. "Now you're changing your mind. This is the only time I have to socialize with people my age."

Taylor walked to the register and fumbled through her knockoff Prada satchel for the overpriced calculator her children bought her for Mother's Day. She lifted the register enough to remove the receipts hidden in an envelope beneath it. "You would've had more time if your grades were better," Taylor told her daughter. She put the receipts in two different piles and started to add the sales for the day. "Like I said, you and Rayven can hang tomorrow. You two see each other every day. One day is not going to damage the friendship."

Joi pouted. "I've been working here for almost two months, and I haven't been able to leave on time yet. It's not fair."

"Consider this preparation for the real world."

The latest Fantasia ringtone caught Joi's attention, and Taylor looked at her with a raised brow.

Joi sighed and sucked her teeth, upset that her mother was ruining her plans. She stomped off to a corner for better reception and privacy. Stripping herself of a foul attitude, she answered her phone in a mature and sultry voice. "Hey, handsome."

"What's up, Boss?" he asked. "I've been out here for thirty minutes. When you coming out?"

"Just relax, big man. We're not going to miss the movie," she said, hoping his agitation would subside. She feared her days of being his girlfriend were numbered. How much longer would he tolerate being kept a secret? Markus deserved a companion without so many restrictions attached. It was a surprise she was able to avoid having sex with him for so long. But Markus insisted he would wait until she was ready, and Joi loved that he was so patient.

Joi talked to Markus until he relaxed.

When she hung up the phone, Taylor was staring at her with an unsettling glare. "What's wrong?" she asked. She pushed the calculator aside. "Who was that?"

"Rayven. She's waiting for me downtown," Joi lied again, trying to control her impatience. If she pressed too much, Taylor would force her to stay at home for the night.

"Rayven, huh?" Taylor queried.

Before Joi could reply, the customer from earlier walked back inside the store. "Taylor?" she said, her smile friendly and wide.

"H-Hey, Chairese. How are you?" Taylor stepped around the counter and greeted the woman with a short embrace. "I haven't seen you in years."

"Yeah, you know how it is. You get married, have a few kids, and try to maintain a job in between all that. I miss you and the girls. I'm so glad I bumped into Kara at the mall. She told me you still had the store, so I had to come check you out," Chairese said in one long breath.

Joi zipped her jacket and tried to exit the store as

Chairese talked, but didn't get far. Taylor blocked her path with her foot, not once taking eyes off Chairese. Annoyed, Joi moaned aloud and stepped aside.

Oblivious to their actions, Chairese continued to ramble about people she'd seen and places she'd been since she last saw Taylor. "I was in earlier and saw some nice clothes. This cute young lady put my stuff up . . ."

Leah joined the trio and held Taylor's hand.

"Oh, is this your daughter?" Chairese continued. Standing side by side, there was no doubt Leah was Taylor's offspring.

"Yes, this is my baby, Leah," Taylor finally had a chance to say.

"She's beautiful. How are your other children? I've never met your boys and—"

"My sons are with their father," Taylor told her. "And that's my oldest daughter, Joi."

The dramatization that followed could have won an Oscar nomination. Chairese's jaw dropped, and she leaned back on the brink of falling then slapped her hands on her face. "She's the spitting image of Jerome," she said, enunciating each word carefully.

This was the first time Joi could follow the conversation without feeling like she was on a ride at an amusement park.

"Did Kara tell you I saw him last month? He looked good, girl. Chicago must be treating him real good." Chairese picked up speed when she looked at Joi. "You've grown up so pretty. Do you visit your dad much in Chicago? I hear he and Renee—"

"Chairese!" Taylor bellowed, and Leah jumped. "You said you left some clothes up front?"

Joi thought she was hearing things. *Did this lady say I looked like my father? Did she say his name was Jerome?* "Excuse me, ma'am," Joi said, her voice sullen and low. "What did you say?" The look on Chairese Gunter's face told Joi that a secret had escaped her lips. "What did you say about my father?" Joi asked again.

"She said his name was Jerome. But Daddy's name is Lance," Leah corrected.

Confused and shaken, Joi turned to Taylor. "What is she talking about, Mother? Is that man my father?"

"I-I-I'll come back tomorrow," Chairese said, her eyes apologizing as she swiftly backed out of the store.

Joi's cell phone buzzed, and she pretended not to feel the vibration. "Mother, can you please answer me?" she pleaded.

Taylor covered her forehead with her hands and called on Jesus several times in a row.

"Mother?" Joi said with authority. and a sensitive Leah started to cry.

"You're talking too loud," Taylor bounced back. "There are customers in here. And you're upsetting your sister."

"Daddy . . . or Lance . . . he . . . he isn't my *real* father?" questioned Joi.

"This is the last time I'm gonna tell you to lower your voice," Taylor yelled, the veins in her neck popping out. She walked to the corner where all of the new shipments were delivered and pretended to read the labels.

Joi could tell she was only buying time, but there was no more time to waste. It was almost five o'clock. She headed to the boxes as well and stood close to Taylor, leaving minimal space between them.

"You're really pushing it," Taylor stated, her index finger pointed in Joi's face.

"Is that man my real father?" Joi pressed one more time. She searched her mother's face for a sign that Chairese Gunter was wrong but found none. What she did find was an emotion she'd never seen Taylor display. Pain.

Taylor looked at Leah, the child's eyes longing for a response as she nibbled on the pretzel she originally bought for Joi. She could hear Linda asking the customers to leave, citing that there was a family emergency.

Taylor waited until the store was free of strangers. "I think we need to talk about this tonight at home."

"Does he know about me?" Joi wanted to know.

"I wanted to tell you, but this situation is more complicated than—"

"Explain the situation to me then, Mother. I'm old enough to understand," Joi interjected.

Although her face didn't show it, Joi's heart was aching. Her entire life had been a lie. Taylor looked Leah in the eyes again then at the floor, shame written all over her face.

"Mother, please say something," Joi demanded.

Linda took hold of Leah's hand and pulled her away. "Leah, why don't you come in the back with me?"

Hesitantly, Leah followed.

Taylor inhaled deeply and stumbled through a number of responses and eventually gave up talking altogether.

It was then that Joi knew Jerome was, in fact, her biological father. Her eyes blinked vigorously to keep from shedding tears. All of the feelings she suppressed for years had been explained with the slip of a stranger's tongue. She always felt the love between her and her mother was forced, not natural like a mother-daughter relationship should be. It was just the way things were, and as Joi grew older she accepted it. But now she understood that it was a past affair that blocked them from forming a bond.

Joi's throat tightened as she spoke. "So was I an accident? You didn't really want me?"

"Don't be silly, Joi," Taylor said. "Of course I wanted you. I loved Jerome, but . . . our timing was wrong."

Joi felt her mother touch her hand, and she flinched. "Did you ever tell him about me?"

"This really is something we should talk about at home."

"I can't believe this," Joi hollered, her world rapidly

closing in around her. Humiliated and feeling betrayed, she turned around abruptly and bumped into the edge of the counter, jabbing her ribs and knocking Linda's Starbucks cup onto the toffee-colored carpet. "How could you do this to me?" she cried and ran out of the front door.

Halfway down the street, Joi paused to control her sudden downpour of emotions. She looked behind her, hoping to find Taylor standing in the middle of the sidewalk, but Taylor wasn't anywhere to be found. Joi wiped her face and fluffed her braids with her hands. She didn't want Markus to see her in this state. Joi inhaled and exhaled slowly, trying to avoid another crying spell.

Regaining her composure, she continued down the street and around the corner. As she neared Markus's 2005 Volvo, she turned around one last time, expecting to find her mother running after her. But she wasn't there.

Markus started the engine when he saw her, signaling for her to get in. "C'mon, Boss. We're gonna miss the first half of the movie," she heard him yell.

Joi opened the car door and slid into the passenger seat. She fastened her seatbelt, not realizing she hadn't looked at Markus once.

"What? No love for the man who's been sitting in the car all this time?" he asked.

"Of course," she said, leaning over to kiss his right cheek.

"That's better," he replied, unaware of her mood. He scanned through a few tracks of an old Fabolous CD already in play and settled on track number four, "Make Me Better," a song featuring the talented crooner Ne-Yo on the hook. He turned the radio up so loud, Joi could feel the bass pulsating through the car, causing her seat, the dashboard, and the speakers to jump with each beat.

When Markus finally pulled off, people stared at them, several young kids singing along and bobbing their heads.

Joi stared out the window as they traveled en route to the expressway. At a stoplight, a little girl about four years old was crying over a stuffed teddy bear she had dropped in a puddle of water. The man next to her, probably her father, picked it up and tried his best to clean its wet fur. Despite his attempt to please her, the little girl refused to accept the wet and muddy stuffed toy. She cried harder until her father picked her up and whispered something in her ear. As he rubbed the back of her head, she whimpered softly and sucked on her thumb.

When the light changed, Joi could see the father carrying his daughter inside a card shop, perhaps to buy some kind of acceptable replacement. She sighed aloud.

Markus turned down the music. "Hey, you all right?"

Masking her hurt, Joi faced him. "Would you mind if we skipped the movie tonight?"

"What's going on? You and your mom fighting again?"

"Sort of," she answered. "I know you want to go, but I wouldn't be good company." Joi lowered her head, afraid that Markus would see the tears forming in her eyes. "Can you drop me off at Rayven's house?"

Markus rubbed Joi's leg, and it soothed her. His touch always felt good, but this time it felt . . . safe, like he could shield her from the pain she was feeling.

"No problem," he simply stated.

Joi grabbed his hand and squeezed it tight. "Thanks for understanding."

As Markus carefully merged onto I-76, Joi smiled and placed her left hand over his. In that moment, she knew that he really cared about her.

Chapter Seven

~ *Taylor* ~

When Chairese walked into the store, Taylor's past flashed before her eyes. At fifty, one would think life had matured a person, both in their thoughts and lifestyle. In high school, Chairese was labeled *gossip queen*. She talked way too much and almost always at the wrong time. Why they ever became friends, only the angels in heaven could say. It was amazing really. Chairese was still the fast-talking, news-seeking woman Taylor knew several years ago.

"Is that man my father?" Joi had asked.

Taylor opened her mouth to speak, but nothing came out. She looked at the customers browsing the aisles, trying their best not to stare. Taylor wanted to disappear, but Leah was standing next to her with innocent eyes, waiting for an answer. *God, what do I say? Do I tell her that I disobeyed your commandments and ended up getting pregnant by a married man?* Although it was the truth, the words were hard to say. Joi deserved an honest answer, but Taylor couldn't bring herself to expose her faults. No, she was not going to admit any wrongdoing. Not now and certainly not in her boutique with everyone watching.

"I-I-I'll come back tomorrow," Chairese said, as she backed out of the store. The other customers soon followed suit at Linda's request.

"Jesus," Taylor cried, "Jesus, Jesus." She didn't know what else to do. Jesus was the only one who could save her now. She grabbed her clip-on ponytail and smoothed its mane. Silently, she cried, *Why is this happening?* To avoid shedding real tears, Taylor moved around the store and Joi followed, demanding to know the truth.

Joi cornered her in the shipping section of the store and asked, "Does he know about me?" Unable to move without applying force, Taylor was shocked at her daughter's gumption. *When did she become so bold? She should put this much aggressiveness into her schoolwork,* she thought as she tried to move out of Joi's way.

Realizing that Joi wasn't going to give up, Taylor had to think of something to say. She tried to explain the situation as best she could. "He was an old friend and . . . we were young and . . . we thought it best that we . . ." Nothing Taylor tried to say felt right, so she eventually opted to keep quiet.

Unsatisfied with Taylor's attempts, Joi stormed out, slamming the glass door with such power, the mannequins in the window display shook. Taylor should have stopped her, but she couldn't move. The shame of her past immobilized her and rendered her speechless. She stared at the door until her vision blurred and reality set in. Joi was not coming back into the store.

Leah crept up behind Taylor and tapped her arm. "Here, Mother," she said and handed her a warm bottle of water that she kept under the counter.

"Thanks, baby," Taylor replied and rubbed her eyes.

Though Leah was being thoughtful, Taylor wasn't thirsty. She took the water from Leah's shaking hand and hugged her. "Let's close up early, sweetie. How about we grab some cheese steaks for dinner?"

Dressed and ready for an evening church service, Lance dried dishes as he listened to Taylor's account of what happened in the store for the third time, while she washed the dishes from dinner. Even though he would be late, Taylor asked him to stay until all of the dishes were clean.

"Don't get so worked up, Tay," he said and grabbed a plate from her hand before she threw it on the dish rack. "We knew she was going to find out one day, right?"

"Yes, but we were supposed to be the ones to tell her." Taylor lathered another plate with soap and scrubbed it clean. "We agreed to tell her *after* she graduated."

"Things don't always work the way we want them to," Lance said, keeping a close eye on the clock. He wanted to get to church before praise and worship ended. As an usher, most of his labor was spent seating people before the sermon began. "For whatever reason," he continued, "God has chosen this to be the time."

"I wish God would've given me some kind of warning," Taylor stated and immediately recalled the still voice that whispered in her ear a few nights ago. God had indeed given her notice. She rinsed the last plate and gave it to her husband to dry then looked at the clock above the wooden cabinets. "Where do you think she is? It's been over two hours. I tried her cell a few times, but she didn't answer." Taylor let the water out of the sink then twisted the dishrag until it was no longer dripping wet.

Lance moved to the other side of the kitchen and cut a huge slice of Taylor's famous lemon pound cake. Avoiding eye contact on purpose, he said, "She's with Ray. She called while I was getting dressed."

Taylor dried her hands on her pants leg. "What do you mean, she called? And why are you just telling me?"

"I-I didn't—"

Taylor snatched the towel off his shoulder and threw it on the drying rack. "You know how worried I've been, Lance. How could you not tell me she called?"

Shoving half the cake in his mouth, he mumbled, "I'm sorry, Tay. I figured I'd give you both time to calm down. She'll be home soon. Rayven's sister is going to drop her off."

Taylor picked up a jug of Tide from the floor and carried it to the laundry room behind the kitchen. She wanted to scream, but that wouldn't have changed things. She placed the detergent on a shelf above the washing machine. Lately, Lance had shown more concern for Joi than his own wife.

"Mad at me?" Lance asked when he entered the shed.

Taylor couldn't answer him. If she opened her mouth, an argument would have ensued. She aligned the laundry essentials and sanitizers on the shelf so that the labels faced her.

"I'm sorry, Tay." Lance touched her forearm to get her attention and defended his actions. "Joi was upset, you were upset, and I was in the middle. If I told you where she was, you would've tried to call Ray's mom or gone over there and—"

"You don't know what I would have done," she snapped and marched around him.

Lance held on to her hand as she walked by. "Okay, I made a bad call. But both of my favorite women are hurt. I was wrong and should've told you she was safe."

"Yes, you should have," she replied. "I was worried sick."

Lance pulled Taylor close to him. "Please forgive me. I'm tired of all the bickering between you two. I thought you both needed a break."

Taylor pouted like a child. She was tired of all the turmoil, too. And her home life was starting to affect her job. Lance wrapped his arms around her, and she let her guard down. Though at times they differed in opinion, she loved him. And, more importantly, she knew Lance loved her, too. Not many men would marry a woman pregnant with another man's baby. "Sometimes I worry too much. But, lately, Joi has me on edge all the time."

"As long as I'm your husband, you don't have to worry at all. That's my job," Lance replied. "Everything will be fine. There's nothing we can't handle together. God will give us the strength we need." Lance let go of his wife and buttoned his usher jacket. He took a few steps, and the jacket popped open.

"A little snug, huh?" Taylor teased.

"It was that cake." Lance sucked in his stomach and buttoned the jacket again, this time holding it in place.

If she did nothing else, Taylor made sure that Lance was fed on a regular basis, treats and all. She didn't want his mother criticizing her for being an "independent" or "new millennium" woman. Excluding Friday and Saturday nights, unless Lance had a desire to cook, Taylor made dinner.

"You and the boys better go," she said. "You'll miss all of the service. I hate that Leah and I aren't going with you."

Leah was just as concerned about her sister and begged to stay home. Knowing how much she cared about Joi, Taylor and Lance allowed her to miss family night service.

"You'll be at the next one," Lance said and planted a kiss on his wife's lips. "Being here when Joi comes home is more important. The boys and I should be back before eleven," he said and left the kitchen.

* * *

Taylor poured water into a small teapot and placed it on the stove. A good cup of green tea with honey was what she needed. As the flames warmed the bottom of the pot, she sat down and reorganized the miscellaneous items on the table: the salt- and pepper-shakers, the sugar bowl, and the stack of *Jet* magazines. Just as her mother had done, Taylor gathered the tiny books together and put them into one pile next to the napkin holder. It was silly to hold on to such an old and odd tradition, but it was hard to let some memories go.

The house, which originally belonged to her mother, had been the birthplace of many rituals: some fond— singing by the Christmas tree, others melancholy—the nights she cried because of something her father had done. Taylor thought the memories of her childhood in the house would die the day she buried her mother, but God worked a miracle. On her third wedding anniversary, Lance surprised her with the deed to the house. How he managed to pull that off was still a mystery, but words would never be able to express her gratitude.

Recalling all the positive contributions Lance had made in her life, Taylor felt a bit remorseful. She didn't pity Lance. She genuinely loved him. But there was a time when her heart preferred the affections of another man, a man whose passionate feelings for her dwindled over time. Jerome.

Lance's family never understood what he saw in Taylor that was so special. But it wasn't for them to understand. God knew Taylor needed someone of his character and magnitude. God had spoken to Lance's heart, allowing him to see beyond her faults and straight to the treasure she harbored inside. Taylor suspected her in-laws accepted their union for Lance's sake. Since he was the only boy, Gram and her daughters depended on him greatly.

The in-laws were kind enough, never speaking to her

too harshly, and they treated her children well. Taylor supposed that was all that really mattered. Every now and then a snide remark or gesture of insensitivity would creep through, but she had learned to ignore such behavior. Besides, Lance seemed to be immune to the way they treated her. Every time Taylor complained, he'd insist she was exaggerating the facts.

All Taylor wanted was to feel like a part of the family. Having lost her mother when she was in her early twenties, and her father months after Joi was born, Lance's family was all Taylor had. That's why she'd taken their subtle criticisms for so many years. She believed they'd eventually grow to love her unconditionally. After fourteen years of marriage, she was still waiting for that prayer to be answered.

The teapot whistled, and Taylor rushed to turn off the fire. She poured four tablespoons of honey into her cup then headed upstairs to wait for Joi. She should be arriving home soon, and Taylor wanted to prepare for the conversation. She walked upstairs slowly with her tea in hand and, with each step, anticipated the many questions Joi would ask.

"Mom," Leah called from inside her bedroom when Taylor reached the top floor.

Tired and worn out from worry, Taylor had almost forgotten that Leah was home. She stood in her doorway and chuckled softly. With a faux fur shawl draped over her shoulders and her hair pulled back into a bun, Leah resembled an old woman. "Yes, baby," she said.

Leah's toes caressed the furry throw rug beneath her feet. "Did Joi call?"

Taylor blew into her mug then answered, "Not yet."

Leah frowned then looked down at the book in her hand. "Daddy says that other man is Joi's father, but not mine and the twins'." Using her finger as a temporary bookmark, Leah closed the book. "That makes us half-sisters. That doesn't matter really . . . does it?"

This was going to be more difficult than Taylor had imagined. "Of course not. It means that you have a different *biological* father."

"Does Joi have other brothers and sisters?"

Taking a deep breath first, Taylor responded, "Yes, but that doesn't change anything."

Leah looked at her mother, her eyes full of wonder. "Were you married to him?"

Toying with different ways to respond, Taylor couldn't come up with one that seemed appropriate. She wanted to lie, but she had already caused enough damage with her secrets. "No. We were never married." Taylor prayed Leah would accept that answer without wanting to know more. She blew into her cup of tea again then took a tiny sip and swallowed hard. "What I did hurt a lot of people, especially Joi. I should have told her sooner."

Leah reopened the book in her hand. "She'll come back, won't she?"

For a reason Taylor didn't understand, Leah idolized her older sister. "Joi will be home soon. Don't you worry."

Taylor closed Leah's door and headed to her bedroom. She pushed the door open and felt along the wall for the light switch before entering. Too many times she had walked in and jabbed her foot on an object on the floor or bumped into a piece of furniture.

Moving around the dreary and cluttered room, she searched for the set of lounge clothes she'd recently washed. She sighed as she placed her tea mug on top of the bookcase that was now positioned in front of her vanity. Taylor couldn't wait for Lance to repaint the walls a brighter and more vibrant color. The current mocha walls were drab and boring. It was time for something brighter, to add a little spice.

Amid the congestion there was one area Taylor kept spotless, an area designated as a place for worship and prayer. Unable to find her more comfortable clothes, she unbuttoned her blazer then picked up an old and worn Bible from her nightstand. She cleared a path to her quiet place, careful not to step on the loose tools Lance had left on the floor. Once settled in her special chair, Taylor kicked off her ankle boots and slid her slightly swollen feet into the fuzzy slippers beneath the seat.

She could've kicked herself. Had she heeded the advice of her good friend, Kara, and left Jerome alone, she wouldn't be in her current predicament. God had also given her a way out plenty of times, but she ignored every one of them. Taylor shouldn't have let Jerome in her apartment that last time. She had just given her life to Christ and had walked away from a car accident practically unscathed. But that afternoon she was full of pain pills. That, coupled with her emotional state and the deep feelings she had for Jerome, her flesh couldn't resist him. Now she had to reap the consequences because of her lust for a man that rightfully belonged to another woman.

Taylor threw her head back and closed her eyes. "God, what am I going to do with my daughter?"

Carrying two plastic bags of groceries in one hand, and a baby carrier in the other, Taylor struggled to get her screaming five-month-old daughter into their apartment. She kicked the door closed with the heel of her new Nine West boot and dropped the groceries on the floor. Quickly, she unfastened Joi's straps. Humming the tune to an old gospel hymn, Taylor rocked her firstborn in hopes that she would settle down. But her cries persisted. She didn't know what was wrong. Before climbing the stairs to her third-floor apartment, Taylor had tried to give Joi a bottle of milk and had checked her di-

aper, but Joi refused the food, and her bottom was as dry as a bone.

With Joi hanging over her shoulder, Taylor rushed into the kitchen and found a clean pacifier. By this time, Joi had cried so hard, she was hyperventilating and turning varying shades of purple. Taylor struggled to place the pacifier inside her mouth. She tried to hold it inside several times, but Joi continued to push it away firmly with her tongue. Taylor couldn't take it anymore. The squeals of her child pained her heart, and she fought back tears. She needed to call someone with experience. But who? Kara was in Ghana doing mission work with the church, and her friend Sherry was not used to taking care of infants. Taylor called Lance's cell, but got the voicemail. Over Joi's cries she left a brief message. "Call as soon as you can."

Taylor walked into her bedroom and sat in a rocking chair, holding her wailing daughter close to her chest. She hoped the rocking motion would soothe her, but again she was wrong. Joi's frets intensified. She stared at her daughter. Thin whelps spanned the length of Joi's right cheek. Too afraid to clip her fragile and tiny nails, Taylor blamed herself for the marks. Feeling like an unfit parent, she started to cry. If only her mother were still alive.

There was one more person she could call. Her father. Although they had only recently reconnected after many years of separation, he was the only relative she had left. Hysterically, she explained the problem to him when he answered the phone. Unsure of what to do himself, he gave the phone to his wife.

Taylor's stepmother diagnosed the situation immediately. "Sounds like she may be teething. Do her gums look swollen and red?" she asked.

Without delay, Taylor lifted Joi's upper lip and examined her gums. No wonder the baby was screaming. Her gums almost looked inflamed. Taylor sobbed into the phone. "Yes, they are. What should I do now?"

"Well, ol'-school mothers would use a touch of brandy. That'll numb the throbbing instantly. But you can also use some Anbesol."

Anbesol. Taylor knew she didn't have any brandy. She had given up drinking when she found out she was pregnant. But she remembered using Anbesol for her wisdom teeth. Gently, she lowered Joi inside her crib and kissed her. She raced into the bathroom and tore apart her medicine cabinet, surfing through all kinds of old medications, shampoos, toothpastes, and Q-tips. Taylor thought she'd hit the lottery when she found the barely touched tube of Anbesol. "Found it!" she yelled into the phone, happy that Joi's pain could possibly end soon.

"Okay. If it's not the children's kind, use a very small amount and rub it on her gums. It might take a minute for her to settle down though," her stepmother added.

Grateful for her wisdom, Taylor said, "Thanks so much." She hung up the phone and did as she was instructed.

As predicted, Joi settled down, and her eyes grew heavy. Finally at peace, Taylor whispered into her daughter's ear, "You wore yourself out, sweetheart."

Looking at Joi, Taylor wondered if she had made the right decision. Choosing to have a child alone was selfish. She had never admitted it to anyone, not even her best friend, but Taylor chose to follow through with the pregnancy for the wrong reasons. She thought for sure Jerome would change his mind and move back to Philadelphia. But despite bearing his only daughter, Jerome still chose to be with his wife, the woman, in his words, he no longer felt connected to.

While Joi was asleep, Taylor put the groceries away then sorted the mail. Shuffling through it with speed, a slight smile crossed her face when she recognized Jerome's handwriting on an envelope. She traced the letters of his scripting and said a quick prayer.

Since Taylor was seven months pregnant, he had faithfully sent child support. A part of her looked forward to the contact each month. Although he sent nothing but a check, there was a slither of hope that he'd insert a note saying he missed her and was on his way back.

Taylor tore into the letter with high hopes, just as she did every month. But there was nothing different inside. Just the same Chicago-themed check. No note. No request to see a picture of their child, and nothing that asked how she was doing. Jerome didn't even know his daughter's name. The only thing that was different was the number of the check.

Taylor dropped the envelope, and the check fell to the floor. She stood over her daughter's crib and cried, her tears falling rapidly on Joi's chubby legs. How could he deny such a precious gift? Taylor placed her hands in the prayer position. "I hope I haven't ruined Joi's life," she cried. Growing up without a father was hard. She knew that firsthand. "God, please don't hold my sin against my baby."

Taylor's intercom buzzed, and she wiped her eyes. Outside of her window she noticed Lance's car parked on the opposite side of the street. Pulling herself together, Taylor ran to the front room and hurriedly ran her fingers through her hair before buzzing him in. As soon as she opened the door, Lance handed her a small paper bag. "I thought one of these might help," he said.

A bottle of Children's Tylenol, a tube of Baby Anbesol,

and a round teething ring were inside the bag. Taylor looked at Lance and smiled. Jerome may not be the man and father Joi needed, but Taylor realized that God had sent one that could be.

Taylor opened her eyes and held tight to her Bible, rocking to her own rhythm, until she heard the squeak of the front door. She could tell by the soft footsteps that it was Joi, and regardless of the late hour, it was time to talk.

Chapter Eight

~ *Joi* ~

Joi inserted her house key in the door and jiggled it three times, a trick she had finally mastered by watching her mother. She lifted the knob and pushed hard on the old wooden door, and it creaked. Again, nothing unusual. She had begged her mother to buy a new door and lock. It was becoming embarrassing, but Taylor refused every time she asked. The house had at one time belonged to the grandmother Joi never knew, and Taylor wanted to preserve as much of it as she could.

With the door half-open, Joi turned back toward the street and yelled to Rayven, "I'll see you tomorrow."

Seeing that she was safe inside, Rayven and her sister nodded and drove away.

It was only ten-thirty, and the first time Joi had ever been home before her midnight curfew. As she walked through the vestibule, Joi crept by the family room, expecting to find Taylor lounging on the sofa, but the room was empty. She walked lightly to the stairs and listened for any noise—the TV, radio, or telephone conversation—but heard nothing. With any luck, Taylor was asleep.

Proceeding up the stairs, her long and muscular legs silently skipped two at a time. Joi couldn't see around the slant in the hallway, but hoped that Taylor's door was closed. To be sure, she tipped down the hall, careful not to disturb her. As she passed the bathroom, her knee bumped into the clothes hamper, and she lost her balance.

Joi bit her lip and waited. Certainly Taylor heard the hamper thump against the wall. She counted to ten before taking another step then softly inched a few more paces to the end of the hall. Her hand barely touched the door-knob when she heard her mother's door open.

"Is that you, Joi?" Taylor called from her room.

"Yes," she mumbled. Taylor's slippers dragged on the carpet, and Joi knew she was headed her way.

Still wearing the burgundy pants suit she'd refurbished a week ago, Taylor stopped in front of the bathroom. "It's late, but I think we should talk," she said and pulled at the bronze, scalloped buttons that Leah had picked out from a fabric store on South Street.

Joi wanted to ask if it could wait until tomorrow, but at sixteen she had to do what her mother wanted. She pushed her bedroom door open, and her nose wrinkled. The apple and cinnamon plug-ins barely covered up the musty scent from the clothes piled in the middle of the floor. Joi cracked one of her windows just enough to circulate fresh air without cooling the room. Washing clothes was at the top of her list of things to do after church tomorrow.

Taylor apprehensively walked inside Joi's room, stepping over CD cases, pens, books, and magazines. Joi could tell she wanted to say something, but held back. Since she'd started working at the store and going to the library every day, there was no time to tidy her room to her mother's specifications. Joi removed a mound of clothes from the chair in front of her desk and dumped them on the bed.

"I don't know how you think straight," Taylor said and took a seat in the now empty chair.

Joi didn't feel like responding. She took off her shoes, flung them in the corner then leaned against the wall next to a life-size poster of Sheryl Swoopes, a daily reminder that she could one day be in her shoes.

"I don't know where or how to start, but I know I have to be honest. So I'm just going to say it," Taylor began. "Jerome was married, and I knew it. What we did was wrong. But I really believed he was going to leave his wife."

Joi could tell her mother was nervous. Taylor had paused a number of times in order to catch her breath and regain composure. Not once during her explanation did she look Joi in the eye.

"When I got pregnant," Taylor continued, "I didn't know what to do. Jerome had moved to Chicago, and I needed to move on." She crossed her legs at the ankles. "Despite what Jerome and I did, I believed that you were a gift from God, so having an abortion was not an option."

Joi slid down the wall. She couldn't believe her mother had been involved with a married man, the woman who fervently preached about doing the right thing. Joi didn't know which was worse, the secret Taylor kept from her, or knowing that she was the product of an affair. She took off her socks, rolled them into a ball, and added them to the growing pile of dirty clothes. "Does Daddy know about Jerome?"

"Yes," answered Taylor, her leg bouncing at a slow and steady beat. "But he isn't to blame. I was the one that wanted to keep this a secret."

Joi heard Taylor's words, but how could she not blame both of them? They let her live a lie for so many years. "Were you ever gonna tell me?" she asked.

"We were trying to wait until you were eighteen."

Understanding her parents' rationale was difficult at times. Telling her at eighteen would not have lessened the shock or the pain. Joi fiddled with a piece of lint on the floor, contemplating whether or not she should ask questions about Jerome. She decided it was worth a shot. "Do I look like him?"

"Afraid so. It's almost uncanny how much you favor one another."

Joi crafted her next words carefully. "When you look at me, do you see him?"

Unsure of where the conversation was heading, Taylor stared straight ahead. "Your looks don't have to remind me that you're Jerome's child. My heart knows that."

"Is that why you treat me different?"

Taylor was perplexed. "What are you talking about?"

Joi was nervous, but this was her chance to put her feelings on the table. "You may not notice, but I do. You don't spend a lot of time with me . . . like you do the twins and, especially, Leah."

Puzzled, Taylor loosened her blazer. "Where is all this coming from? I did plenty of things with you when you were Leah and the twins' age. But you're older now and into sports. You know I don't know a lot about basketball."

Taylor's response was not satisfactory. "What about the tickets for the Nutcracker? You didn't even ask if I wanted to go," Joi replied.

"Leah likes ballet. I didn't think you'd be interested in traveling to New York with a bunch of preteens," Taylor explained. "I wouldn't ask Leah to go to a Sixers game with you and your friends."

"I would've gone to be with you and Leah," Joi retorted, her face growing warm with anger. "Is it because I don't wear skirts and dresses? Or that I prefer to wear my hair in braids rather than get a perm every month? You don't even come to my games anymore."

Taylor interrupted Joi's attack. "All of my children are different, and that's okay. It doesn't mean I love one child any more than the other. And I go to your games when I can. It's hard to get away from the store during business hours." Taylor tapped the floor rapidly with her foot. "I have three other kids to divide my time between. I'm doing the best I can."

"You own the shop, Mother," Joi said, trying to maintain a respectful tone. Although she was encouraged to express her opinions, she was taught to do so calmly and in a manner that didn't designate blame. Lance, more so than her mother, stressed peace in their home. "You take off a whole weekend to go to a pageant with Leah, but you can't spare a few hours once a week to be in the stands for me?" Joi asked, surprised at the words that came out of her mouth. "And what about the sneakers I wanted last month?"

"That's enough, Joi." Taylor stood to her feet. "You didn't need another pair of sneakers. You have fifty pairs thrown around in this junky room. If you cleaned up or organized a little better, you'd know that."

Joi threw her hands in the air and let them fall into her lap. "You told me you didn't have any money, but then Leah showed up with a new gown for her pageant."

"She needed that to be in the show. You knew we were saving for that dress," Taylor responded defensively. "You act like I never do anything for you. You need things for basketball that the other kids have to give up luxuries for, too. I didn't know I had to keep a record of who gets what around here."

Joi was silent. Her point had gotten lost. She didn't mean for the discussion to turn into an account of all that Taylor had done for each of her children. She just wanted her mother to see that her love was not evenly divided amongst her daughters and admit the reason why.

"You need to stop focusing on all that you feel you missed out on and how bad you think I'm treating you, and thank God that He gave you parents like me and Lance." Taylor walked to the door. "You're blessed, Joi. You're kidding yourself if you believe Jerome would've been half as good as we are."

"You didn't give him a chance to be a father to me," Joi fired back. If Lance were home, she'd be in trouble. Joi knew she had gone too far with her questions but couldn't help herself. Her pain was great, and she was determined to make Taylor understand that. "Did you ask him to stay away?"

Taylor ignored her and faced the door, her hand firmly hugging the knob.

"I want to meet him," Joi said matter-of-factly.

Taylor spun around. "What?"

"I want to meet my real father," she repeated.

"Okay, look, enough is enough. I know you're upset with me, but I'm not going to tolerate too much more of your mouth," Taylor bellowed. "And I don't know where Jerome is, so let this be."

"What about that lady from the store today?" Joi asked, refreshing her mother's memory. "Maybe she knows where to find him."

Taylor stared at Joi long enough to make her feel uncomfortable. "I'll see what I can do," she said and left the room.

Joi sat on her half-made bed and hugged the stuffed zebra Markus had won at a college festival. She didn't pray as much as she should and, in her mind, for good reason. It seemed like the more she prayed for her mother's love, the tougher she was on her. Even though she thought her prayers went unanswered, Joi did believe in God. He had given her a gift. With no formal training or mentor to guide her, she picked up a basketball one day and out-scored children who had played the sport for years. God was the only logical explanation for her talent.

Joi squeezed the stuffed animal with all her strength and begged God to make an exception. "Please bring my real father to me," she whispered. For some reason, she believed Jerome would make a difference in her life.

* * *

The stench in the McDonald's ladies room was strong, but the few women gathered in front of the mirror didn't seem to mind. Joi covered her nose and mouth with her hand, and kicked open the door of an empty stall. The lock was broken, so Rayven had to hold it in place. In record time, Joi relieved herself of the liter of water she'd consumed over the last hour, taking as few breaths as possible.

It was Friday night, and Joi had come up with a plan to get her out of the house for most of the evening. She was supposed to be with Rayven rehearsing a presentation for an upcoming English project. With little argument or debate, Taylor had made this night an exception and al-lowed her to go to Rayven's house to practice the assign-ment. Since their conversation last week about Jerome, Taylor had not been as stringent with her rules. Joi be-lieved it was an effort to avoid further confrontation on the subject.

Joi and Rayven had studied together on many occa-sions, so there was no need for Taylor to confirm the arrangement with Rayven's mother. The toughest part of Joi's plan was convincing Rayven to go along with it. All she had to do was ask for permission to go to what many high school students had labeled "Club McDonald's" on 40th Street. This was not an unusual request for the girls on a Friday night, so Rayven's mother agreed to let them go. Tonight, however, the girls used McDonald's as a decoy. They were actually going to Markus's new apartment. He and his roommates were hosting a housewarming, and Joi was determined to be there for the celebration.

"Remember, we can't stay late," Rayven tried to whisper as she held the stall door in place. "My sister is going to meet us back here at eleven-thirty."

Joi flushed the toilet with the bottom of her baby blue Timberland boots then pushed the door open with her elbow. "I know," she said, not wanting to say more than absolutely necessary.

"We better get moving," Rayven urged. "We have to walk three blocks to get to his house from here."

Joi gave her a short reply. "One second." She wanted to get a good look at herself before walking into Markus's new place. This was the first time she'd get to actually meet some of his friends. It was important that she make a good impression.

The same young ladies were still in front of the mirror competing for their own space, primping and prodding at their faces and hair. They laughed and chatted about the fine men seated at various tables as they complimented one another's outfits.

Joi couldn't wait any longer. She wanted to leave the foul smelling space before it seeped into her clothes. She recognized one of the girls from a church outing and tapped her shoulder lightly. "Excuse me. Can I just get a quick look?"

All three girls looked at Joi as if she had asked a rude question, but got the hint that they were taking too long.

"Sure," one girl said, and in unison they perched imitation designer bags on their arms and pranced out the door.

"How silly did they sound?" Rayven laughed when the

bathroom was clear, her hand covering her nose. "I sure hope I don't sound that desperate." She checked that the tiny curls in her urban Mohawk cut were in place as she strained to get a glimpse of her face through the tarnished mirror. Next, Rayven smoothed on another layer of a bronze-colored eye shadow.

"You don't," Joi affirmed.

Bending and squatting at odd angles to get better views of their long and fit bodies, Joi and Rayven made certain they were presentable enough for a college party. When they were satisfied, the girls rushed out of McDonald's and charged down Walnut Street as best they could without breaking into a sweat.

A small mound of college students were gathered on Markus's porch, socializing when they reached his apartment.

"Eleven-thirty," Rayven reminded Joi as they grew closer.

"I know, Ray. Just be cool. We won't be late," Joi responded and slowly walked up the concrete steps, searching for her boyfriend or any familiar face.

The girls tried to make their way inside, but they were stopped by a five-foot six, brawny guy wearing fraternity paraphernalia. He introduced himself as Wayne and bragged about being a third-year engineering major.

Before the girls could state their credentials, they were whisked away by Markus.

"Make sure you bring the one with the Mohawk back," Wayne yelled as Joi and Rayven followed Markus inside.

"He lives upstairs," Markus said to Rayven. "He's one of the smarter brothers in the building. Just your type," he joked.

Rayven twisted her top lip. "Not really. He's all right-looking, but way too short."

The girls shared a laugh. Meeting boys they were attracted to had been a challenge since they were in ninth grade. Standing at heights of five-nine and five-eleven, they were either too young or too tall for the men they wanted to pursue.

Markus gave the girls a tour of his new place and introduced them as "good friends" to his two roommates. When the tour concluded, members of the football team had entered, all wearing matching jackets, and Markus told Joi to make herself at home. "I need to tend to some of the other guests for a while," he said.

Not knowing what to do, Joi and Rayven decided to leave the smoke-filled domain and mingle with the people outside.

Wayne, or Too Short, as they had tagged him, gravitated to Rayven almost as quickly as her feet hit the porch. "Can I talk to you, beautiful?" he asked and grabbed her hand.

Rayven jerked it away, pursing her lips to decline his advance, but Joi responded before she had the opportunity to. "Go ahead," Joi insisted. "I'll be sitting by the dee-jay table when you're done."

Rayven squinted her eyes in disbelief, and Joi walked away giggling to herself. She wanted Rayven to have some fun for a change. Maybe Too Short could help her relax. They only had an hour before it was time to leave.

A full moon overshadowed the front porch, and Joi was drawn to its beauty. Sitting alone on an old railing and staring at the sky, she sipped on the same lemonade for the last twenty minutes. Markus had surfaced once since leaving Joi's side, and had handed her the drink currently in her hand. She had tried to mingle, but quickly realized she had little in common with the folks in attendance. They discussed politics, statistics class, rent, professors, and studying for finals. Besides her casual denim attire and her interest in sports, she had very little to contribute.

She was too embarrassed to mention that she was in high school, so she shied away from talking at all.

She took off her jacket and placed it over the railing. For November, the weather was surprisingly warm. The leaves on the trees had yet to turn colors and fall to the ground.

Glancing across the porch, Joi noticed Rayven's eyes roll every time Wayne whispered something into her ear. Joi knew she was in for a mouthful later. Rayven had tried to escape him several times, but wherever she moved, Wayne moved with her.

Surrounded by empty beer bottles and clouds of smoke, Joi wondered if this was what college life would be like— total freedom to do as you pleased. She didn't drink and couldn't stand the smell of cigarettes, but the taste of freedom was pleasing to her senses.

Through the window of Markus's first-floor apartment, she spotted him sharing a smoke with some friends. Feeling her stares, Markus turned around and winked. She blew a kiss his way and jumped off the rail in hopes that he'd come to join her.

Instead, two girls, one of whom she recognized from pictures in Markus's old dorm room, headed her way. He had explained that the girl was a very close friend, just one of the crew. She and another girl stood next to Joi, and shared Buffalo wings from a small bowl. They smiled politely then talked to one another as if she weren't there. The girl from the picture lit a cigarette and grabbed a Heineken bottle from the cooler beside her.

Joi watched the young college woman, somewhat amazed. She couldn't have been over the age of twenty-one. Joi had never seen a female that age drink anything stronger than an ice-cold Dr. Pepper.

After standing next to Joi for several minutes, the young

woman finally initiated a conversation. "So, how do you know the guys?" she asked.

"Markus is my boyfriend," Joi stated proudly.

"Oh," the girl said, a look of surprise and confusion on her face. She turned and asked her friend, "He and Eboni broke up?"

"They broke up months ago," the friend replied, her fingers covered with Buffalo wing sauce.

"Really? She was such a nice girl."

Joi didn't like her response but played it off. She swallowed a large amount of her warm drink and looked back inside the house. Markus was no longer in view.

"I'm sure you're a nice girl, too," the girl replied, though Joi felt her response was phony and insincere. "I'm Nyemah," she said. "Markus and I have lots of classes together." She paused long enough to puff her cigarette. "He's a cool dude."

A questioning look crossed Joi's face. If Nyemah was such a good friend, shouldn't she know about Joi? Joi pretended she was glad to meet her. "My name is Joi," she replied.

Nyemah chugged quite a bit of her alcoholic beverage then stared at Joi. "You gonna nurse that lemonade all night?" She waved the beer bottle in front of Joi. "You ought to try some of this."

"I'm good." Joi politely swatted the bottle away.

Nyemah lost her balance, and in just enough time to rescue her from falling down the steps, Markus appeared. "You need to sit down for a minute, sis," he said. "You're gonna hurt yourself." Making sure Nyemah was stable before letting her go, he held tight to her arm. "Joi can't drink. Ain't that right, Boss? I have to keep my basketball star healthy." Markus flashed a winning smile, and Joi blushed.

"A little beer never hurt anyone," Nyemah said and laid

her almost empty bottle on the edge of the deejay table. She placed her cigarette in between her lips and bounced up and down to an old Nas hit.

"Pay her no mind. You don't have to do anything you don't want to," Markus said and put his right arm around Joi's small waist. "C'mon, let's go inside."

Joi tossed her lemonade in the garbage pail below the porch, grabbed her jacket and followed her man inside to his bedroom. In the bright light, Markus looked even more handsome, his naturally wavy hair and thick eyebrows dark as coal. Posed in the doorway, the collar of his button-down shirt was flipped up, his jeans sagged, and his Timberlands was without a scratch. He looked like a model for a hip-hop or urban magazine. An average height for a man, Markus towered over Joi only a few inches. Model Tyson Beckford was no match for her baby. If he had asked her to drink with Nyemah, she would have. Markus could've talked her into almost anything.

Joi admired Markus's new dwelling. Now that he had his own place, the two of them would have more time together alone.

Markus had decorated his room similar to what his dorm room had been, same black and grey color scheme, same position of the furniture, and same framed pictures.

Joi walked over to his window and tripped over a blue Burberry knapsack. "This is cute," she said, picking it up from the floor. "I've never seen a blue one." She placed the bag on the closet doorknob. "Where you'd get it?"

"It was a gift," he answered. "You okay?"

Her nervousness must have been apparent. "I'm fine. Why?"

Markus shut and locked the door then walked over to her. "I saw the way you looked at Nyemah," he replied and kissed Joi's cheek.

"She's interesting."

"She's cool," Markus replied and sat down on his bed. He tapped the space next to him. "Crazy, but cool. You'll learn to like her."

Joi smiled as she sat next to him. His statement made her happy. It insinuated that she would be around for some time. "I heard someone say that you were going to be a guest host on Power ninety-nine," she said.

Markus rubbed her thigh. "Yeah, I'm excited about that. I get a chance to showcase my skills."

Markus gently nudged Joi backward, and she lay flat on the bed. Slowly, he positioned himself on top of her.

Going along with the flow, Joi initiated a kiss. Tasting remnants of whatever Markus was smoking, she turned her head away, and he eased up just a little. Joi turned to her side, and her top raised enough to show the tattoo on her back.

Although Markus had seen the tattoo before, he traced the words with his pinky and said, "This is nice." Normally, Joi didn't mind his touch, but tonight it felt different, more sensual. "We've been kickin' it for a while. I think we might be ready to . . ." he stated and reached up the back of her shirt.

Markus didn't have to finish the sentence. Joi knew what he was implying. Now that he had his own room, it was only a matter of time before they'd begin a more intimate relationship.

"You're not ready for me," she toyed and removed his hand. But the truth was that Joi wasn't ready for him. She was still very much a virgin.

Markus chuckled low and kissed her again. "Are you on the pill?"

Joi's eyes widened. "No."

"I think it's time you get some, don't you?"

Joi didn't know what to say. Perhaps his intoxicated

state was the root of his sudden aggressive manner. Going on birth control was serious. She hadn't even considered it until now. She inched away from Markus and stared him in the eyes. She was afraid to tell him no. With his good looks and charisma, he was bound to find someone to take care of his needs if she wouldn't.

"Who's Eboni?" she blurted, hoping the topic would dissuade them from pursuing the birth control issue.

Markus pushed himself up and leaned on one elbow. "She's an old girlfriend. Why?"

"She goes to Saint Joe's, too?"

"She used to. She transferred to some school in Maryland last semester. Haven't seen her since." Markus rolled on top of Joi again and kissed her neck. Softly, he spoke into her ear. "She's history. You're the one that I love now."

Did he say he loved me? Hearing those words, Joi succumbed to Markus's embrace. Although nervous, she caressed him back.

Eventually, the situation became too intense. Markus's breathing increased, and his hands wandered into unchartered territory. Joi couldn't have gained control of the situation if she tried. *Jesus*, she prayed silently.

Knock, knock, knock.

Engrossed in the moment, Markus ignored the pounding on the door.

Knock, knock, knock.

"Joi!" Rayven yelled over the loud music.

Relieved, Joi wiggled from beneath Markus and said, "I better get that." She straightened her clothes and rushed to open the door.

Rayven pushed her way inside. "I knew this was a bad idea," she raved. "Guess who just walked in?" From the look on her face, Joi thought it might be Jesus Himself. Rayven paced the floor, stopping briefly to stare at Markus lying on the bed. She then looked at Joi, her eyes saying she knew what they were doing. "Linda is here. You know how close she is to your mother. What if she calls her?" Rayven asked frantically. "My soul's going to burn for lying to my mother."

"Don't exaggerate, Ray. Did she see you?" Joi asked.

"She might have, but I ran back here so fast, you would've thought I was Superwoman." Rayven walked briskly from one end of the room to the other. "God is trying to tell us we don't belong here."

"Calm down, Ray," Markus barked from the bed, clearly angry that his mood had been busted. "There are so many people in this apartment, she probably didn't even see you."

"Let's go," Rayven demanded and pulled Joi by the arm. "Maybe we can get out of here unnoticed. We don't have much time before my sister comes looking for us at McDonald's anyway."

"I'll call you tomorrow," Joi said to Markus, praying he wasn't too mad, but thrilled that their previous activity had ceased.

Carefully, the girls maneuvered through the dark room full of people. They were almost home free, until Wayne stepped in front of them, spilling some of his beer on Joi's jacket. "Leaving so soon?" he asked Rayven. "Can I call you later?"

Rayven sighed. "I have to hurry. I'm going to miss my ride."

"Get her number from Markus," Joi interjected, and Rayven popped her shoulder.

"I'll do that," he yelled as the girls rushed down the porch steps.

When they reached the bottom step, Joi wrapped her jacket around her waist. As she tied the sleeves into a knot, she looked back at the apartment for the last time that night, and through the semi-fogged window, her eyes locked with Linda's. Joi quickly turned around and pulled Rayven's arm. Together they sprinted back to McDonald's, not once stopping to catch their breath.

"Thank you, Jesus. We still have seven minutes," Rayven exclaimed, panting heavily once they were safely inside the restaurant. "Whew, that could've gotten ugly."

Joi didn't want to tell Rayven that Linda spotted them. That would only send her into a panic attack. "I don't know why you're so worried. Your sister is cool. Mother is the one we need to be afraid of," Joi told her.

"I don't want to take any chances. Want something to drink?"

"Just some water," answered Joi.

When Rayven went to the counter to get their drinks, Joi pulled out her cell phone and sent Markus a message. She wanted to make sure she hadn't lost him for good.

Minutes later, he texted back: *Call u n the morn. I luv u.* Joi felt warm inside. *Ditto,* she replied back.

Yes. Thank you, Jesus. She prayed Linda wouldn't ruin the evening by telling her mother.

Joi walked into the house a few minutes after midnight. Taylor was awake in the family room watching an old Denzel Washington movie. "Hey," Joi said as she passed her mother and made her way to the stairs.

"Finish your project?" Taylor asked.

Not interested in a lengthy conversation, Joi simply said, "Yes," and continued to her room.

"Joi?" Taylor called.

"Yes," she said, holding on to the handrail. Joi feared Linda had called her mother.

Taylor walked into the next room and partially up the stairs. She sniffed the air a few times. "Have you been smoking?" Taylor moved even closer, and Joi backed away. "And drinking, too?"

"We went to McDonald's after we finished working on the report," responded Joi.

"You went to McDonald's?"

"Yes, McDonald's," Joi said, upset that she had to repeat herself. "I guess I stayed in their bathroom too long."

"You don't reek of an odor that strong from being in a bathroom too long, Joi." Taylor climbed one more stair. "I know you weren't at Rayven's, so where were you?"

"We did go to McDonald's," Joi stressed.

Taylor climbed another stair, separating them now by only one step. "I'm only gonna ask you one more time."

Joi had never been hit by her mother, but something in the way Taylor looked at her said that tonight might be the first time. She backed up the next stair and stuttered through a different explanation, praying Taylor didn't know the truth. "R-Rayven's sister s-stopped at her f-f-friend's house before b-bringing me home."

"A friend's house, huh?" Taylor asked, her face saying she didn't believe one word. "Let me see what you and Ray worked on tonight?"

Joi rolled here eyes and whipped her backpack off her shoulder. It was a good thing she had something to show. Taking a thick blue binder out of her bag, Joi showed her mother the rough draft. "This is the report," she said then flipped through some of the pages. "And these are the notes."

Taylor snatched the binder from her hand and read the pages in more detail. Not yet satisfied, her eyes shifted from Joi to the binder several times. "Did you have something to drink or smoke?"

"No," Joi snapped.

Taylor slammed the binder closed. "I don't believe you."

"I didn't have anything," Joi said with an attitude, then called her mother's bluff. "You can ask, Ray."

"You knew you weren't supposed to leave Rayven's house. You're strictly prohibited from anything unrelated to school until your next report card," Taylor reminded her. "I don't know what your problem is, young lady, but I'm tired of it." Taylor threw the binder at Joi, and it fell on her foot. "Your father will deal with you when he gets back from Gram's." Fuming, Taylor marched down the steps and back into the family room.

Joi sighed with relief. Linda had not called; otherwise Taylor would've mentioned it. Joi glanced at her watch. It was just after midnight. *I'll be asleep by that time*, she said to herself then picked up her binder and stormed off to her bedroom.

Chapter Nine

~ *Taylor* ~

Taylor's internal alarm went off as it did every morning at seven. Stumbling out of bed, she bumped into the treadmill Lance bought a few years ago for Christmas. Neither one of them had used it all year. He was supposed to move it into the basement, but was waiting on a friend to help him. Taylor rubbed her shoulder and pushed the exercise machine closer to the wall and out of her way. If Lance didn't get their bedroom together by Christmas, she was going to make the changes herself, even if it meant hiring people to do it for them.

The movement had not disturbed her husband at all. Judging from the deep bass of his snores, Taylor knew he was tired. He'd been working nonstop on Gram's house for some time, and his lack of sleep was beginning to take its toll. It was after one o'clock when he had dragged himself in the house last night. Taylor had tried to explain Joi's latest episode while Lance changed for bed, but as soon as his head hit the pillow, he was sound asleep.

Taylor used the light coming through a small slit in the curtains as a guide to her prayer corner. She and God had a lot to talk about this morning. If Joi was going to make it through high school while they lived under the same roof, Taylor was definitely going to need God's help. She read another chapter from the book of Judges then communed with God in silence.

Thirty minutes later, muffled voices outside her door interrupted her sacred time. The twins were awake. Almost every Saturday they thought of a new prank to try on their sisters. Their routine usually ended with one of Taylor's daughters chasing the twins through the house or yelling for them to stop. As she listened to the patter of feet tromp down the stairs, Taylor concluded her prayer session. It was time for the weekend to begin.

She got up from her chair and leaned over an old TV stand to reach a robe hanging off the closet door. Unable to grab it, she leaned in further and almost fell, causing the stand to roll into the bed.

Lance snorted a few times before his snores stopped completely and he opened his eyes. "Morning," he said, his voice groggy and deep as he lay on his back.

"Morning," she replied as she tied the belt of the robe around her waist. She removed the scarf on her head and fluffed her short curls. Standing over her husband and rubbing her silk scarf on her arm, Taylor said, "You must've been really tired. You fell asleep on me."

Lance grabbed the extra pillow on the bed and stacked it under his head. "I had a long day."

"Do you remember anything I said before you dozed off?" she asked.

Lance thought for a minute, then covered his face with his hand. "Was it about Joi?"

"It's been about Joi for the past two months," she told him. "I really need you to talk her. What do you and the boys have planned for today?"

Lance cleared his throat. "I'll be at Gram's most of the

day. I want everything done before Thanksgiving next week."

Taylor lifted the shades to let some natural light into the room and dropped her scarf on the dresser. "Can you make some time for her?" she asked. "We need to address this. She's really getting out of hand."

"Okay," Lance said and sat up, "but can you give me all the details again? I only remember the part about a party."

Taylor circled the room, throwing knickknacks and clothes out of her way as she recounted the story. She may have exaggerated a few points, but she wanted Lance to understand that their style of discipline was not working for Joi.

"I'll pick her up from work today. Maybe we'll go out to eat or something," Lance said and lay back down.

"Thank you," she said and changed the subject. "I talked to Gram yesterday. I'm going to make the pies this year." Taylor didn't mention that she practically had to beg her mother-in-law to allow her to do so. "So I'm going to get the shopping done this morning. Linda's gonna take Joi to work and Leah to dance for me. Then I have a meeting at church at eleven. Oh, I need you pick up Leah, too."

"Sounds good. I'm sure Gram would love to spend some time with her," he replied and buried his head under the covers for a few extra minutes of sleep.

"I'll have the twins come get you when breakfast is ready," Taylor said and closed the door behind her.

Faint noises coming from Joi's room caught Taylor's attention as she walked down the hall. The twins were in their room entertaining one another with jokes they'd made up, and Leah was watching television. Who was Joi talking to?

Curious, Taylor walked lightly on her feet to Joi's door. She must've been talking to someone on her phone. It wasn't even eight o'clock. From the nature of her high-pitched laughs, Taylor could tell that a young man was on the other end of the line. Joi was not banned from talking to boys. She was sixteen. It was unrealistic to believe that she didn't have male friends. But at this hour on a Saturday morning? Who and what was so important that the call couldn't wait until after she at least had breakfast?

Taylor put her ear close to the door, hoping to hear tidbits of the conversation. Maybe she'd learn the truth behind the streety smells Joi brought home yesterday. Eavesdropping was wrong, but she knew Joi would never be honest about last night. Placing her fingertips on the door, Taylor pressed her left ear against the wooden frame.

"Hey, Mother," Taylor heard from behind and jumped. She pushed herself away from the door and turned around slowly, her face flushed with embarrassment.

In Superman pajamas he'd yet to outgrow, Tyrell stood less than a foot away. "Can we spend the night at Gram's tonight?"

"It's okay with me. But ask your father," she said, praying he wouldn't question her actions. Using her knuckles, Taylor tapped Joi's door, and seconds later it swung open. With untamed braids and crusty eyes, Joi stared at Taylor as if she was invading her private space.

Tyrell poked fun at his oldest sister's appearance and ducked behind his mother for safety. Shielding her son, Taylor looked at Joi and said, "Linda's coming to get you this morning."

"You're not going to work?" Tyrell asked. "Are you coming to Gram's with us?"

"Not this time, sweetie. I need to pick up a few things for Thanksgiving. Your grandmother wants me to bake some pies," Taylor answered, her eyes glued on her daughter. Something about her wasn't right.

"Ummm. I can't wait for your sweet potato pie. Can you put caramel on top?" Tyrell requested and freed himself from Taylor's protection.

"Yes," she replied then shifted her full attention back to Joi.

With the cell phone wedged between her ear and shoulder, Joi pulled up her striped flannel pajama pants and asked, "What time will she be here?"

Joi's nonchalant attitude was bordering rude, but Taylor let it slide. "About an hour."

Resuming the conversation with the person on the other end of the line, Joi turned around, and her pajama bottoms dropped a little, exposing a small portion of her lower back.

Taylor blinked several times. The foreign image painted on Joi's skin had to be a figment of her imagination. She rubbed her eyes. Maybe there was something clouding her vision.

Joi tried to shut the door, but it wouldn't budge. Taylor had stopped it with her hand, chipping two of her freshly manicured nails. "Lift up your shirt," she commanded calmly.

"Let me call you back," Joi huffed then flipped her cell closed. She tugged at her baby tee, trying to cover herself completely.

On impulse Taylor raised the top herself and gasped. She knew her daughter *couldn't* have a tattoo. But a basketball the size of a silver dollar was etched on Joi's lower back with the words *Boss Lady* scripted underneath. "When did you do this?"

"A few weeks ago," Joi said as if she'd done nothing wrong.

"I don't know what's gotten into you." Taylor studied the image closely, checking for any sign of infection or swelling. The flames that emerged from the left side of the round basketball showcased someone's fine artistic ability. "What on earth possessed you to do this?"

"Everyone on the team got one," Joi responded, infuriating Taylor even more.

"I don't care what the team decided to do. You didn't have my permission to mark your body," Taylor yelled. "If this is what you're going to spend your money on, I guess I'll have to take control of that, too."

"I don't see what the big deal is. Nobody's even gonna see it."

"You can't just do what you want to around here. You're still a child, and until you become an adult and no longer living at 5032 Walnut Street, you have to live by the rules." Taylor tried her best not to shout. "You can't just do things behind my back and expect to get away with it."

Joi threw the phone on her bed and walked to the corner of the room. "Just like you couldn't get away with keeping Jerome a secret," she mumbled under her breath as she gathered toiletries from her closet.

"Watch yourself. You're not too big for me to use a belt," Taylor said, though Joi knew her mother's words were a harmless threat.

"Have you spoken to Jerome yet? It's been a week," Joi said as she tossed her toiletries in a small purple, plastic basket.

Taylor had not even attempted to contact him, praying that Joi would eventually forget about it. "No, I haven't. But what I do know is that you're making your life here more difficult than it has to be. If you want to be on punishment for the rest of the year, so be it. And another thing . . ." Taylor kicked the clothes in the middle of the floor aside. "If you keep this up, you're gonna find yourself watching your basketball games from the bench."

"What's the problem in here, ladies?" Lance said from the doorway, catching both women off guard. "It's too early for all this commotion."

Taylor looked at her husband with fire in her eyes. "Your child has a tattoo."

Lance looked at Joi, disappointment on his face, and

she lowered her head. "Go ahead, show him," urged Taylor. "Your precious angel thinks she can do whatever she wants. What she needs to do is clean up this dirty room. It takes two seconds to put clothes in the hamper," Taylor said, annoyed at the mess.

Purple basket in hand, Joi stepped away from her closet and rested all of her weight on her right hip. "I didn't think it was going to cause so much of a problem."

Taylor grew impatient and lifted Joi's shirt. "Will you look at this?" she said to Lance.

"Taylor," Lance said. "Why don't you let me—"

"You don't pay attention to me anyway. It's not like you really care about what I do," Joi snapped.

"Joi!" Lance yelled in a tone he rarely used, and rushed to stand in between the two females.

"I've had about enough of your mouth and nasty attitude," Taylor replied sharply. "I think missing a few games is what you need. Maybe then you'll have a change of heart."

Joi threw her miniature basket on the bed, her body soap and lotion falling on the floor. "You can't do that, Mother. The team needs me." Joi looked to Lance for assistance.

"I can, and the team will be fine without you."

"Tay," Lance said and reached for his wife's waist, "let's talk about this later. Leah is going to be late for dance class."

"Everything is later with you. You need to deal with her now," Taylor enforced. She and Lance had agreed not to disagree in front of their children, but she was fed up.

"You're gonna mess up the team's balance if I can't play," Joi cried.

"Spare me the drama. This wouldn't be an issue if your grades were better and you hadn't come home smelling like beer and, God only knows, what else," Taylor responded.

"I can't wait to leave this place!" Joi yelled and picked up the fallen objects from the floor. "You might as well put bars on the windows."

Taylor's neck snapped. "If this is what your teen years are going to be like, it certainly will be a prison around here, sweetheart."

Lance had had enough. He grabbed Taylor's hands and pulled her toward the door. "You're going to make the other kids nervous with all this chaos."

"Daddy, can you talk to her?" Joi pleaded. "The team needs me to play."

Frustrated, Lance looked back at his daughter and said, "Just get ready for work."

"Things are never fair when it comes to me." Joi pouted.

"You should have talked to us before—" The tunes of a Chris Brown song coming from Joi's cell phone interrupted him.

"Don't even think about answering that," Taylor said and charged to Joi's bed to get the phone before she had a chance to. "I'll hold on to this for a while."

Joi looked at her father, and he shrugged his shoulders. "I have to agree with your mother on that one. Sorry, Boss."

"I can't believe you're doing this, Mother," Joi said, obviously devastated. "Can I at least see who called?"

"Not a chance," Taylor answered, appalled. "And we'll talk more about that tattoo when I get home tonight."

Joi folded her arms. "I don't want to go to work today."

"Too bad," Taylor remarked, shocked at her daughter's boldness. "And that's non-negotiable. In the meantime, you need to make sure your shirt covers that rising flame on your back." Taylor stormed past Lance without looking at him and exited Joi's bedroom.

The twins, who had been standing by their door listening to the argument, pretended to clean their room as she walked by. "One of you, get in the bathroom now!" Taylor yelled.

"But Leah has dance class. She has to go in first," Dennis replied timidly.

Taylor hesitated and sighed. "Well, somebody needs to get in there soon!" She continued down the hall and slammed her bedroom door behind her, letting out a moan loud enough for everyone in the house to hear. Taylor plopped on her bed so hard, she heard a spring pop. *God, please help me! What am I doing wrong?*

Taylor's eyes fell on the family portrait hanging on the wall. That picture was starting to get on her nerves. She got up from the bed and snatched it off the wall then stuffed it in the back of her wardrobe closet. She stayed in the closet, Joi's cell phone in her hand, and scrolled through her contact list, looking for any unrecognizable names.

"Now you're violating her privacy?" Lance asked.

Taylor had not heard him enter the room. "There's no privacy in this house," she answered. She flipped the cell phone closed and surfed through her clothes for something to wear.

Lance walked inside the tight space, making it difficult for Taylor to view all her options. She looked down, his ashy feet in plain view, and made a mental note to buy more Eucerin. It was the only lotion strong enough for his skin during the fall and winter months.

"I agree that getting the tattoo was wrong," Lance began, "but there has to be some other way to reprimand her. We can't keep using basketball as a threat."

"Then you tell me what to use. Basketball is the only thing she responds to," Taylor stressed. "If you keep defending Joi, she's going to run all over you, and we'll have more than just bad grades and tattoos to worry about."

Afraid to admit things weren't going as he had hoped, Lance said, "It's not going to get to that point. I'll talk to her this evening and try to get to the bottom of everything."

Taylor reached for a multi-colored knit sweater she had purchased at Marshalls and grabbed a pair of light denim Calvin Klein jeans. "Communication may have worked for you and your sisters, but not all kids respond to that. What Joi needs is a good lashing."

Lance knew his wife was upset, so he didn't press the issue any further. He walked out of the closet and turned on the television.

Clothes in hand, Taylor went through her extensive nail polish collection and chose a color to match her outfit. Next, she opened the closet that housed all of her handbags—Dooney and Bourke, Gucci, Louis Vuitton, and her all-time favorite, Coach. She chose a black leather Via Spiga clutch to match the shoes someone donated to her store, and which she later bought. She gathered her things in her arms and proceeded to the door.

"Before you go, I think we need to pray," Lance said.

Stubbornly, Taylor looked to the ceiling. She knew it was the right thing to do, but she wasn't in the mood to pray with her husband.

At the moment, he felt like the enemy. "Tay," Lance said, "if we don't seek God for help, there won't be any peace in this house for a very long time."

Taylor turned around slowly. She loved that Lance wanted to seek God for guidance, but wished he'd give her some time to get her mind in the right place. She placed her clothes on the bed, and Lance stood to his feet.

"By the way," he said as he took her hands, "and this is my thinking, not Joi's. I'd like you to consider giving Joi her phone back."

"You've got to be kidding me," Taylor remarked.

"I know what you're thinking, but I'm not taking her side. I just think she needs to have her phone in case of an emergency," he explained. "She travels to and from the library every day."

Lance was right, but Taylor didn't want to admit it. "I didn't have one at sixteen," she argued.

"You grew up in a different time. Can we not debate about this right now? We both have a lot to do today." Lance bowed his head. "Let's pray."

Taylor tried to concentrate on her husband's requests to God, but was distracted by her thoughts. She would give the phone back as her husband asked, but not before Joi understood who the real boss was. Things were about to get a lot tougher for her.

There were about fifty people inside the meeting room at New Life Baptist Church when Taylor walked in. She didn't like being late to the women's retreat committee meetings, but she had a lot on her mind. Since Joi found out about Jerome, the relationship between them was even more strained than before. To make matters worse, she wanted to meet him.

Taylor wasn't prepared, nor was she ready, to open that can of worms. She had promised Jerome that she wouldn't interfere in his life anymore than she already had. Although Jerome was just as much at fault for the affair, Taylor accepted most of the blame. She knew he was married and forced the relationship anyway. No matter how many times she prayed, Taylor couldn't shake her guilt.

Taylor spotted her friends in the front of the room. As officers of the planning committee, she and her friends always sat next to the first lady's table. Sitting in an available chair, she dropped her tote bag on the floor. "Good morning, ladies," she said, her eyes puffy from the tears she had cried in the parking lot.

"Rough morning?" Sherry asked, noticing the redness of her eyes.

Friends since junior high school, Sherry knew more about Taylor than anyone alive. Taylor thought marriage would change their bond, but their friendship had stood the best and worst of times.

"I had to make sure Joi was ready for work, Leah for dance class, the twins for a weekend at their grandmother's. I'm shocked I don't have on one blue and one red shoe."

"I don't miss those days," Kara offered with a grin.

Of the three, Taylor was the only one with school-aged children. Taylor and Kara met as SEPTA drivers for the city of Philadelphia over fifteen years ago. Their friendship was unique in that Kara and her husband were once good friends with Jerome and his wife. The entire situation caused a strain for everyone, and after Joi was born, Kara made the decision to sever all ties with Jerome's family. It was sad that a long-term friendship had to end. Kara wouldn't even accept the role of godmother to Joi. And Taylor agreed not to so much as whisper Jerome's name in her presence.

"It gets harder as they get older," Taylor said without realizing the sadness in her tone. She took out a notebook with last month's minutes in them and placed it on the table.

Kara leaned over and touched her hand. "Well, you made it, and there's still three minutes left before we officially start. The first lady's not even here yet."

"Believe it or not, I look forward to these meetings." Taylor sighed. "This may sound strange, but I actually get to rest when I'm here. There's no one screaming, 'Mother, can I have this,' or 'Mother, can I do that.' Or my all-time favorite, 'Mother, that's not fair.' "

"No one told you to have all those kids," Sherry teased.

The only one without children, partly because she didn't marry until the age of forty-two, Sherry believed that babies were raised best when their parents could run after them without gasping for air. Although Sherry did not want to bear children, she claimed Taylor's as her own.

"If you're still thinking about adoption, you'll see what I mean," Taylor added.

Sherry shook her head and laughed. "I don't think so. That ship has long sailed off to sea. Watching you and Kara has been plenty enough for me over the years. Between the two of you, I'm good."

"Well, feel free to come and get your goddaughter whenever you want. Her hormones have kicked in, and I'm about ready to put her out." Taylor laughed to keep from crying.

With her children well over twenty years of age, Kara had already experienced the "puberty blues." "This too shall pass." She chuckled. "It's just a phase, my dear. Stephanie used to act up, too. More so than the others. She couldn't wait to get out of the house, and I couldn't wait to see her go. But when she went away to college, I must have received a letter *every* week. And we talked on the phone every day."

"And they're best friends now," Sherry noted.

"Trust me when I say it took lots of prayer to get where we are today," Kara said. "Prayer and Advil. That girl was something else."

As the ladies continued to share stories about their children, one of the members, dressed in a fancy copper-colored suit, walked across the room and greeted them. Just from looking at her, one could tell that she was a true Southern belle. Having migrated from Georgia, the way she glided across the room was classy and pristine. "Sister Belle, I had to come over and give you a compliment." Her Southern drawl was slow. "I went to a sorority meeting this morning and almost everyone there commented on my suit. Do you have a business card or something I can hand out at the next meeting? The ladies were enamored with the design."

Taylor beamed at the possibility of new patrons. She reached into her clutch and pulled out her last ten cards. "Please let them know they're welcome anytime I'm open." Taylor took the opportunity to give a sales pitch. "Did you tell them that everything is gently used? I only accept the best. Just because the merchandise is previously owned doesn't mean it has to be ragged or unusable. *Thrift store prices without the thrift store appearance* is my motto."

"How long have you been around?" the sixty-something woman asked.

"Since my sixteen-year-old was in the womb."

"That long? Are you only located in Chestnut Hill?"

"Yes," Taylor replied, "I only have one store."

"You're sitting on a goldmine, Sister Belle. You should really consider opening a store in South Philly. I think you'd get much more business out there."

That goldmine remark sounded good to Taylor.

The lady dug in her purse and pulled out a business card. "Here's the name of a really good realtor. You should give her a call. She belongs to Sharon Baptist over near West Philly, but she knows a lot about commercial buildings downtown."

Years ago, Taylor considered opening a second shop, but her mother-in-law suggested she wait. The twins were only three years old at the time, and Gram had convinced Taylor to believe that adding another responsibility would be too much to handle. Hoping to gain Gram's love and remain on her good side, she agreed.

"Thank you," Taylor said. "I really appreciate your kind words and your support."

"Step out on faith," the Georgia peach replied and strolled back to her seat.

The light rumblings and side conversations in the room

came to a lull when the first lady walked in with a posse of female deacons. Gracefully, First Lady Robinson passed by the tables, greeting the members within range and waving to those she couldn't physically touch. Her cocoa skin looked flawless, and no matter what the situation, she always had an aura of peace surrounding her. "Good morning, ladies," she said, her voice raspy from a recent cold. "Sorry I'm late. My house was a little hectic this morning."

"No problem. We're all enjoying this fellowship," Sherry assured her.

"That's good to hear," the first lady responded. "Kara, do you have a minute to look over some figures before we begin?"

"I sure do," Kara answered and left the table.

Taylor watched them converse and tried to recall a time when her life was at peace. For the most part, her life had been filled with extreme emotional highs and lows—no in-betweens. Oddly enough, the one time she felt most at peace was after her car accident seventeen years ago. She was restricted to a hospital bed for over a week, suffering a broken leg and other minor bruises. The days she spent lying in the bed soothed her spirit. It was hard to explain, but she knew that God had touched her.

Just a year after the accident, Taylor joined New Life, started her own business, and had a baby. She'd been running non-stop ever since.

"You don't look like yourself, diva. What's up?" Sherry asked Taylor.

Taylor inched her chair closer to her best friend and quietly gave her a summary of the events that had transpired since they last talked.

As always, Sherry listened carefully. "You're better than me," she said when Taylor was done. "You let Jerome off way too easy. Always did. Call him! Let him explain himself for a change. He can't have my godbaby all upset."

"Your godbaby is too grown," Taylor said. "Besides, Jerome is doing the best he can, considering—"

"Considering what?" Sherry interrupted. "Don't give me the husband, father and poor old Renee scenario. He and Renee have been together long enough to handle this, and his kids are old enough to understand what happened."

Sherry was right, but Taylor felt the need to defend him. "He hasn't missed sending a check since I told him I was pregnant."

"You sound like he's doing you a favor. Money isn't the only way to raise a child."

"But it sure helps."

"You need to stop this madness and call him," Sherry said bluntly.

"I can't just spring Joi on him."

"You're not. Joi isn't a secret to him. Let him figure out how to tell his family. Joi is upset, and this isn't fair to her," Sherry said. "She wants to know who he is, and she has that right."

Knowing it was a weak excuse, Taylor said, "I don't know how to reach him in Chicago."

"His family is in Philly," Sherry snapped. "I'm sure Kara knows how to find him."

"You know she's not giving up his number, and I'm not gonna ask for it," Taylor said quietly.

Sherry sighed. "Then hop on over to his brother's house. He still lives in Yeadon, doesn't he?"

"I think so, but I can't get Brandon involved."

Sherry sucked her teeth. "You're too nice."

Taylor glossed over last month's meeting notes. With so many things already on her plate, this was something she definitely didn't want to deal with. "I know God doesn't give more than we can handle, but I feel like this is my fault. I feel like an avalanche is coming." Taylor scribbled on the piece of paper in front of her. "It's even starting to mess with my marriage."

"I'm not a minister like Kara, but I do know that God wouldn't punish you for something you did so many years ago. How does that saying go? He washes our sins away and makes us clean as snow. Something like that. You know what I mean."

Taylor smiled. She could always count on her friend for a good laugh. "But seriously," Sherry continued, "you're punishing yourself too much. If this is eating you up, do something about it. Calling Jerome gets my vote."

"What's going on?" Kara asked when she returned to the table. From the look on their faces, she could tell something was wrong.

Taylor knew she couldn't tell Kara the truth, so she said, "Thanksgiving at the in-laws this year."

"Really? That's not so bad, is it? It would give you a break."

Always the one to give the women a reality check, Sherry spoke up, "Now you know the Belle women are still mad at Tay because of the wedding."

Recalling the day Taylor and Lance exchanged nuptials, the friends tumbled over in laughter.

Initially, Lance's mother and his sisters were in charge of planning a traditional church wedding. After months of making decisions and attending meetings, Taylor decided that the process was too overwhelming. There was too much to do for a bunch of people she barely knew or never met. The only relatives she had at the time were her father's second family, and she wasn't that close to them at all.

One night during an argument over the guest list, Taylor exploded and called off the extravaganza. After a heated discussion with her then fiancé, Lance, they agreed that they should exchange vows in a more intimate setting. Together they chose a secluded island in Jamaica. There were to be no bridesmaids, no groomsmen, no expensive dresses, and no huge reception. Just close family and friends coming together to celebrate Taylor and Lance's union. But much to Taylor's surprise, her soon-to-be in-laws showed up at the ceremony wearing matching lavender gowns and sequin sandals, and insisted they be escorted down the aisle.

Taylor put her foot down when Gizelle, the youngest sister, asked if they could stand behind Lance during the ritual. To this day, any mention of the wedding was followed by a frown.

"Good morning, and sorry for the delay. I think we're ready to get started," a deaconess said from the front of the room, and the ladies controlled their snickers. "But first, let's open with a word of prayer."

As the deaconess prayed, Taylor replayed the conversation she had with Sherry. Contacting Jerome made sense, but there was no way it was going to happen. Taylor refused to interfere in his life again. Jerome had rejected her one too many times. She wasn't about to let him reject their daughter. Joi had a tough exterior, but her heart was fragile. If Taylor could do nothing else, she wanted to protect Joi's heart.

From the moment Taylor laid eyes on her firstborn, all of the bad things in her life seemed to disappear. When the nurse placed Joi in her arms for the first time and her tiny eyes opened, nothing but joy filled Taylor's spirit. She had prayed that Joi would bring peace and happiness to the lives of everyone she encountered. Though it didn't feel like it lately, Taylor believed that Joi would one day live up to her God-given name.

Chapter Ten

~ *Joi* ~

Joi was on the floor of Taylor's office surrounded by boxes. She was so upset, she ripped each one open with her bare hands. Joi didn't feel like being at work today, but had no choice. So that she wouldn't interact with any customers and ruin their day, she volunteered to count and shelve the new merchandise delivered by UPS that morning.

She couldn't believe she'd slipped up after going weeks without her tattoo being noticed. She tagged the new feather and beaded winter hats inside the box and tossed them in a small cart. When she was finished with the last hat, she rolled the cart to the front of the store. Linda was busy helping a customer choose between two very different scarves—one salmon-colored and plain, the other a montage of pale colors.

Although Joi didn't ask, Linda excused herself and left the customer to help her unload the cart. Joi was nervous. She had a feeling Linda was going to ask her about the party.

"So," Linda began, "been to any good parties lately?"

Joi tried not to look guilty as she spoke. "Rayven's sister took me and Ray to a housewarming," she lied. "We didn't stay long though."

"Hanging out with college folk, huh?" Linda responded in a joking manner. "College parties are fun, but then I enjoyed myself in high school, too."

The customer Linda was helping earlier signaled that she needed help, and Linda nodded to let her know she would be right over. Before rushing off to the customer, Linda looked at Joi. "I wouldn't be in such a hurry to grow up. Life only gets more complicated, especially when it comes to men."

Without saying too much, Linda had let Joi know that she knew she was at the housewarming. And after running into her at the Penn step show, Linda probably figured out that she was dating someone older. She wondered how long Linda would keep the information from her mother.

Joi arranged the remaining hats haphazardly on the display case and returned to the back room. Quickly, she dialed Markus's number. No answer. She hung up without leaving a message and decided to call Rayven.

"Where've you been?" Rayven asked right away. "I've been calling you all morning."

"Mother saw the tattoo," she informed her. She wanted to tell Rayven about her conversation with Linda, but knew it would only make her anxious.

Rayven laughed nonstop. "I told you this was going to happen. You should've gotten the temporary one like me. It looks just as good."

"That thing doesn't last longer than a week at a time."

"Yeah, but my mom's not mad at me."

Joi wasn't in the mood for a lecture, so she changed the

subject. "Can you call Markus and tell him that I'll meet him at his apartment? Tell him I'll catch the bus down there." In case of an emergency, Joi had programmed Markus's number in Rayven's cell phone.

"Are you even sure you can go? Mrs. B didn't put you on punishment?" Rayven asked. "I can't picture her letting this one slide."

"She took my phone and said I couldn't play ball anymore. She didn't say anything about me not hanging out after work." At least Joi hoped Taylor wasn't going to trip. "Tell him if I'm not there by seven then I couldn't get away."

"Okay, hit me back later if you can," Rayven replied.

The other line clicked, and Joi feared it was Taylor calling. "Okay, I better go. Don't text or call until I tell you it's safe." She hung up without saying goodbye and held the receiver until the phone rang a couple times, that way her mother wouldn't know she was on the phone.

"Second Chance," Joi said after the third ring. "How can I help you?"

"Hey, Joi. This is Aunt Gizelle. How are you?"

"Hey, Auntie," Joi said, her tone lifted. Gizelle was her favorite aunt. Although Joi overheard her mother say that Gizelle was spoiled and too outspoken, Joi thought she was great to be around. "Are you coming down here today?"

"I wish I could, but I have a lot of running around to do for Gram. I'll see you on Thursday though," she replied. "Is your mother in?"

"No," Joi answered flatly.

"Do you know if she started making the pies yet?"

"She said something about it this morning, but I wasn't really paying attention." Joi kicked a new box to the center of the floor. "Should I have her call you?"

"Have her call my cell please, doll. Tell her it's important."

Joi promised her aunt that she would give Taylor the
message and hung up. She opened a box filled with deco-
rative socks. "Three more hours before I can leave," she
whispered as she separated the socks into groups.

Chapter Eleven

~ *Taylor* ~

In jeans that made her look and feel ten years younger, Taylor sashayed into her store. She always took pride in her appearance. Just because she was fifty didn't mean she had to dress the part of an old maid. Polyester pants that hovered above the ankle and handmade sweaters had no place in her wardrobe. As a child she wasn't able to afford designer clothes, but she managed to put together great ensembles using hand-me-downs and thrift shop bargains. That's where the inspiration for Second Chance came from. There was no reason why those who had little money to spend couldn't look their best.

"Hi, Mrs. Belle. Done shopping?" Linda asked from behind the men's rack of clothes.

Taylor looked around the store. For a Saturday afternoon it was empty. "Hey, Linda," she replied. "Been slow all day?"

Linda folded her last sweater and headed in her mentor's direction. "Not really. This is the first chance I had to straighten up since we opened."

That pleased Taylor, especially since all day long, she'd been seriously considering opening a second shop.

Linda had been an employee at Second Chance since her senior year in high school. In the four years that she had been there, Taylor had no complaints. Linda was a hard and dependable worker, something difficult to come by these days. She loved the business just as much as Taylor and was the perfect protégé. Last year, Taylor convinced her to take some business classes at a local community college. It was Taylor's hope that Linda would one day run the shop completely, especially since Joi was not interested. And if she opened a new store, Linda was going to play a vital role in its development.

As Taylor surveyed the store, everything was set the way she liked it; everything but the new hats. She knew that was Joi's doing. Taylor walked over to the shelf and played around with different combinations until she was satisfied. When her work was done, she stepped back and admired her creation. The church women were going to love the new collection of winter hats.

"Is my child still here?" Taylor asked. She'd been preoccupied with so many things, she'd forgotten to tell Joi about dinner with her father.

"She's been in the back all day with the inventory," Linda said. "She's been pretty mellow."

I bet she has, Taylor thought.

"Trouble with a boyfriend or something?" Linda asked.

A loose thread dangled from one of the new hats, and Taylor wrapped it around her finger then yanked it. "You know something I don't?"

Linda lowered her voice. "Oh no," she said. "I saw Joi at a step show with a group of her friends. I thought one of them was a boyfriend."

"She hasn't mentioned anything to me yet," Taylor responded, her suspicions confirmed. "Besides, she's too young to have man problems."

"Then I'm sure it's nothing." Linda walked to the dressing room and gathered the clothes left on the bench. Customers often threw the clothes they didn't want there after trying them on. Linda put the items back on hangers and returned them to the appropriate rack.

"I'll be in the back if anyone needs me," Taylor announced and headed to her office. Joi was standing by her small locker when she walked in.

Without looking at her mother, Joi zipped her jacket and threw her backpack around her arm. "I finished all the boxes," she said and closed her locker.

Where did Joi think she was going? Had she forgotten about the tattoo? Or the party she'd gone to last night? "Your father is picking you up today," Taylor stated firmly.

"I can catch the bus to Rayven's," Joi said, as if she was entitled to do as she pleased. "We wanted to go over the report one last time."

"Not today." Taylor walked to her desk and turned on her computer. "And this is not a debate," she added before an argument ensued. Taylor took off her coat and placed it on the back of the chair at her desk.

"We have to present Monday morning. I want to make sure we do a good job," Joi replied with a straight face.

Taylor almost laughed aloud. Who was Joi fooling this time? Taylor wasn't about to let her go out again so she could run off with Rayven's sister to another college party. Plus, they had to talk about the tattoo she so boldly had carved into her back. Taylor logged onto her email account as if Joi wasn't in the room.

"Mother, why—" Joi began, but Taylor cut her off.

"I don't want to hear it, Joi." Taylor didn't look at her daughter, but knew she was full of attitude and biting her bottom lip. "Your dad will be here by five. That's less than an hour from now."

Joi huffed and fell into the reclining chair behind her. She took a textbook out of her backpack and pretended to read it.

"While you're waiting," Taylor said, "can you go clean the windows up front?" Taylor waited a few seconds, but Joi didn't budge. Annoyed, she looked away from her computer screen. "I'm going to ask you one more time nicely. Then God help me, but I'm going to take off my belt, and I mean it, so don't give me a reason."

Promptly, Joi got up and threw the book in the chair. If she bit her lip any harder, she'd draw blood. Taylor watched her push the cleaners around in the storage cabinet and tried her best not to speak. They were both emotionally charged. Joi slammed the cabinet door, and Taylor winced. Joi had one more time to work her nerve.

Joi trudged out of the room, and Taylor massaged her temples. Headaches were becoming too common whenever she dealt with her oldest child. The music coming from her new system was not helping the throbbing in her head either. Tye Tribbett was great when she was in the mood for hand-clapping and foot-stomping praise. But at the moment she needed something soft to speak to her spirit. She rifled through her compilation of CDs and settled on "Thy Kingdom Come" by CeCe Winans. As words of exhortation belted from the renowned singer's soul, Taylor let the music take her mind to a more serene place.

"Mrs. B," Linda interrupted. "I'm sorry to bother you, but here's the mail from last week. I took care of the important notices. Also, Joi wanted you to know that Gizelle called. She wants you to call her cell."

Why couldn't Joi tell me herself? Lord, I'm two seconds off that child. "Thanks, Linda," Taylor responded glumly and took the mail from her hands. Linda was a godsend and the only employee she trusted to handle daily operations.

"No problem. You want anything from Starbucks? I think I'm gonna run down there before things pick up again." Linda grabbed a granola bar from the snack tray.

"No, thanks. I've had enough coffee products for today," Taylor replied as she sifted through the mail. Wrapped in a separate rubber band were personal letters, usually from customers expressing their appreciation and gratitude for a service well done. Near the end of each month, Taylor could also rely on an envelope from Jerome. This one was early. She took the check out of the envelope and was surprised to see a message in the memo line. *Happy Holidays.* The check he'd sent at the beginning of the month for November also had a pleasant greeting. She didn't know what his sudden one-line phrases were about, but she was glad Jerome had stopped being so cold.

Joi ran back into the office and shoved the supplies inside the cabinet. "Daddy's here. He's taking me to Red Lobster," she said, and quickly gathered her belongings. She didn't even give Taylor a chance to say goodbye.

Taylor placed Jerome's check inside her clutch then picked up the phone receiver and dialed Gizelle's number. Whatever she wanted, Taylor had a feeling Thanksgiving dinner was involved. "Hey, Gizelle. You called me earlier?"

"Yes, I tried your cell, but kept getting the answering machine."

"I was in a long meeting this afternoon. What's up?"

"I wanted to catch you before you went to Pathmark. I talked to Mom, and we think you should let us handle everything this year. I can make the pies. It really won't be a problem," Gizelle stated.

Taylor put her hand over the receiver and ground her teeth together before responding. She had just gone through this with Gram the night before. "Really, it's not a problem. It's my pleasure to contribute."

"Well, I already bought most of the ingredients. You can bring some beverages if you want. You know how much our boys run through soda and juice." Gizelle had two teenage boys, one a freshman in college but still living at home, the other only thirteen.

Taylor was determined to stand her ground. The Belle women were not going to leave her out this time. "I went shopping this morning as well, and I have *all* the ingredients. I really don't understand why you won't let me—"

"It's no big deal," Gizelle blurted. "We just thought you'd like to sit back and enjoy yourself for a change. We know how busy you are every day."

"I'll enjoy myself by making my pies," Taylor noted.

Gizelle didn't say anything for several seconds. If Taylor could see through the phone, she'd probably see her sister-in-law making all kinds of offensive facial expressions. "No problem," she finally said. "I'll save the sweet potatoes for another time. See you Thursday."

Without meaning to, Taylor slammed the phone on the hook. "This is nothing God can't handle," she repeated silently. One day she was going to have a heart-to-heart with the Belle women.

Taylor wanted to call Lance, but from experience she knew he'd say, "You're overreacting." Then at the next family gathering, his mother and sisters would act funny toward her.

Taylor picked up the receiver again, but this time called Kara. Although Taylor had no problem encouraging herself, there were times when she needed an extra boost.

"Hey, Taylor. I was making my dinner list for Thursday and was just thinking about you," Kara said when she answered. "What's up? The Belles driving you crazy?"

Taylor sighed. "This time, it's not just them. You have a few minutes to talk?"

"Sure. Why don't you come to the church? I'll be here for a while," Kara said without hesitation.

Seated in a cold metal folding chair in Kara's office, Taylor belted out her problems—Lance, Joi, the in-laws, the business, and lastly Jerome. Jerome had been a taboo topic, but considering all that had transpired, Taylor needed to share her feelings with someone who knew him just as well as she did.

"Everyone keeps telling me not to torture myself, but the bottom line is I brought all this on myself. I had just given my life to Christ, and as if salvation meant nothing, I fell back into bed with him *again*. What kind of person does that?"

"A human being," Kara replied. "You're not the only person to slip up. You think I was a saint? I was still smoking like a sailor, remember? It doesn't matter how long you've been saved, you're gonna mess up sometimes. That's why we need God. He pulls us back on track when we do fall, and He doesn't make us feel guilty about it." Kara walked to the front of her desk and sat on the edge. "You really need to stop punishing yourself over this, especially now that Joi knows the truth."

Taylor couldn't stop the tears that flowed down her cheek. "I know, but that can be hard to do when your teenage daughter challenges your every move."

Kara handed her friend a box of Kleenex. "Sometimes the lessons we have to learn come through our children, and we learn to fast, pray harder and longer, and do all we can to force our flesh to submit to God. And that's not a bad thing. God just wants us to totally depend on Him."

"I pray every morning, and I meditate on a different scripture every month." Taylor wiped her eyes. "I'm trying to stay in His will, but I feel like, if I'm not careful, I'm going to lose it." Taylor blew her nose into a clean tissue and balled it up inside her hand. "Besides my children," she continued, "Lance is one of the greatest gifts God has given me. But lately there's been a lot of tension between us, and his family only talks to me when it's absolutely necessary." Taylor threw her hand in the air. "And I still don't know what to do about Jerome. I do know I can't let Joi continue to act like she has no sense."

Kara picked up her Bible and crossed her legs. She flipped through the pages searching for an appropriate passage to share. "You know, the more thrown at you, the greater the blessing in the end. Are you familiar with generational curses?"

Taylor used her tissue to dab her runny rose. "I've heard of them. Why?"

"Well," Kara said, preparing to read a scripture. "Exodus 34 talks about curses being passed through generations of children because of their father's sin. It says here that generational cur—"

"What does that mean?" Taylor interrupted. "Are you telling me that my children and their children are doomed because of me?"

Kara placed the Bible on the desk. She could tell Taylor was becoming even more upset, and that was not her intent. "No, that's not it at all. I believe these curses are very real, but I also believe that God has given us the weapons needed to break them. Besides wearing the full armor of God—"

"Wait a minute, Kara. Let me get this straight. God has cursed Joi's life because I had sex with a married man *and* before I was married? If I recall correctly, your daughter Stephanie was born out of wedlock and seems to be doing just fine."

"That's not what I'm saying to you. You're blowing this out of proportion." Kara tried her best not to become testy. "If you look at the situation with your mother and father, and then with you and Jerome, you have to be honest with yourself. There are some pretty significant similarities there. All I'm trying to convey is that you need to recognize that certain patterns keep repeating. Then you can specifically rebuke the cause and break the cycle." Kara hesitated.

Taylor's expression had changed from sorrow to anger.

"Maybe curse was too strong of a word to use. I'm not trying to hurt you or point fingers, I—"

"You know what?" Taylor stood up and grabbed her leather coat from behind the chair. She'd heard enough. "I know you're ordained and all, but I don't need Minister Kara quoting scriptures to me right now. I came here for my friend, someone that used to help me sort out my problems and inspire me to do better. I didn't come here to learn that I—no, excuse me, my parents—single-handedly cursed the entire Kimball line."

"I'm always a minister, Taylor. I can't just erase that because we're good friends," Kara replied. "I'm not going to say what you want to hear. Maybe you should turn to God for what you need and not me. You can't depend on me or anyone else to help you feel better."

Taylor zipped her coat and placed her clutch under her arm. She didn't want to be disrespectful in God's house, so it was best she leave before things got out of hand. What bothered Taylor the most was that Kara had hit a nerve. If in fact she was living through some kind of curse or destructive pattern, it would explain why she had yet to forgive herself for the affair with Jerome.

Taylor walked to the door, her heels hitting the tiles with great force. "

Taylor, wait!" Kara said, chasing behind her. "Taylor, wait a minute! Will you let me at least apologize?"

Taylor stopped at the door when Kara grabbed her arm.

"Can you please give me another minute?"

Taylor sighed and closed the door. "Only a minute," she said.

Kara walked to her desk. "You have to remember that I was there with you from the beginning. I supported you and Jerome even though I didn't agree. That was hard for me, too. The situation was wrong, and I can't dance around that anymore," she expressed. Then feeling compelled to help, Kara scrolled through her Rolodex and stopped at Jerome's name. "But," she continued as she scribbled Jerome's information on a purple sticky note, "I am still your friend. I didn't mean for you to take this so harshly." Kara handed the note to Taylor. "I believe this can be the start of a new season for you. I'm not Joi's godparent, but I love her and don't want to see her suffer."

Taylor took the note. "Thank you," she responded and turned to leave.

"One more thing," Kara said. She walked to her personal library and pulled out a small book, *The Prayer of Jabez*. "This was a craze several years ago, but it richly blessed my life. When put in a challenging situation, pray for increase—an increase in love, success, and peace."

"Increase," Taylor repeated. She took a deep breath and said it again and again until she felt her mood mellow out. "Thank you."

"You're a strong woman who believes in the Lord," Kara pointed out. "Hold on to that. God will never take you to a place that He can't carry or take care of you."

Taylor knew Kara meant well, but sometimes her words were too powerful to take in one sitting. "I'll give you a call soon," she replied and left.

* * *

Surprised to see Lance when she walked in the house, Taylor took off her shoes and left them by the door. She'd take them up later. "I thought you'd be at Gram's all day," she said. "Are the kids here?" The house was too quiet.

Lance sat up and lowered the volume on the television. "Joi's upstairs. The rest of them are still at my mother's. I'm going back over there, but I wanted to wait until you came home."

Taylor hung her coat in the closet then sat on the sofa next to her husband. He placed his arm around her. "How did things go with Joi?" she inquired. "Did she open up to you?"

"I think we have an understanding. She's gonna try and do better from now on."

"That's yet to be seen, Lance," Taylor remarked. "I just know I can't take too much more of her attitude."

Lance kissed the top of her head. "I think she knows that."

It felt good to cuddle in Lance's arms. "Did she tell you she wants to see Jerome?"

"Yes," Lance said. "And why haven't you taken any action?"

Besides fear, Taylor had no other excuse. Now that she had Jerome's phone number, she really had no reason, other than the fear of rejection, not to call.

"What are you afraid of? Jerome isn't going to take her from us, if that's what you think."

"You have all the answers, don't you?"

"I know my wife."

Taylor rested next to her husband until the program on the television ended. "You better go before Gram calls. I know she's had enough of the boys by now."

"The kids are fine, but you're right." Lance stretched and kissed Taylor one more time before leaving.

Once he was gone, Taylor reached into her clutch and pulled out *The Prayer of Jabez*. Jerome's check fell out, and she stared at it for a while. *Maybe he's softened up and is ready to talk.* She placed the check back inside her purse. "Increase," she said to herself then pulled the purple sticky from the back of the book.

Taylor reached for the house phone and whispered, "Increase," three more times. She convinced herself that she was doing the right thing and dialed Jerome's number.

Chapter Twelve

~ *Jerome* ~

A crew of three-year-old infants jumped around Jerome's legs as he held a piñata above him. "I wanna be first!" they yelled, one, sometimes two at a time, each vying for the strings hanging from the dangling object. Jerome wasn't moving fast enough for their sugar-filled bodies.

Piñatas weren't the same as when he was a young boy. He remembered swinging a lightweight bat at a colorful horse in hopes that he'd be the one to crack it open. Today, the variety of piñatas ranged from childhood heroes to favorite cartoon characters. Children didn't use sticks and bats anymore to claim what was hidden inside. All they had to do was pull the right string. Sadly, the new-age piñatas had turned into a game of luck and not skill or athletic ability. Renee had purchased a fish named Nemo, a popular character created by someone at Disney. Jerome didn't think there was anything extraordinary about the fish, but the kids seemed to love him.

Jerome tried to control the miniature crowd, but had little success. The kids were anxious to start the game and couldn't contain their excitement. If his daughter-in-law hadn't rescued him, the kids would've attacked Nemo in two seconds flat. Jerome stood back and watched the children take turns. His grandson was definitely leading the pack. Jerome was proud to be a grandfather. His three-year-old grandson had already exhibited an interest in sports. Although his grandson didn't understand the game, on football Sundays they'd sit together, shouting at the television screen on bad calls and poor plays, and cheering when their team scored a touch down or intercepted the ball.

His only granddaughter sat on the steps, peering through the banister. She was only two, but already mature like her grandmother. "Pop-Pop, phone," she called too softly and ran to Jerome's cell lying on a table.

Jerome saw her running his way with the phone in her hand. Even her running was feminine, her long corduroy brown skirt lightly dusting the floor. "Thanks, princess," Jerome said, and she smiled, melting his heart. The number on the screen was foreign, but Jerome recognized the 215 area code. Someone from Philadelphia was calling.

"Jerome speaking," he said, wondering if it was a relative or old friend.

"Jerome?" a female replied.

He almost gasped. It had been years, but he could never forget the voice of the woman who almost cost him a marriage. "This is he," Jerome responded more professionally than before. He quickly excused himself then drifted to an isolated area of the basement.

"This is Taylor," she said. No explanation for her call was needed. The awkward silence that followed her greeting spoke volumes. She wanted to talk about their daughter. "I got your number from Kara," Taylor said.

This had to be serious. He hadn't heard from Kara or

her husband Harold in a few years. "How can I help you?" he asked.

"I think you know why I'm calling," Taylor began. "I know we agreed not to do this, but . . ." Taylor paused long enough to gain control of her emotions. "I need some help."

The tremor in her voice told Jerome that she was desperate. A dozen things ran through his mind, and in a matter of minutes, he'd narrowed his choices. Either Taylor needed more money, or their child was sick. Whatever the reason, this was not a good time to talk. Renee was on her way downstairs carrying a tray of fresh baked cookies. "I'm at my grandson's birthday party," he answered. "Can I call you later?"

"No, you can't. Your daughter—Joi is her name by the way—wants to meet you."

Perplexed, he asked, "She knows about me?"

"A friend blurted it out before I could stop her. I hadn't seen her since Joi was seven," Taylor explained. "She thought Joi knew."

Renee handed each of the guests one huge turkey-shaped cookie and set the leftovers on the table. She looked at Jerome, her eyes questioning the nature of his call.

Looking down at the carpet, he pretended to wipe at a stain with his foot. The last thing he wanted was for Renee to suspect anything.

Tired of waiting for an answer, Taylor said, "After all these years, meeting your daughter is the least you can do."

Jerome couldn't respond. What could he say? She was right. He thought about the recurring dream. Maybe this was God's way of reminding him to act. But as he watched Renee head toward him, his jaw tightened.

Taylor continued to speak, despite his silence. "She got

a tattoo a few weeks ago. She missed curfew a few times. And I think she may be drinking." Taylor paused only to catch her breath before continuing to rant. "I can't keep an eye on her twenty-four seven. I have other kids that need my attention. I have a business to keep up with, not to mention a husband who needs me, too. I don't know what else to do."

The mid-seventies temperature of the room suddenly felt like ninety degrees. Jerome's armpits started to sweat, creating small circles underneath. He nervously wiped his forehead. "What makes you think she'll listen to me?"

"You can at least try," Taylor said. "I'm at my wits end here."

Renee wrapped her arm around Jerome's waist. Inconspicuously, he lowered the volume on his phone so that Taylor's words could not be heard.

"Did you hear me?" Taylor sharply asked. "She doesn't listen to me anymore, Jerome. Her grades are just average, and her mouth . . . that mouth is out of control."

She got that honest, he thought as Taylor rambled on.

Renee rubbed Jerome's chest and handed him the cookie in her hand. "It's Saturday," she whispered. "Don't let the job stress you too much, Jay. Don't forget this is your grandson's party."

Renee released her husband and returned to the guests. Years ago they'd promised one another not to let work interfere with family events and special occasions.

"I wish I knew how to help," he said when Renee was out of hearing range. "If things are as bad as you say, Joi is not going to want a stranger telling her what to do. I'm positive she resents me just as much."

"She wouldn't have asked for you if that was the case," Taylor retorted.

Guilt set in, but he couldn't promise anything yet. "Maybe you and I should set a time to talk after the holidays."

Renee helped their granddaughter dress the popular Addy American doll she carried everywhere. He loved his family and didn't want to risk losing them.

"You don't know what life has been like this school year," Taylor cried. "I have prayed, considered counseling, prayed some more, threatened to take basketball away, prayed again. Jerome, I'm all tapped out. She doesn't listen to me."

Basketball? Did Taylor say our daughter played ball? Jerome didn't know Joi, didn't even feel a connection between them. He'd never even seen a picture of her. That was his fault. Still the time was not right. "I want to help," he said, "but I'm not sure what I can do."

"You can't be serious," Taylor said.

Without looking directly at his wife, Jerome could sense Renee staring. "I need to get back to my grandson. We'll plan to talk soon," Jerome said and abruptly disconnected the call.

"You okay?" Renee asked when Jerome approached her.

"Nothing I can't handle on Monday," he said solemnly, and tried to enjoy the rest of the evening with his family and friends.

Jerome sat in front of his computer, once all the kids and adults were gone. He finally had the basement all to himself. It was one in the morning, but he couldn't sleep, thinking about Taylor and the daughter he chose to alienate. Jerome typed in different combinations of key words in search of information about his daughter. If she were a basketball player and any good, there should be something in the system about her. He hit the return button and was surprised at the number of results displayed on the screen.

—Joi Belle scored 25 points to lead Engineering & Science to a 75-33 win at Ben Franklin. Since the season began, the Engineers have beaten all opponents by at least 30 points.

—Joi Belle is a 5-11 jumping jack forward from Engineering and Science . . .

—Joi Belle might arguably be the best power forward to come through North Philly in the last decade.

For the next hour, he read every article he found pertaining to Joi, and swelled with pride. She was good. According to the recruiters and reporters, she was better than good. A permanent smile now on his face, Jerome searched the Internet for good action shot photographs. Image after image, he was surprised how much she favored him. In many of the pictures, they could almost pass as twins.

Jerome had just about decided on one to download when he reached a picture of Joi and her stepfather, Lance. His right arm was wrapped around Joi's shoulder as they hoisted a trophy in the air together. Lance sported the grin of a proud poppa, and Jerome couldn't help but think he should've been standing in his place. If only God had made him a better man . . .

Jerome remembered Lance from the days he worked at the SEPTA depot. He wasn't shocked Taylor had married him. Lance was a decent man then, and if he'd been taking care of his daughter all this time, he was a decent man now. It pained Jerome to know that Lance had filled the shoes he couldn't, but there was no room for resentment sixteen years later. He was just glad God blessed Joi with a father figure.

"Jerome?" Renee said softly as she crept into the basement. "You okay?"

Jerome casually minimized the browser before he turned around. "I couldn't sleep and didn't want to wake you," he said.

"It's almost two o'clock, honey. You won't be able to get up for church. You want me to make some tea or something?" Renee offered. "That might put you to sleep."

Jerome's eyes burned from staring at the computer for so long, and he rubbed them. "I can give it a try. My eyes are getting heavy."

"Then you need to come on up to bed. I'll put a cup of water in the microwave for you," she said and headed back upstairs.

Jerome waited until he heard Renee leave the kitchen before revisiting the pictures of Joi. He made two selections, one of Joi blocking a shot, and the other of Joi and Lance. That was to remind him of the mistake he had made. He hit the print function and waited.

He leaned back and realized that his dream of having a professional athlete in the family might finally come true. Determined not to miss another stage in her life, Jerome checked Joi's basketball schedule online. Her next game was in three days. He had to see her in action for himself. Without thinking it through, he logged onto his United Airlines account and booked a flight to Philadelphia.

* * *

Jerome had been sitting in a plane on a runway at O'Hare International Airport for over forty minutes. Light drizzles tapped the window, and he focused his attention on the sky. The clouds were sparse and spread apart. It was ten o'clock in the morning, but the overcast skies made it look and feel like it was evening. Jerome wasn't spooked or squeamish when it came to planes, but he knew this was an indication that inclement weather was ahead and possibly a long, bumpy flight.

Ding.

"At this time turn off all cell phones and electronic devices," announced one of the flight attendants over the intercom.

Jerome pulled out a magazine from the pouch in front of him and flipped directly to the back. Though it was a short flight, sometimes he could catch a movie, short sitcom, or History Channel documentary. Scanning the list of selections, Jerome's eyes paused on *Batman Forever,* and instinctively he grinned. The last time he'd watched that movie, he was lying next to Taylor.

Jerome rang the buzzer to Taylor's apartment without feeling an ounce of guilt. He felt compelled to say goodbye. He owed the other woman in his life for the last two years at least that. He walked up the flights of stairs slowly, waiting for any sign that he should turn around. Thoughts of his beautiful wife should have been enough to make him stay away, but they weren't. Jerome had to see Taylor one more time before he moved to Chicago.

Taylor's door opened mid-knock. He could tell he had awakened her, by the lines imprinted on her face and the way her hair sat up on one side. Yet, even in denim cut-off shorts and a cast up to her thigh from a recent car accident, Taylor's natural beauty was still evident.

"What do you want?" she said, full of attitude.

"I wanted to say goodbye."

"I guess I should feel privileged." Taylor leaned on her crutch and pursed her lips.

Jerome should have known he would've been met with her special candor. "I didn't come to argue."

"Then why are you here?"

"Look, can I just come in so we can talk?"

Taylor seriously thought about Jerome's request then opened the door wide.

As she hobbled to the couch, he could hear her mumbling under her breath. Jerome didn't want their last encounter to be unpleasant, so he didn't bother to ask what she was muttering. "I'll be leaving in a few days, and I wanted to spend some time with someone I care very deeply about," he said and sat in a chair across from her.

With head-rolling and neck-twisting action, Taylor said, "It's too late for that. You made your feelings very clear when you chose Renee over me."

Jerome was ready to respond, but she wasn't finished.

"You practically ignored me at the depot the other day. Do you have any idea how that made me feel? Is that how you treat someone you claim to have deep feelings for?"

Jerome didn't know what else to say, so he got up from his seat and sat next to her. "I really am sorry things turned out this way. But . . . I have kids and—" Jerome tried to put his arm around her, but she rejected him.

"Spare me, Jerome. I've been hurt enough. I know you love Renee. And what hurts the most is that I still have feelings for you."

Tears streamed down Taylor's face, and he rubbed her arm.

"The kids are with their cousins tonight, and Renee is already in Chicago. Let's just enjoy our last night together." Jerome wiped her wet face with the palm of his hand. "Let's watch one of your Batman movies. That always makes you feel better."

"I don't know about that," she said softly.

Jerome reached for her again, and this time Taylor did not stop him.

"This doesn't feel like a good idea," she added.

"It's only a movie. It'll be like old times . . . when we were friends."

"Okay," she said with little hesitancy. "I started watching one this morning in my room. You'll have to go get it."

"Why don't we just watch it in your room?"

"Oh, I don't know about that. I think we should—"

"Don't be silly," Jerome said. "You'll be more comfortable in your bed than on this old sofa." He helped Taylor to her feet and guided her to the bedroom. Once she was settled, Jerome situated himself comfortably next to her on the bed. It felt like old times.

Minutes into the movie, they started to kiss. Jerome's arm found its place around her full hips, and she caressed the top of his head. As much as he wanted to stop . . . as much as he should have stopped . . . Jerome couldn't control himself.

"Flight attendants, prepare for take-off," the captain said, and Jerome snapped back into the present.

The engine revved up, and Jerome sat back in his seat, closing his eyes until the aircraft was in flight. Hindsight was always 20/20. He and Taylor should have spent their last night together in the living room, although there's no guarantee the outcome would've been any different. He was ashamed of what he'd done, but couldn't wait to get a glimpse of his daughter.

Located in North Philadelphia, only a short walk away from Temple University's main campus, Jerome walked into the Engineering and Science High School. The school looked very different from the days he'd visited with his Murrell Dobbins team. He hardly recognized it when he pulled into the parking lot. Originally an elementary school, Engineering and Science was now a magnet school for students interested in science and technical fields. It felt good to know that his daughter was smart. Back in the day, not just anyone could attend the school. Students had to apply and be accepted. He couldn't imagine that they'd lowered their standards.

Jerome found it hard to believe that Joi had bad grades, as Taylor had said during their brief phone conversation. Coaches usually demanded more from their players, especially coaches at magnet schools. It could be that Taylor exaggerated. From what Jerome remembered, she'd always been a bit high-strung.

Engineering and Science resembled a private college campus. A great deal of money had obviously gone into renovations. The gymnasium was a far cry from the old-fashioned court he used to play on. The new one actually had a place for people to sit.

Preferring to stand, Jerome positioned himself close to the main doors. He had made it in time to see most of the first half, and the Engineers were already up by twenty-five points. Wearing dark glasses and a long coat, he felt more like a private detective or talent scout. Amidst the crowd, Jerome scanned the audience quickly for a Taylor and Lance sighting, but there was no sign of them. Relieved, he concentrated on the game.

In a number three jersey, Joi bounced the basketball near the sideline. Even without her last name ironed on the back of her shirt, Jerome could've easily identified her.

With four seconds left on the shot clock, Joi charged to the basket and was fouled. Next to Jerome, a young student shouted, "That's the way to do it, Boss!"

Behind the student another child yelled, "You show 'em, Boss!"

Jerome smiled. *Imagine that, my daughter's the Boss.* Only the good players had nicknames. In his day, Jerome was called *Smoke* because it was said that he'd leave his opponents choking on his fumes.

By the fourth quarter it was clear the Engineers were

going to win, so Jerome left before the final buzzer. He had to meet his brother at the Chipotle on City Line Avenue.

Having not seen his brother since their family trip to Hawaii a year ago, Jerome had forgotten how much Brandon favored their mother. His brother now completely bald, Jerome wondered when and if his hair would start to shed, since he was the oldest.

Jerome rubbed the top of Brandon's head after a quick hug and joked, "You look like Mom, but I got her hair."

Brandon pushed Jerome's hand away. "Be careful what you say. It only took a few months for me to get this way. Your luck could change before the spring, my brother."

Jerome massaged his full beard. "No matter how we change, the Thomases always look good."

"Let's eat, man," Brandon replied and led Jerome to the front counter. "I'll have the carnitas bowl with extra rice and black beans," Brandon told the server.

Jerome looked at his brother. "Bowl?"

"Yes," Brandon answered. "I'm trying to cut back a little every day. Jocelyn's been on my case."

Jerome shook his head. "I'll have the fajita burrito with pinto beans, please."

The brothers continued down the line, ordering their choice of salsa and other toppings. "You can hold the guacamole, but can I have extra cheese?"

"I thought you were cutting back?" Jerome asked.

Brandon laughed. "I said a little every day."

The server placed the brothers' meals in a tray, and the cashier started to key in the cost. Brandon pulled out his wallet, but Jerome stopped him. "I got this one," he said and handed the cashier a credit card.

Brandon didn't argue. "Whatever you say. You are the big brother."

Jerome and Brandon filled their cups with soda, Jerome a regular Pepsi and Brandon a Diet, then sat at an empty table by the window.

Brandon mixed together the ingredients in his entrée. "So, what brings you to town on such short notice?"

"You're not going to believe this," Jerome began as he cut his grand burrito in half. "I got a call from Taylor a few days ago. Our daughter's been inquiring about me."

Brandon dropped his fork, and it landed on top of his meal. "I knew this was going to happen. Have you seen her yet?" He picked up his fork and wiped the sour cream off the handle with a napkin.

"I went to her school today. She plays ball, and she's pretty good. They call her, *Boss*," Jerome gloated.

"Well, she's got honest Thomas genes then," Brandon mentioned. "How did you two get along?"

"She doesn't know I was there."

Brandon shook his head. "So, you were stalking her?"

"I felt like it. But God's been tugging on my heart to do this for some time."

"Well, I'm just glad everything is finally out in the open," Brandon replied, his mouth full of rice. "What's her name?"

"Joi," he said with pride.

"You need to bring Joi by to meet her cousins. You know we'll welcome her into the family." Brandon washed the rice down with a sip of his Diet Pepsi. "How is Renee handling this?"

Jerome coughed. "That's the thing. Renee doesn't know yet."

Brandon eyed his brother. "When you plan on telling her?"

"I'm trying to hold off until after the holidays, but I don't know for sure. Every time I look at her and think about all the sacrifices she made for me, I-I freeze up."

"Man, if Jocelyn finds out that I've known all these years and didn't say anything, I'm in trouble. Remember what happened when she found out about the affair? You had her following behind me for months. She thought I was cheating on her, too," Brandon said. "I can't be a part of this lie any longer, man. I love you, but you've got to own up to this."

Jerome was surprised at his brother's remarks. Up until this point, Brandon had never criticized him. "I know, I know. I just need to find the right moment."

"Being quiet is easy for you, but what about Joi? Waiting isn't going to change her feelings; it might even make them worse. You have no idea what she's going through right now," Brandon said. "The same goes for Renee. Does she know you're here?"

"No, I told her I had to work late." Jerome suddenly lost his appetite. Renee hadn't questioned him. She didn't even let on that she suspected he was being dishonest. More than anyone, she understood the need for him to work late hours occasionally.

"Jerome, you've got to stop. One lie leads to another, and before you know it, you're caught up."

Although Brandon was right, Jerome didn't know how to take his brother's toughness. Lies were like an infectious disease. "I don't want to lose my wife," he said and finished his soda.

The two men sat for a while in silence, toying with their food like children. "Let me suggest you tell her in the presence of your pastor." Brandon was only half-joking. He knew Renee was not going to accept this without someone getting hurt. He prayed it wouldn't be his brother. "So, how long are you staying?"

Jerome took a small bite of his burrito. "I just came for the game. My flight heads back at five after sevem."

* * *

The music in Joshua's bathroom blazed through the top floor. When Jerome came in last night, Renee was asleep. He couldn't recall the last time she'd gone to bed that early, but thanked God she did. It prevented him from telling more lies. Jerome stared at the ceiling and realized that he'd made it through two nights without having a dream.

Joshua's shower shut off, and five minutes later the music ended. That was Jerome's cue to get up and begin his day. Suffering from a mild case of jetlag, he considered staying home. It was the day before Thanksgiving, and Renee had a lot of things to do. Maybe he could help out around the house, do some of the things she'd been begging him to do for months, like replace the wobbly toilet seat in the downstairs bathroom, oil the squeaky hinge on the guest room door, and put in the new light fixture in the dining room.

Jerome got out of bed and put on his robe. The house was freezing, but he knew not to touch the thermometer. Once Renee got the oven going, he'd appreciate the coolness. He walked downstairs, slightly dizzy from his travel, and entered the kitchen. A bowl of fresh cut melons and grapes were on the table. He ate a few pieces of melon and took a small stem of grapes. In the basement, he heard Renee counting out loud to one of her Donna Richardson tapes. He walked down the steps and stopped midway.

"Hey, honey," she said, keeping up with the exercise mogul on the television. "Want to join me?"

"No, I might go to the gym later. I'm thinking about calling in to work." He popped a few grapes inside his mouth. "Maybe I can hang that new light in the dining room."

Renee stopped moving, sweat soaking through her workout gear and dripping from her hair. "That would be nice."

"Just want to do my part," he replied.

Renee smiled then resumed her moves. As she jabbed the air with her fist and kicked it with her foot, Jerome imagined those would be the moves she'd use after he told her about Joi.

Chapter Thirteen

~ *Joi* ~

Joi sat in the clinic next to Rayven eyeballing the posters covering the walls, each with a different message promoting safe sex. She'd heard about this place from one of her teammates. It was one of the few places in the city that serviced teenagers without parental consent. Joi's stomach felt like it was turning in circles. With the exception of something called the HPV virus, she had some knowledge of the sexually transmitted diseases on display from her health course at school. Sitting across from her with a belly the size of an eight-pound bowling ball was a young girl not much older than Joi. She couldn't help but to stare. The thought of being a parent at her age was frightening. It was hard enough babysitting her siblings and getting them to obey.

Rayven, who had been unable to relax in her seat, nudged Joi's arm. "We've been in here for thirty minutes. I thought you had an appointment. My mom will be looking for me in an hour," she whined. "I'm supposed to help with the potato salad for tomorrow."

Joi bit her lip to keep from answering. If there was someone other than Rayven she trusted, Joi would have asked them to accompany her. But Rayven's presence only heightened Joi's current anxiety.

Noise from the front door caught everyone's attention. A mother in her early twenties walked into the clinic pushing a stroller. As she walked to the front desk, two small children trailed behind her, two boys dressed the same, but one noticeably older than the other. When the stroller stopped moving, the baby inside screeched.

On cue the mother rocked the stroller back and forth, and almost immediately, the crying baby calmed down. "Hold on to the handle," she instructed her other children, while she signed her name on the waiting list.

Spotting the floating balloons in the corner, the youngest boy started toward them, but his mother was quick. She dropped the pen in her hand and grabbed his thin arm. "You have to stay next to me," she ordered, but the little boy tried to break free from his mother's grasp. When he couldn't get away, he cried and fell to the floor.

Rayven leaned close to Joi's ear. "Are you sure about this?"

Joi looked straight ahead at a poster about the AIDS epidemic. "You ever think about doing it? You and Chris were together a long time."

"Of course," Rayven replied. "Chris was a nice-looking boy, but I knew better. This may sound corny to you, but I want to wait for marriage. I don't want to risk having any babies before my time." Rayven remembered where she was and talked softer. "When he got tired of begging me for some, he found a girl that would."

The thought of Markus leaving Joi for another female unnerved her. He made her happy, and she was determined to hold on to that feeling for as long as she could. "I'm sure I don't want any babies either," she said. "That's why I'm here. It's the mature thing to do, right?"

Rayven scoped the room. The number of young women

waiting for their name to be called was appalling. "That doesn't mean this is something you should be doing."

"Aren't you mad Chris left you?" Joi didn't mean any harm. It was just that Rayven and Chris were together for almost a year. When he left her for another classmate, Rayven didn't shed one tear or express any sadness. Joi wasn't sure she could've been as strong. She'd never had a real boyfriend before Markus and was certain her heart would break if they parted ways, especially because of another woman.

"I'm worth waiting for. Don't you think?" Rayven replied, and Joi smiled with little enthusiasm. "I'm waiting for my one true love."

Joi thought about her mother's situation and wondered if she thought Jerome had been the one. "Does true love even exist?" Joi asked. "If it did, so many people wouldn't be filing for divorce or breaking up."

"Yes, Doubting Thomas. It does exist. People are just impatient. As soon as something goes wrong, they're ready to jump ship. But God says that love is patient. So when I meet my one and only, I'll know him because he won't pressure me," Rayven noted. "Is that why you're doing this? Is Markus pressuring you?"

"No," Joi answered quickly, staring at the mother with the three kids. "Markus told me he loved me."

"And you believe him?" Rayven asked, surprised that it could be true. "It's been what . . . four months?"

Joi kicked the cement floor with her boot. She loved Rayven, but sometimes her Sunday School training was too wise for her own good. At times she could be more like a mother than a friend. But Joi respected her honesty and knew she meant well. "He's been good to me," she said.

Rayven looked around the waiting room. "He's been good enough for *this?*"

"Well, we do study together, *and* he shows me some good moves for the court."

"Please." Rayven rolled her eyes. "You don't need his help with basketball. You're three times a better player than he is. *You* need to be the one giving *him* some tips."

Agitated, Joi asked, "Why all the questions? I thought you liked him."

"Markus is cool, but I think you're moving too fast."

"Is it too far-fetched to believe that he might actually love me?"

"Anything is possible. But I'm not sure that's the vibe I get from him. You also need to remember that he's in college. You're not worried about other girls being with him?"

Immediately the name *Eboni* came to mind. Markus had said it was his ex-girlfriend. "Well, I'm only getting information today. My mind is not made up yet."

"Why do you have to subject yourself to taking a pill *every day*? He's not going to use a condom?"

"I want to make sure nothing gets through," Joi said, slightly smiling to lighten the mood.

"If you wait until you're married, you wouldn't have to worry about that," Rayven charged back.

"I'm not old enough to marry, Ray," Joi remarked, half-jokingly.

"My point exactly," she replied and crossed her legs. "Did I tell you that Wayne guy called last night?"

Joi was glad she changed the subject. "Too Short? What did he have to say?"

"I didn't answer the call. He left a message," Rayven said. "You tell Markus I'm gonna get him."

The crying little boy from earlier ran down the aisle and bumped into Rayven's leg before he fell. He had gotten hold of a balloon when his mother wasn't looking and was trying to get away from her.

Rayven helped him to his feet then tied the balloon around his fragile wrist. "That way you won't lose it," she told him. The child kissed Rayven on the cheek and gave her a hug. She hadn't expected that.

The mother of the boy came over and yanked his hand. "Thank you," she said. "This one can't sit still long enough to save his life."

Rayven sighed when they walked away. "They're cute when they're not yours and you don't have to take care of them for eighteen years." Rayven played with the strings hanging off her shirt. "I won't hound you with any more questions about this. But remember . . . God will always provide a way of escape. Then the choice is up to you."

"Joi Belle," a middle-aged nurse bellowed from the corner of the room.

Joi quickly jumped to her feet.

"You can come this way."

Joi followed the nurse through the double doors. Once they were both on the other side, the doors clicked, and Joi nervously looked behind her. No one seemed alarmed. The click was just to assure the medical professionals that the doors were secured. Joi felt like she couldn't turn back if she wanted to.

The nurse led her down the narrow hallway, Joi's knees knocking together with each step. A bulletin board full of baby pictures from past and present patients decorated the bland white walls. Joi grabbed her stomach and prayed she wouldn't have a picture to contribute to the wall anytime soon.

"This will be your room. I'll be back shortly to check your vitals," the nurse said.

Joi stood at the door and swallowed hard. She was entering a new world. As she stood there staring at the models of human genitalia and posters describing the stages of pregnancy, Rayven's words resonated in her mind. *Was Markus really worth all of this?*

Chapter Fourteen

~ *Taylor* ~

The wrought iron storm door was the first change Taylor noticed about her mother-in-law's house. "That's beautiful," she told Lance as they walked inside. The next thing she noticed was the upgraded fireplace with wooden panels and marble floor. Lance's Home Depot work experience had clearly paid off. Gram's house was definitely ready for sale.

Lance's two sisters and their families were already in the house when Taylor arrived. As requested by Gram, her children needed to be there before the other guests showed up. Gizelle's oldest son relieved Taylor of the pie cases she was carrying and took them into the next room. The kids ran upstairs to join their older cousins, and Taylor admired the rest of Lance's handiwork. The new paint job and moldings, coupled with the natural shine of the cherrywood floors, did wonders for the room.

"Wait until you look upstairs," Lance said and helped Taylor out of her coat.

"Let me say hello to Gram first," Taylor said. She didn't

want to start out the day on wrong foot. "But I'm loving this. Now you know I expect the same for our house."

"Anything for you, sweetheart."

As Taylor approached the kitchen, she noticed her pie trays sitting on a serving table. Next to them, she also noticed that someone had baked two additional pies—one apple and the other a peach cobbler. She knew that was Gizelle's work of art. Taylor took a deep breath and mouthed, "Increase my patience."

"Happy Thanksgiving," she announced when she walked into the kitchen, where the Belle women were hard at work preparing for dinner.

"Thanks, baby," Gram said. She stopped stirring the pot of gravy and gave Taylor a kiss.

Crystal, Lance's older sister and a replica of Gram, brushed small amounts of butter on her homemade rolls, and Gizelle cut chunks of cheddar and Colby-Jack cheese for her vegetable and cracker trays. Both sisters returned the holiday greeting and continued their assignments.

Taylor studied the upgraded kitchen—granite countertops, dual and deep porcelain sinks, stainless steel dishwasher, refrigerator, and oven. Although she wanted to maintain her mother's home in its original form, she was having second thoughts. "The kitchen looks great," she said.

Gram dumped a small amount of flour inside the gravy pot and stirred it vigorously. "My boy sure outdid himself."

"What can I help with?" Taylor asked. She loved to cook too, and missed the opportunity to bake more than just the three pies.

"Let's see," Gram said, scanning the numerous items still needing attention. "Why don't you finish the lemonade?"

Making beverages wasn't exactly what Taylor had in

mind, but this wasn't her house, and she wasn't in charge. Taylor accepted the task and sat next to Crystal, who was now slicing mushrooms and green peppers for a chopped salad.

Lance and Joi poked their heads in the kitchen and smiled. "This is how I like to see my women," Lance teased.

"You better get out of here before we give you something to do," Gram said.

"We ought to make you do something," Gizelle remarked. "Thanks to you, my baby wants a tattoo."

Taylor frowned. Was there anything Lance didn't tell his family?

"You know my daughter's a trendsetter." Lance patted Joi on the back.

"I guess it could've been worse," Gizelle stated. "My son knows I don't play. I wish he would come in my house with a tattoo. He'd need more than Jesus to tear me off him."

To keep from commenting, Taylor squeezed the lemons as hard as she could. Gizelle was not going to get under her skin today.

Crystal, a single mother of three adult children, turned to Taylor. "My kids pulled fast ones on me all the time."

For lack of anything better to say, Taylor replied, "It was a team decision. They thought it was a cool thing to do."

"The whole team got one?" Gram asked Joi. "Lord, I pray you won't be like those players whose bodies are covered in ink. I hear those things can be addictive."

"Don't read so much into this, ladies. She won't get another one." Lance looked at an obviously annoyed Taylor and winked then turned to Joi. "Ain't that right, Boss?"

Taking the matter a little too lightheartedly for Taylor's taste, Joi dragged out her response. "I promise I won't get another one."

"Well, let us see it," Gizelle said, and Joi glanced at Taylor. "Oh she might as well model it, Tay. We all know it's there. Besides, you never know, I might get one," she joked.

Taylor didn't find anything funny, but gave her child the go-ahead. Joi lifted her shirt and posed, and all eyes fell on her lower back.

Gram walked away from the stove to get a better look. She placed the glasses that hung from a chain around her neck on her eyes. "What's that say? Boss Lady?" Gram touched Joi's back. "Why'd you get those flames?"

" 'Cause I'm on fire, Gram," Joi replied proudly, and Taylor moaned softly.

"Child, you don't have to mark yourself to prove you're good on the court. People can see your talent when you play. You kids are something else," Gram said and went back to the stove to check on her candied yams.

Lance interrupted the moment. "Okay, you've all seen it. Now, Joi, let's go before the store closes."

Gram lowered the flame on the stove and looked at Taylor when they were gone. "I can't believe how fast she's growing up. You better keep a good eye on her."

Without realizing it, Taylor threw the lemon in her hand on the table. She poured a cup of sugar into the pitcher and stirred it until all the grains had dissolved. "Lance and I are trying some new things, but I think we've got it under control."

"Gram is just looking out for her grandchildren," Gizelle said in response to Taylor's defensive manner. "Joi told me that she had a midnight curfew. That's pretty late."

Taylor hated being in the hot seat. She wanted to broadcast information about Gizelle's sons, but held her tongue. She would not stoop to her level. At least not today. "Joi works at the store on weekends, and as a reward, she is allowed to spend time with friends." That was really none of their business, but she resented being picked on. "She goes to a friend's house or to a movie, but a reliable source always brings her home, if that's what you're concerned about. I don't let her catch public transportation after hours."

Taylor couldn't believe she was defending her daughter. They still hadn't made amends, but the Belle women didn't need to know that either. "Things could be worse. She could be using my car and having accidents." Taylor cut her eyes at Gizelle. Her son had taken her brand-new Maxima without permission a few weeks ago and ran into a parked car. According to Lance, that wasn't the first time he'd done that. It was also the main reason why Gizelle was so firm on chauffeuring her thirteen-year-old around and enforcing an early curfew.

Gizelle looked as if she was ready for battle. "The older your children get, the more supervision they need."

Taylor didn't mean to, but she snapped. "Sometimes the tighter the rein you put on your kids, the worse they become. It's been my experience that kids whose parents are too strict rebel."

"I thought I was gonna lose my mind when my husband died," Crystal butt in.

Of the three, she was the least confrontational.

"It's amazing how different your kids can be," she added, "and what works for one doesn't always work for the other. Even after raising my girls, I felt like I was still learning how to be a parent to my son. Being a mom is hard."

Gram silenced all of the women. "All I had to do was put my children in Jesus' hands. It wasn't always easy, but I have no complaints."

Taylor got up from the table and placed the finished lemonade in the refrigerator. She didn't offer to help with anything else. She was ready to leave their presence.

"Well," Gizelle started again, "I went to Joi's game on Tuesday. She had thirty points. Lance told me her father used to be that good, too." The room grew silent, and Gizelle dumped a mound of crab dip in the center of her appetizer trays. "Have you spoken to him lately?"

"Gizelle!" Gram bawled.

Crystal got up from the table and poured herself a glass of cranberry juice. She didn't want any part of the conversation.

"What?" Gizelle asked, as if she had said nothing wrong. "Joi told me she knew the truth. So it's no secret anymore. And it's about time."

Taylor wanted to explode. Gizelle knew Taylor hadn't heard from Jerome. Why was she instigating? *Increase*, Taylor said to herself, though she wanted to scream it out loud. She hadn't realized Joi and her aunt were so close.

Gram tapped Gizelle's back and said, "That's enough. It might be a blessing that Jerome hasn't been around. Now, let's stop chatting and get ready. Everyone should be here in an hour." She turned around and opened the oven. The turkey was almost a nice golden brown. Gram based the huge bird one last time then said, "This is the last time I'll be in this house for Thanksgiving. Let's try to be thankful for all the good years we've spent here."

Lance entered the kitchen carrying a bag of onions. "You still need these?" he asked Gram, unaware of the tension in the room.

Gram wiped her hands on her apron and kissed her son. "You're a lifesaver. I almost forgot I asked for them."

Lance dropped the bag in an empty space on the counter and stood next to his wife. "Ready for that tour?"

Lance had no idea how ready Taylor was. Walking two steps ahead of him, Taylor prayed she'd be able to get through dinner without harming Gizelle.

Chapter Fifteen

~ *Jerome* ~

After a hearty Thanksgiving Day dinner, Jerome napped on the couch in the family room. He was supposed to be watching his grandchildren while their mothers were cleaning up the kitchen. But after ten minutes of spinning them in circles, he had fallen dizzy himself and needed a break. Thankfully, Joshua was standing by to relieve him. Tired from all the energy he'd burned the day before and early this morning getting the house ready, it didn't take long for him to drift off to sleep. Nor did it take long for a new dream to begin.

Wearing an old basketball uniform, Jerome moved back and forth trying to get attention. He was wide open and ready to take a shot. Waving his arms up and down, he didn't understand why no one would pass him the ball. He tried clapping, but no one flocked to him. Out of nowhere, Joi ran down the court, a number of opponents around her, making it difficult for her to shoot the ball.

"Joi, toss me the ball," Jerome yelled.

Joi stopped, dribbling the ball in slow motion.

"Joi," he repeated, "toss me the ball!"

"I can't," she uttered.

Confused, Jerome stopped pacing the court and asked, "Why not?"

"I can't depend on you to take the ball to the hoop," she said. Joi dribbled around him and went for the basket, despite the number of people guarding her. "I can't depend on you," she said as the ball flew through the hoop.

Jerome jumped up and looked around the room. Renee and his daughters-in-law were still in the kitchen, and his sons were in the basement playing with the Wii box. Grabbing his cell from the coffee table, Jerome went into the bathroom upstairs. He searched his contact list for TB, the indentification under which he stored Taylor's number. He hit the connect button and let the phone ring. When Taylor answered, he said, "I know I'm the last person you want to hear from, but . . . I'm ready to meet my daughter."

* * *

Jerome stood by the window in the lobby of Houlihan's on City Line Avenue waiting for Joi to arrive. He was twenty minutes early. The bumper-to-bumper traffic from the Philadelphia International Airport into the city was no longer as hectic as it used to be on a Friday evening. While he waited, he called in to his office to check on Melanie. She had volunteered to wrap up a few last-minute details for an upcoming meeting with their boss. She had proven to be a huge asset to getting the plans for Future Ballers underway. He was glad Mr. Usiskin offered her services. He was worried that her flirtatious manner would get in the way, but thus far he'd been able to maintain a professional relationship between them.

"Hey, Mel," he said when she answered. "Renee will be

stopping by the office to pick up some colored folders I left on my desk. She's going to proof the budget this weekend for our meeting."

"Aww. How sweet," Melanie replied.

"That's my better half," Jerome said. Renee did not put up a big fuss when Jerome suggested he spend a weekend with his brother. She knew how much he missed his hometown. "She should be there before six. Is that okay?"

"I'll stay until she gets here," Melanie offered. "It's the least I can do for a super team leader."

Jerome saw Lance get out of his car and walk up the ramp to the restaurant. Joi trailed closely behind him. Lance had not changed much; maybe a few extra pounds and his crowning baldness. He had expected to see Taylor, but she had called to say that plans had changed.

"Wonderful. Don't hesitate to call me if there are any problems," Lance said to Melanie and disconnected the call.

Anxious, Jerome opened the door as they approached, letting the cool air fill the lobby, much to the chagrin of some of the waiting patrons. "This beautiful young lady must be Joi," he said as she walked through the doors, her closed-mouthed smile saying that she too was nervous.

Joi looked back at Lance, as if asking for permission to speak. The moment had to be awkward for her.

Jerome couldn't help himself. He reached out for Joi and hugged her. "It's so good to finally meet you," he said. Joi barely hugged him back. Jerome prayed it was her nerves that made her seem distant.

Jerome looked at Lance and extended his right hand. "Good to see you, man. It's been a long time."

"Same here," Lance replied and shook his hand.

"Joining us for dinner? I know that Taylor couldn't make it—"

"She got stuck at work," Lance cut in. "I'll have to give

you a rain check. Our other kids are waiting in the car. I'm just dropping my angel off." Lance kissed Joi on the cheek. "Your mother will come get you. Just give her a call when you're ready." He looked at Jerome before leaving. "Nice seeing you again. Enjoy dinner."

Joi stared at Lance until he was in the car. Jerome didn't know how to initiate the conversation, which was unusual. He was a social kind of guy. But he'd never been in a situation like this before. "Well," he finally said, "let's see about getting a table."

Looking at Joi up close was like staring into a mirror. Her thick, perfectly arched eyebrows and long, chiseled legs were all traits she received from Jerome's lineage. The small space between Joi's two front teeth was the only trait that visibly connected her to Taylor.

As Jerome and Joi sat in a cozy booth, his heart wept for all the years he missed: her birth, first tooth, first walk, step, smile. He should've been the one to teach Joi how to ride a bike and dribble a ball. But he wasn't. He couldn't be.

Initially shy, Joi warmed up to Jerome by the time the waiter brought out their main entrées. Joi sat across from him and skimmed through her life as if she was on an interview detailing highlights of her basketball career and other noteworthy achievements. To his listening ear, she had a good life. Taylor and Lance had done a good job of raising her. It was hard to believe that the eloquent and soft-spoken girl before him could be capable of all Taylor had claimed.

He didn't know her well, but he was already proud to be her father. He was proud of all his kids. God had truly blessed him. With his past, he'd expected to get double for all he had done to his parents and his wife. But they were all doing well—one a doctor, another a journalist, Joshua a future CPA, and his only daughter, a strong contender for the WNBA. Who would've thought? Jerome had started grooming his grandson for a future in sports, but now maybe he'd get to nurture his daughter's career. *God sure does work in mysterious ways.*

The waiter came by the table and refilled the water glasses. Jerome removed a lemon wedge from a plate in the middle of the table and squeezed it into his water, something he learned from Renee. "Lemons cleanse your system," she had said one day. Being a creature of habit, Jerome drank a big glass of lemon water after every meal. He leaned back in his seat fully satisfied. The night was coming to an end. There was still so much to learn about Joi. One dinner was not enough time.

Without being too assertive, Jerome asked about the tattoo.

Joi looked surprised. "Mother told you about that?"

Joi had called Taylor *Mother* all night. She explained that Taylor liked that better than *Mommy* or *Mom*. It sounded more sophisticated.

"The whole team got one," she said. "We did it together."

The concerned parent in Jerome wanted to know where the tattoo was located. He prayed it wasn't in a place that would attract the opposite sex.

"It's a basketball . . . on my back," Joi replied.

Jerome smirked. He was silently pleased to know that Joi was a team player. But it was wrong to go behind Taylor's back. He remembered the time he let Reggie get braids at thirteen. It was cool for boys his age, but Renee had a different standard for her children. Even though Renee made Reggie take the braids out, Jerome had to listen to her whine and fuss for days.

"I won't lecture you," Jerome said. "I'm sure you've heard enough from your mother."

Joi looked relieved. "I guess she told you about my grades, too?"

"She did," he affirmed, and Joi picked at the vegetables on her plate. "I just have one question for you," he said. "Do you want to go pro one day?"

"Yes, I want to be like Sheryl Swoopes," she replied with enthusiasm.

Jerome could tell she really meant it. She was much more passionate than his sons ever were. "Well, to be *better* than Swoopes, you've got to keep those grades up."

"I'm doing better."

Jerome thought for a minute. "I don't normally like to do this, but . . . what if I give you twenty dollars for every A you get on your report card?"

"Twenty dollars?"

"That's not enough? If you get five, that's a hundred bucks."

"Then I guess you should put it in writing." Joi smiled, her mouth closed, hiding the gap.

Joi was sharp and witty. Jerome liked that. "Okay, I'm going to challenge you even more. What about fifty dollars for every A in your core classes—history, math, science, and English?"

"Deal," she agreed, and they shook hands.

For the next fifteen minutes, Jerome talked about his family in detail. He used the pictures in his wallet to familiarize her with each family member.

Joi stared at each picture carefully, especially the one of her brothers. "I wish Mother would've let us meet earlier," she said.

"It wasn't your mom that did this. Did she tell you I was married at the time?"

Joi nodded.

"I was afraid that I would lose my family if they knew. So I asked her to keep this a secret."

Joi looked disappointed. "Does Renee know now?"

"Afraid not. But I plan to tell her in January."

Joi was silent as she studied a picture of Renee. "She's pretty," she said and returned the picture.

"She is. I think you'll like her," he said. "Why don't you keep the one of the boys and maybe this one of me."

Joi giggled at Jerome's high school photograph. He kept it in his wallet to remind him of his youth, but now it seemed appropriate for his daughter to have it.

Joi placed the pictures inside her coat pocket and shared more information about her siblings, her best friend, and her boyfriend.

"Boyfriend?" Jerome didn't know how to handle her having a boyfriend. He didn't believe in double standards, but he didn't want some knuckleheaded boy messing with his daughter either. Not mentally, and especially not physically. "You have a boyfriend?"

Reluctant to answer, she said, "Mother doesn't know yet, but yes, I do."

"I'd like to meet him." Jerome wanted to see the boy that won his daughter's heart. "Why don't you invite him out to play a game or two tomorrow. Me and him against you and Rayven. Is he any good?"

Joi laughed. "Markus can play a little, but he isn't in town. He went to New York with his roommate this weekend. He won't be back until . . ." Joi stopped mid-sentence and bit her bottom lip.

"He has a roommate?" Jerome asked. "How old is this boy, Joi?"

Joi didn't say anything.

"Is he not in school?" Jerome continued to query, his tone now more serious. He didn't want to scare or frighten Joi in any way, but she was too young to have a boyfriend out of school. "Exactly how much older is he?"

"Let's just forget about it. You're only gonna run and tell Mother."

Jerome could see the attitude now. Joi's eyes rolled, and her body language changed. "I won't tell her, but that means you have to be honest with me." Jerome wished he hadn't said that, but it was the only way to gain her trust, and he needed Joi to open up.

They sat across from one another in silence, Joi calculating her risks, Jerome trying to maintain his cool.

"He's a sophomore in college," she mumbled.

Jerome dropped his hands heavily on the table. "I have to be honest with you. I'm not keen on a college boyfriend. No wonder you haven't told Taylor. She would crush both you and the boy."

Jerome figured this was the reason for the recent string of behaviors Taylor had been complaining about. If the boy could affect her grades and performance in school, then he might eventually affect her game. Jerome wasn't going to sit by idly and let that happen. "I hope he . . . Markus, doesn't interfere with basketball. Relationships can do that."

Joi gave Jerome the same look Taylor used to whenever he asked something she didn't want to discuss. "Nothing is going to get in the way of basketball, Jerome. You don't know this, but I am serious about my game."

Being called by his first name was not Jerome's choice, but he allowed it. That was the price he had to pay for abandoning her.

Joi added, "I'm not going to put my spot on the team in jeopardy for anyone."

"He's a little old for you, don't you think?"

Joi finished the last of her mustard-encrusted salmon fillet then threw her fork on her plate. "You can't just walk into my life for the first time and tell me what's good and bad for me. You don't even know me."

"Hold on, Joi. I used to be Markus's age. I'm not saying he's anything like I was, but at his age, many boys aren't interested in being faithful to one woman. I don't think this is a good idea."

"I'm not trying to be disrespectful, but Markus isn't like you or most boys. He hasn't cheated on me."

That stung. Jerome took a sip of his lemon water. "No need to get upset. I'm just speaking out of concern. How long have you two been together?"

Joi twisted her lips. "Since the end of June."

"Have you met his family or friends?"

Joi stared at him.

"If he is really serious about you, he'd care enough to bring you around the people he's closest to." He could tell Joi was highly bothered by his questions.

"I've met some of his friends. We're very happy," she snapped.

"Good," he fibbed. "I hope that means he's being faithful."

Joi pushed her plate away and glanced around the room. Jerome didn't want to upset her, but he was disturbed. He had been young once, and the thought of Joi spending time with her boyfriend was unsettling.

Jerome feared what she might say, but he had to ask. "This may be out of line . . . but you haven't been intimate with him, have you?"

Joi rolled her eyes. "You are out of line."

"I just think you're too young. You'll have plenty of time to be an adult. I mean, if you get pregnant or something, your life will change drastically. I know you don't want to make things difficult . . ." Jerome stopped himself. He was sounding too fatherly. It was too soon for that. "Maybe I'm reading too much into this. I'll just have to meet Markus when he is in town. I'm told I have a good antenna when it comes to these things."

"Whatever, Jerome," Joi interceded. "You can't preach to me about what's right or wrong. Your family doesn't even know I exist."

Ouch again. Jerome wasn't exactly a good role model in this area, but he was determined to try and make her see his point. He wasn't about to let some hormone-happy punk derail Joi's dreams.

"Don't you think I care about what happens to me and my future?" she continued.

The waiter returned to the table and picked up the empty bread basket, and Jerome welcomed the interruption. "How was your meal?" he asked.

"Everything was good," Jerome stated. "Thanks."

The waiter reached his long, bony arms across the table and removed the empty plates. "Will you be interested in dessert?"

"I think I've reached my limit, but if my daughter wants something—"

Joi shook her head, and the waiter grinned. "All right then. I'll be back with your bill."

"I'm leaving on Sunday, but I hope you know that I plan to be around as much as I can. You can call me whenever you want or need to. I don't want us to become strangers."

"I should call the home or cell phone?" Joi's sarcasm was strong, just as her mother's used to be.

"It's not my intention to keep this from my family," Jerome said. "As soon as the holidays are over—"

"Whatever, Jerome," she uttered again. "You and Mother are just alike."

Under the table Jerome felt Joi's leg shaking.

"What about my feelings? What if I wanted to spend the holidays with my brothers?" She threw the napkin from her lap on the table and said, "Where is the waiter with the check?"

Jerome played with the salt and pepper shakers on the table. For a moment, he'd forgotten he was talking to a sixteen-year-old. "All I can say is that I am sorry. I sent money to your mother every month since you were a child, so please don't think that I didn't care. I wasn't man enough then to step up, but I promise you, things will be different. This was a big step for me. I pray you'll understand that. I'm trying, Joi. This won't be easy, but I am trying. We'll spend tomorrow together, and I'll come back as often as I can to be with you, but you have got to show some effort here, too. Okay?"

"Okay," was all she had to say.

Chapter Sixteen

~ *Taylor* ~

Taylor pulled off the City Avenue exit and stopped suddenly at the light around the curve. She was so busy talking on her cell phone that she almost rammed into the back of an old Impala. It had been almost two weeks since she and Sherry had a chance to catch up, for which Taylor was most to blame. Between being a wife, mother, and boss, she rarely had time for herself. Life was supposed to be easier at fifty.

"You're good. I would've been the first one at the altar Sunday morning praying for forgiveness," Sherry said in response to Taylor's Thanksgiving Day dinner story. "You let those women get away with too much."

"I do what it takes to keep peace between me and my husband," Taylor responded.

"And how's that working out for you?"

Taylor drove around the curve when the light changed and pulled into Houlihan's parking lot. She parked her cherry Durango behind a string of cars in front of the restaurant and turned on her hazards. "I can't put my foot down now," she continued as she looked for Joi.

"Says who?" questioned Sherry. "It's never too late. You've got to start somewhere."

"You're right," Taylor agreed. "But we'll have to finish this later. I need to go in and find . . ." Taylor stopped talking and leaned forward. Joi and Jerome were coming down the ramp. She couldn't believe how much they favored one another. Even their slow and subdued strides matched.

"Tay?" Sherry called through the phone. "You still there?"

Taylor's cell almost slipped from her hand. "Yes. Yes, I'm here. Just staring at Jerome. He looks good."

Sherry laughed aloud. "Did you expect him to look as old as Frederick Douglass?"

Taylor said nothing. She didn't expect him to look like a senior citizen, but she thought the years would have aged him more than what she observed.

"You've got a good husband," noted Sherry. "His momma and sisters may be nuts, but Lance is a good man."

As Jerome grew closer, Taylor's breathing patterns changed. Sherry was right. Lance was a good man, but that didn't mean she couldn't admire an attractive man. Even one she used to be in love with. "I have to call you back. They're coming," she said and dropped the phone in the cup holder attached to her dashboard. Quickly, she checked her makeup and straightened the brown Coach hat covering her uncombed hair.

Through the passenger window Taylor saw Joi point at the car, and when Jerome looked in her direction, she waved. Before getting out of the car, she smoothed her eyebrows.

"Taylor Kimball," Jerome said as she walked around her car.

"It's Taylor *Belle* now," she replied when she reached the ramp, flashing her three-emerald diamond-cut wedding ring.

Jerome hugged Taylor longer than a normal greeting and spoke softly into her left ear, "Yes, it has been a very long time."

Taylor had pictured their reunion much differently. She was supposed to be dressed in an outfit that could put Beyoncé to shame, and her hair was supposed to bounce like Oprah's. Jerome was supposed to be gray and walk with the aid of a cane. Thanks to last-minute errands, she didn't have time to run home and change before picking up Joi.

Taylor also thought he would be cold, like his many letters, and was prepared to fill his ears with words to make him feel guilty. But as she stared at him, all the years of frustration and resentment were forgotten.

Joi stood beside them, her arms crossed and shivering from the cold. "Can I get in the car?" she asked.

Taylor pressed the automatic starter on her keychain and unlocked the door. "Don't turn the heat up too high," she told Joi as she hopped into the vehicle.

"Thanks for dinner. I'll see you tomorrow," Joi told Jerome before closing the door.

Taylor had to force herself not to stare. "She wasn't too hard on you, was she?"

"She was fine. She's a lot like you," he responded.

"Compliment, I hope."

"Of course."

Taylor felt as if she was flirting and couldn't stop. "She looks just like you."

"I know. I can't believe I have a daughter." Jerome loosened the thin scarf around his neck. "Taylor, I'm sorry it's taken this long."

"No need to explain. I understand. I'm just glad you came to your senses," Taylor said to keep the mood light.

A car swished over a puddle, and water splashed onto Taylor's winter white velour outfit. On impulse, she jumped closer to Jerome, almost touching his side. "I better go," she said and immediately stepped back. "I don't want to be late for my hair appointment," she said, although an appointment was not needed in her niece's salon. "How long will you be in town?"

"Through the weekend," he said. "Joi and I talked about going to Germantown and playing a couple games at the center. Thought it would be nice to take her to my old stomping grounds to see what she's got."

"I don't know, Jerome," Taylor joked. "My girl's pretty tough. They don't call her *Boss* for nothing."

Jerome smiled. "I guess we'll see."

"Well, she usually works on Saturday, but I suppose I can make an exception. Call me and we'll work out the particulars." Taylor looked back at her car. Joi was watching, her eyes carefully examining the situation. "Nice seeing you, Jerome."

"Same here," he said and waited for Taylor to settle inside her car.

Taylor adjusted the heat, unaware of the smile plastered on her face. She watched Jerome walk to the end of the lot and get inside of a sedan rental. He was talking on a cell phone. Taylor wondered if it was Renee he was talking to.

During the span of their relationship, he had often left Taylor's side to be with her. Flashbacks of the arguments and the nights she cried because of Jerome's actions resurfaced, and her heart instantly filled with regret. One day she prayed God would completely erase the memories of that time in her life.

"You're in a good mood," Joi stated.

Taylor snapped her seatbelt into place and turned off the hazards. "I'm always happy when I'm going to get my hair done. I might do a weave this time."

Joi faced the window and tapped the side of her door to a beat only she could hear. Taylor merged her car onto I-76 and navigated to the far left lane and turned down the radio. Taylor hoped Joi was ready to talk about the evening. In an attempt to get some answers, she asked, "How did things go?"

Joi shrugged her shoulders. "I guess he's all right. He said he was sending you money for me for a long time."

Surprised, Taylor focused on the road. Before Joi's young mind could accuse of her of any wrongdoing, she said, "I used a lot of that money when you were small to buy things you needed. When the shop picked up business, I opened a college fund for you."

Joi leaned her elbow along the window ledge, her face expressionless.

Taylor wondered what her daughter was thinking about. The silence was bothering her. "Glad you met him?" Taylor wanted to know.

"Not sure yet," Joi responded. "Did you have to tell him *everything* about me?"

"I mentioned specific things I was concerned about." Taylor prayed Joi wasn't trying to start an argument. The main intent of sharing things with Jerome was to help them deal with their problems, not push them farther apart. "This is what you wanted, right?"

"Guess I'll know better tomorrow," Joi said, making herself more comfortable in the seat.

Taylor didn't push for more information. As she traveled down the expressway, she prayed she had made the right decision when she called Jerome.

In a fresh, long and curly weave, Taylor paraded into the house, eager to model in front of her husband. The new style should last three months, but Taylor doubted she'd make it past Christmas. Having a niece as a personal hair stylist spoiled her. Taylor changed her hair, both in color and cut, more than most women did in a year.

Tinkering with an uneven leg on the dining room table, Lance looked away from his project long enough to notice his wife. "I love it," he complimented as Taylor twirled around. "How was dinner, Boss?"

"Fine," Joi blurted and dashed upstairs.

Lance looked at his wife. "You sure she's okay with this?"

"Someone called on that phone; that's why she's in such a rush," Taylor answered and walked to the kitchen. The truth was she wasn't exactly sure how Joi felt.

In the kitchen, half-eaten cheese steaks and cold French fries decorated the table. She wrapped the food in foil and placed them in the refrigerator. In an hour, one of the twins would come looking for leftovers. The smell of food reminded Taylor that she had not eaten since noon. Not in the mood to cook, she reheated the pepper steak from last night's dinner and sat at the table.

While the kids were busy, she had a chance to catch up on some reading. "Any messages?" she asked Lance and picked up a *Jet* magazine.

"Yep," Lance called from the next room. "Someone named Collette Brown called. Said something about seeing a property downtown."

Taylor moaned internally. She had not discussed her plans with her husband yet.

"Care to fill me in?" Lance asked, now standing in the kitchen in a ragged pair of jeans. He had taken the day off to run some errands for Gram.

Taylor couldn't look him in the eye. "I'm thinking about opening a second store."

"Were you going to tell me?"

"It's just a thought. I was going to mention it," Taylor said. "I wanted to see what was out there first."

"You used to talk to me about your thoughts. What's different this time?" Lance opened the refrigerator and pulled out a pint-sized Pepsi.

"Nothing. I didn't want to make a big deal out of nothing."

Lance twisted the cap off his soda and gulped down half of his drink. "We have money saved for this?"

"A little." Taylor turned the page of the magazine, and it ripped. "I might need to get another loan."

"We're not finished with the last one, babe. Maybe you should think this through some more." Lance finished the soda and threw the can in the trash. "I'm not trying to squash your dream, but we have four kids now, one of which will be off to college very soon."

Taylor refreshed Lance's memory. "Joi has a college fund."

Lance stood up tall, like a professor in a lecture hall. "Joi is not our only child. And scholarships pay for tuition room, and board. She'll need money for other things. She might want a car—"

"Is there a crime in looking?" Taylor didn't feel like being schooled.

"Of course not," he replied. "I only want you to consider *all* your options."

The food on the stove sizzled, and Lance turned down the flame. Taylor had lost her appetite. "I'll let you know how things go tomorrow," she said, hoping the conversation was over.

Lance headed out the kitchen and stopped at the door. "I almost forgot. Gizelle bought tickets to see Rhianna and some other cats in concert. It's her Christmas gift to the kids."

"They'll like that." Gizelle may have had reservations about Taylor, but she loved the children, especially the girls, since she only had boys.

* * *

Taylor sat at the dinner alone, staring at the now cold pepper steak in front of her. She'd eaten only one mouthful. She looked at the kitchen clock. Fifteen minutes had passed since she first sat down to the table. She had a feeling Lance was going to react the way he did. That's why she wanted to wait before telling him. Gram had instilled the notion that Taylor couldn't raise children and have a business at the same time. It didn't matter that she and Lance had managed when Joi was a tiny baby. Sure, there were more children in the picture, but they weren't infants.

Taylor chuckled to herself. Gram was famous for quoting, "Nothing is impossible with God." As far as Taylor was concerned, God made no exceptions. That phrase didn't only apply when Gram thought it was necessary. It was a word applicable to *all* situations.

Instead of putting her barely touched dinner back in the Tupperware container, Taylor dumped it down the garbage disposal. She didn't like to reheat food twice. She washed the few dishes in the sink and, when she was done, decided to give Collette Brown a call. There was no harm in seeing what was on the market.

Upstairs, the kids were all settled in their rooms. The house was quiet, and she was ready to unwind. Lance was awake and reading a newspaper, his reading glasses drooped by the tip of his nose.

Taylor sat on the bed next to him and kissed his cheek. "I'm sorry for not saying anything. But I feel like I need to do this. Maybe God is pushing me to do this." She rubbed Lance's head tenderly. "I promise to keep the family first. Same as I always have."

Lance took his wife's hand. "I'm gonna hold you to that. Just don't keep me out of the loop."

"I made an appointment for tomorrow," she said and hopped off the bed. She hated to ask, but had no choice. "I won't be here when Jerome comes by for Joi. Do you mind?"

"Not a problem. I'll ask Gizelle to take Gram to the market. She won't mind."

As she prepared for the night, Taylor imagined what Gizelle would have to say. Before the week was out, Taylor was sure the Belle women would know about Jerome and the second store. Then, like clockwork, Gram would call with her opinions on the matter, and Taylor would pretend to listen and take notes.

Lance pushed his glasses up so that they sat on the bridge of his nose, and resumed reading the paper. "How is Jerome?"

"About the same," Taylor answered nonchalantly.

"Did you get a chance to talk?"

Taylor buttoned her flannel top, careful not to show signs that she had enjoyed seeing him. "Not long. I was in a hurry to get to the salon."

Lance didn't show it, but Taylor realized this had to be hard for him. After all, she had dumped him once because of Jerome. "I was thinking . . . let's go away for a few days. Maybe Vegas or someplace warm."

"That would be nice," he replied.

Taylor pulled her new long hair into a ponytail and stuffed it under a satin cap. The clutter in the room didn't bother her tonight as she made her way to the prayer corner. As long as she kept Jerome and the Belle women out of her marriage, she and Lance could conquer anything. She sat in her special chair and picked up *The Prayer of Jabez* and turned to page eighteen.

Oh, that you would bless me indeed!

Chapter Seventeen

~ *Joi* ~

Joi held the pictures Jerome had given her at dinner in her hand. Studying each of her brothers' features carefully, she imagined what her life would've been like had she grown up around them. Of the three boys, Joi looked most like the oldest son. Joi least favored the middle son, who resembled Jerome's wife. Joshua, the youngest son, was a cross between his parents. It was hard to believe that he was only a few months younger than Joi.

"Jerome must've been busy that year," Joi joked, though, in retrospect, the situation was not a laughing matter. Conceiving two children in the same year by two different women was disturbing on many levels, which made Jerome's speech on infidelity even more interesting. How could he accuse Markus of cheating, when he obviously lacked control in that area at one time?

Joi switched her attention to Jerome's high school picture. Unintentionally, she laughed out loud. Caressing a basketball with the scowl of a bulldog, Jerome's true character was prominent. She could see why her mother would be drawn to him.

She opened the jewelry box on her dresser, an heirloom passed down from Taylor. It had previously belonged to her grandmother, and Joi kept many of her precious mementos inside it. Old from years of use, Taylor had painted it white and fixed the once-broken lock to make it appear fairly new.

Joi glanced at the pictures one last time. She wondered why Jerome had chosen to stay with his wife. Did he not love Taylor at all? She placed the pictures on top of the ribbon she received in her first All-Star game and locked the box. There was no point in pondering over what could have been or the reasons why Jerome decided to stay with his wife. Jerome and Renee had been together for many years. If an affair couldn't break them up, in Joi's opinion, the love between them was solid.

Although Jerome was more direct than she would've liked for a first-time visit, Joi had to admit, she felt comfortable around him. As long as he stayed clear of her relationship with Markus, they should get along just fine.

Joi knelt by her bedside, and for the first time in years, she prayed in that position. God had finally heard her prayer. *Maybe He loves me after all.* She thanked Him for bringing Jerome into her life. She prayed for her siblings, the ones she lived with, and then the ones she hoped to one day meet. *Please let them accept me*, she mouthed and crawled into bed.

It was getting late. Joi needed to get up early and complete a long list of chores before Jerome came to get her. She connected her cell to the charger and hit the speed dial for Markus. She had not spoken to him since his last final exam.

"Yo," he answered over loud music and constant chatter.

Joi wished she was old enough to party and travel with

him. "Enjoying New York?" she asked, trying not to speak too loudly.

"Missing you," he tried to whisper, but failed.

Joi could hear his friends teasing him in the background. "When are you coming back?"

"Christmas Eve, I think," he answered. "When I get back, are we gonna spend some *real* alone-time together?"

Joi couldn't tell if Markus was drinking or not, like he was the night of his housewarming party. "I made an appointment to get the pills next week." The doctor had told Joi a Pap smear and complete exam was needed before birth control could be administered. Joi had had the brochures and pamphlets for weeks, but her nerves kept her from moving forward. Wanting Markus to believe that she was mature enough to handle the next step in their relationship, she said, "I can't wait to be with you."

Joi had heard detailed stories in the girls' locker room and wanted to fit in, but something inside her didn't feel right about sleeping with so many men. She knew it was a reality for many women and girls her age. Her mother was proof that it was possible to love more than one man, but Joi didn't want that to be her story. Markus was the only one she wanted to give herself to.

"You're all the gift I need for Christmas," he said before being rushed off the phone by friends.

Joi placed her cell on the nightstand and closed her eyes. *God, please show me that Markus is the one.* When she opened her eyes, she reached for the birth control information she kept hidden under her mattress. She'd read through the pamphlets every night, familiarizing herself with all various diseases, side effects, symptoms, and possible complications. There was HIV/AIDS, chlamydia, gonorrhea, herpes, and something called HPV. There were long-term effects to consider, and a small chance that she could still get pregnant.

Joi had most of the information memorized. She thought studying the material daily would ease some of her fears. Instead it only confused her more. In her eyes, it was the female that shouldered most of the responsibility and consequences of an intimate relationship. That just didn't seem fair.

A faint knock on the door broke Joi's concentration.

"Yes," she said and stuffed the information back under her mattress.

"Can I come in?" Leah's tiny voice inquired.

"Sure," Joi responded. "It's open."

Leah walked in dressed in her school uniform, still finely pressed. Even after a full day, Leah's clothes looked as good as new.

"Did you have fun tonight?" Leah sat on the edge of her sister's bed.

Joi could tell she was worried about her having another family. "It was okay."

Leah stretched across the bed. "Tell me about it."

"Well . . ." Joi began, and for the next hour, the two sisters talked until their eyes grew tired.

* * *

With the help of her best friend, Joi was able to finish her morning chores by ten o'clock. The only thing left to do was fold and put away the clean clothes in her laundry basket. "He had the nerve to lecture me about Markus," she told Rayven.

"You told Jerome about him?" Rayven asked as she sorted and separated Joi's socks.

"It slipped out. But he's the last person to talk to about being faithful and loyal."

"Well . . . he almost got divorced," Rayven pointed out. "He might have *something* to share about the subject."

Joi stopped folding the shirt in her hand and gave Rayven the eye.

Rayven laughed. "I'm just saying, he knows firsthand."

Joi stacked the neatly folded t-shirt in a growing pile and grabbed another one from the basket. "He said Markus doesn't really care about me. You think that's true?"

"Don't know," Rayven replied. "He seems nice enough. But who am I to judge?"

A blast from the past came on the radio, and Rayven jumped up. "Chicken noodle soup with a soda on the side. Remember that?" she asked, recalling the simple steps associated with the song.

Joi wasn't much of a dancer, but enjoyed watching Rayven's long limbs try to find some rhythm. "I made a second appointment," she yelled over the music.

Rayven stopped moving. "You really ready for that?"

"I think so."

"Then you're not ready." Rayven continued to dance until the song ended. "Do you even love him?"

Jerome's words came to mind. "I don't think I really know what love is or what it's supposed to feel like. I like being with him. So, in that sense, yes, I do love him. And I think he loves me."

"Well, if you ask me," Rayven offered, tired from the mini workout, "I think you need to do more than *think* you love him before he gets the goodies. You know, like that Ciara song." Rayven was in a silly mood. "Not my goodies," she sang.

"I asked God to make Markus do something to prove that he loves me before Christmas."

Rayven sat back on the floor and finished matching Joi's socks. "Be careful, Joi. My mom said we shouldn't test God. He answers our prayers in His own time."

Joi finished folding her clothes and put them in the appropriate drawers. She was in too good a mood to have a religious debate. She and God finally had an understanding, and Rayven wasn't going to ruin that.

Joi's cell phone vibrated on her nightstand and she raced to answer it, praying it was Markus. No such luck.

"It's your father," Jerome said when Joi answered the line. "I'm on the porch. You guys must be partying or something. I rang the bell three times. You didn't hear it?"

It was strange listening to another man refer to himself as her father, but Joi supposed it was something she needed to get used to. "Sorry, my dad and the twins are in the basement. It's hard to hear down there," Joi explained. "Ray and I are coming down now."

In a Sean Jean sweat suit and leather jacket, Jerome stood on the front porch holding a bouquet of flowers in each hand. The man was fifty-three, but had the mindset and swagger of a thirty-year-old.

"These are for you." Jerome handed Joi the larger arrangement of flowers then hugged her as if it was his last one to give. "Hey, how's my favorite daughter?"

"I'm your only daughter," she said, then introduced him to Rayven.

"It's nice to finally meet Joi's best friend. She's told me a lot about you," Jerome said and handed Rayven the bouquet in his left hand.

"Nice meeting you, too. Thank you," Rayven said, accepting the beautiful arrangement of flowers. "I can't get over how much Joi looks like you."

Jerome swelled with pride. "She is my twin."

"I'll be right back. I need to go get my dad and put these in water." Joi took Rayven's flowers and walked away, slowing down when she realized that she had called Lance *Dad* for the second time since Jerome had been there. She now had *two* dads: one that planted the seed of conception, the other that raised her. From this point forward, her life was either going to be confusing or very interesting.

Chapter Eighteen

~ *Jerome* ~

"Not bad, Boss," Jerome said, out of breath. "Where did you learn how to play?"

"She's a Thomas," Brandon shouted as he tried to guard Rayven. Eager to meet his niece, Brandon had come to the center expecting to win a game. Instead, Joi and her best friend were giving the two brothers a real workout.

Joi dribbled the basketball around Jerome, trying to score another point. This was the second game; the first, Joi and Rayven won by twelve points.

Refusing to lose on his home court, it was Jerome's idea that they try again. So far, he and Brandon only trailed six points.

Jerome was tired and lightheaded, but pressed on. He was on a mission. Joi dribbled faster and moved forward with more power than before. Jerome couldn't believe her strength. He threw his arms in the air, but that did not disturb Joi's flow. As Joi advanced, Rayven pushed back toward the basket with force, and Brandon fell on his back. Automatically, Joi threw Rayven the ball, and it effortlessly sailed through the net.

Jerome bent over, hand on knees, catching a few breaths. He turned around and faced a growing crowd, many of them familiar with the girls' style of play. Others yelled for him and Brandon to retire. Jerome noticed Lance seated on a bottom bench, observing the game. Dressed in old army fatigue, Lance looked as if he wanted to play.

"Hey, man," Jerome called, and Lance hopped to his feet. "My brother's a little dusty. Wanna give him a break?"

Lance explained that he was in the neighborhood, and after dropping the kids off at his mother's, he decided to swing by.

Jerome guessed that had probably been the plan all along.

Without hesitation, Lance tightened his laces and entered the game. The two men tried their best, but they were no match for the dominating youth. When it was all over, the girls had won again, this time by only four points.

"How about dinner tonight? My treat," Jerome said as they headed out the gym.

"My dad, too?" Joi asked and zipped her coat.

"It's up to Lance," Jerome stated.

"That would be nice. I'll call Taylor to see if she can make it, too." Lance reached into his duffle bag and pulled out a hat and scarf set. "Put this on," he said to her. "It was snowing when I came in."

Jerome leaned against the front door and waited for Joi to get situated. Looking at Joi and Lance made him a bit jealous. "Pull your hoods over your head, too," he told the girls. He wasn't trying to compete with Lance, but he wanted Joi to know that he was concerned about her as well. "I don't want you to get pneumonia."

"Okay, well, I guess we'll call you once we're all changed," Lance replied. "We better get going before the snow really picks up."

Jerome hugged Joi one more time then pushed the heavy

door with his arm. Small balls of snow flowed from the sky, and they all darted through the parking lot to their cars.

As Jerome approached his rental, Brandon tugged on his sleeve, and he slowed down. Brandon pointed to a parked car facing them with its engine running. "I think that's Jocelyn," he told his brother.

Between the headlights and the falling snow, it was hard to see clearly. A woman in a long raincoat and holding an umbrella stood next to the car. The umbrella shielded the woman's face from the weather, but her frame almost perfectly matched Renee's. *That can't be her? Why would it be?* Jerome said to himself. The woman started walking in his direction, and he stopped moving when she lowered the umbrella.

"You okay, Jerome?" Joi asked from behind.

Jerome couldn't say anything. Immediately the scripture about Gideon came to mind, and when Brandon's wife jumped out of her car, Jerome knew he'd been caught.

"Is that her?" Renee demanded, now directly in front of him.

"What are you doing here?" Jerome asked, bewildered.

"Since your brother seems to be tongue-tied," Jocelyn said and stepped next to Renee, "Brandon, you tell me what's going on here."

Brandon pulled his wife away, begging her to get inside the car and keep silent.

Jerome stared at his wife, her face wet from the snow. "Renee, I was going—"

"Which one is your daughter!" she screeched, and her voice turned hoarse. "I asked you a question, Jerome."

An instant headache formed, and Jerome looked around him. Lance and the girls were still standing in the snow. "Please, go get in your car," he told them. "Everything's okay here."

Lance motioned for the girls to get in the car, and Renee followed them.

"Which one of you is Taylor's daughter?" she asked, her lips trembling. Had it been a clear and sunny day, she would have known Joi was the obvious choice.

Joi and Rayven looked at one another, unsure of what to do.

Lance blocked Renee from getting close to the girls. "We're not looking for any trouble. Talk to your husband," Lance said and shot Jerome an "I-can't-believe-you" look.

Renee stood still, the snow flattening her long hair. "Renee, c'mon. We can talk—"

Jerome didn't finish his sentence. The sting from Renee's hand across his face stopped him from talking. He hadn't seen her that angry since they'd left Philadelphia years ago.

"We should probably get in the car. You're going to be sick in the morning," he said and wiped his face. "Please, get in my car."

"How long have you known about her?" Renee asked.

Jerome pulled his hat down tighter on his head and stuffed his uncovered hands in his pockets. The better question was, how did *she* know? He had been so careful all these years. Or so he thought.

As Lance's car passed him, Jerome saw Joi staring at him, her eyes full of worry and concern.

Impatient, Renee slapped his achy arm with her umbrella. "Answer me!" she barked.

Brandon jumped out of Jocelyn's car and stood next to his brother.

Unsteady from Renee's blow, Jerome tried to grab her arm, but his hands slid off her coat.

"How could you do this to me again? How could you bring her to this club?" Renee's voice cracked. "You played with our children here."

Jocelyn rolled down her window and begged Renee to get in the car.

"You make me sick," Renee cried and ran to the car.

"Let's get out of here," Brandon said.

"Things done in the dark come to light eventually," Jerome recalled from Pastor Hampton's sermon. *How did she find out?* Nearly soaked, Jerome watched Jocelyn drive away. The happy and blessed life he once knew was about to come to an end.

Jerome drove Brandon home. Jerome wanted to go inside to change, but Jocelyn had made it clear that he wasn't welcome. "Once Renee goes to the hotel, Jocelyn will calm down," Brandon had told him before going inside the house. "I'll call you when it's safe to come back."

The roads were slippery, but Jerome was used to driving in the snow. Mindlessly, he traveled through the city, stopping once at a gas station to fill up the gas tank. As he pumped the gas, he noticed a convenience store across the street. The neon Budweiser sign was calling him, and when the tank was full, he ran to the store and purchased two cans of beer. With one hand on the steering wheel and the other on the brown paper bag, Jerome pulled out of the gas station.

Nowhere to go, he drove through West Philadelphia, down Chestnut Street, past Drexel University and the Amtrak station, straight to Penn's Landing to the hotel where Renee was staying. Having trouble finding a parking spot near the hotel, Jerome circled the block three times then decided to find a spot a few blocks away. There was a public garage down the street, but he wasn't sure how long he'd be visiting Renee. Fees at the garage were outrageous.

Parking his car in an empty space along Second Street, Jerome pulled out a can of beer. Without thinking too deeply, he pulled back the tab and inhaled. A recovering addict, he hadn't consumed an ounce of beer since his youngest son was born. *What am I doing?* Jerome questioned himself. This was not the way God had taught him to solve his problems. He had come too far to relive the dark days of his past.

Before Jerome could convince himself otherwise, he opened his car door and poured the beer on the side of the car. He did the same for the other can and shut off the engine.

Jerome secured his scarf around his face and got out of the car. The Luxury Inn Renee once worked at was only a few blocks away. He braved the cold and walked briskly through the inclement weather. Before he did something he'd later regret, he decided to wait at the hotel until Renee appeared.

The hotel hadn't changed much since Renee was promoted and moved to Illinois. Even her picture was still on the wall beneath the original owners'.

"Can I help you?" a young front desk clerk asked Jerome.

"No, I'm just waiting for my wife." He pointed to her picture. "That's her. Renee Thomas. Have you met her?"

"Yes, sir," the young man responded. "She did a training here last month. She's nice."

"I know," Jerome replied. "I'll just hang around until she comes. She should be on her way."

"No problem," the clerk answered.

Jerome could tell he'd made him nervous, and a few minutes later, the security guard appeared. Unfamiliar with the current employees, Jerome prayed Renee would show up before the guard put him out.

While he waited, he thought about Joi and the worried look on her face when she left the recreation center. He dialed Joi's number a few times and eventually left a message.

Where was she? He waited a few minutes then decided to call Taylor. By now, he was certain she knew what had happened.

"Renee will talk to you once she calms down," Taylor said after Jerome told his side of the story.

"I'm not so sure," he replied. "She hit me pretty hard."

Taylor informed him that Joi had gone to her grand-mother's with Lance. "I'll have her call you in the morning, okay?"

"Mrs. Thomas," Jerome heard someone say, and he turned around, "your husband has been waiting for you."

Renee turned around and looked Jerome in the eyes.

"I have to go now," he said into the phone and hung up.

In clothes more casual than Renee was used to wear-ing, Renee approached him. She must've been wearing Jocelyn's clothes. "Was that Taylor?" she asked. "Couldn't wait to call and tell her what happened?"

"I wanted to make sure everyone got home safe," he said.

"I'm too old for this mess, Jerome." Renee took off her gloves. "Just so you know, I'm leaving in the morning, and then I'm going to California for a few days. Everett needs some help in the head office."

Jerome wanted to give her space, so he didn't argue.

Renee caught the front desk clerks staring and walked to the elevator. Jerome followed. "How long have you known?" she asked as they waited.

"Taylor wrote me a letter some time ago."

Renee shook her head and stepped inside the elevator.

"How did you find out?" he asked.

Renee sneezed then said, "Melanie wasn't sure which folder to give me, so she handed me everything on your desk."

Jerome pressed his lips together. He must have forgotten to put the folder back in the file cabinet. The elevator stopped at the third floor, and he followed Renee to her room. "Can I come in?" he asked.

Renee rolled her eyes. "This isn't Fox News," she said.

"You don't think I want everyone to be a part of our drama, do you?" She walked inside her suite and threw her bag on the bed.

Jerome stayed by the door, and before he could speak, Renee started to talk.

"God helped me through the affair, but I don't know about this, Jerome. A man that loves his wife wouldn't do something like this."

Jerome walked toward her, but she backed away. "We agreed to keep this quiet," he explained. "We thought it was best for everyone. I had hurt you enough."

"I'm not a fragile child or a weak woman. You should know that by now." Renee took off her outerwear and tossed it on top of a leather duffle bag in a chair. "I can't believe you had unprotected sex with her and then came to me in Chicago with a clear conscience." She pulled the duffle bag from under her coat and unzipped it.

Jerome was still standing in the same place.

"The articles I read said she's a junior in high school." Renee took a nightgown from the bag and looked at Jerome. "Is that true?"

Jerome was afraid to answer. "Yes."

Renee's shoulders dropped, and she looked at Jerome with disappointment. "Then she's the same age as Josh? Jerome, how could you?" Renee walked to the mirror by the bathroom. She pinned her hair with a few bobby pins and put on a shower cap.

Jerome found it hard to speak. This was Renee's time to vent.

She slammed a bar of soap in the sink and asked, "How many times have you been here to see her?"

"Just once. I wanted to see her before I told you."

"What's wrong with you, Jerome?"

"I did this to save us. I didn't believe you'd forgive me."

A look of disgust crossed Renee's face. "You and Taylor

deserve each other." Renee snatched a washcloth and towel from a rack and walked into the bathroom. "I guess you finally got your basketball star," she snapped and slammed the door behind her.

Jerome stared at the door until he heard the shower run. He sat on the bed and waited for her to come out, praying that she'd forgive him.

When Renee was done, she opened the bathroom door. Wrapped in a large white towel, she looked at her husband. "You need to leave. You can't stay here tonight."

"Renee, I don't want to leave—"

"Brandon is expecting you," she said and closed the door again.

Jerome didn't want to push any further. They would talk when she got back from California. He pulled himself together and left the hotel. When he reached his car, he cried and apologized to God for his procrastination.

Jerome woke up the next morning at Brandon's house with a headache and an aching arm. After he showered and dressed, he called Joi to assure her that he would not be a stranger. He just needed time to work things out with his wife. Joi understood and said she looked forward to his next visit.

In the kitchen, Jocelyn stood over the stove monitoring sausage links.

Brandon was seated at the table, reading the morning paper. "Good morning," he said to Jerome. "How did you sleep?"

Jocelyn looked Jerome's way, but did not speak.

"Good," he said. But the truth was, Jerome tossed and turned half the night.

"I made some fresh coffee," Brandon said. "And I bought a huge can of creamer just for you."

Jerome smiled. He'd been drinking coffee, half black,

half cream, for years. "Thanks, man." He tipped around Jocelyn and poured himself a cup before sitting at the table.

The timer for the oven chimed, and Jocelyn removed the biscuits inside. She turned off the burners on the stove and tossed two plates on the table. "Breakfast is ready. You'll have to serve yourself." Jocelyn placed two pieces of sausage and a biscuit on her plate and walked out the kitchen.

"She's been like that all night. I'm surprised she made us breakfast," Brandon said when she was gone.

"I apologize for bringing this into your home."

"I'm glad it's finally out in the open. Now we just need to figure out how to deal with it." Brandon got up from the table and made him and his brother a plate. "You want some of everything?" he asked.

Jerome looked at the stove. Jocelyn had made grits, eggs, sausage, and biscuits. "Yes, I am pretty hungry." He sipped on his coffee. "Renee was pretty upset last night."

"Can you blame her?" Brandon handed Jerome a plate of food.

Before Jerome could say anything, Jocelyn came back into the kitchen and poured herself a glass of orange juice. She slammed the refrigerator and faced Jerome. "How could you ruin your marriage?"

"Jocelyn," Brandon said, "you promised to stay out of it."

"Somebody's got to say something," Jocelyn snapped.

"That somebody doesn't have to be you, sweetheart," Brandon sang.

For the next two minutes, Jerome listened to Jocelyn rant about his responsibility as a husband and father.

Brandon sat by and let his wife say her piece. When she was upset, there was no stopping her.

Jerome stared straight ahead in order to appear as if he

was paying attention. Involuntarily, the fork in Jerome's hand fell to the floor, and a sharp pain raced up his left arm. No one had noticed that he was in pain. He tried to get up but almost immediately fell back into his seat. He placed his hand over his chest and tried to speak, but he couldn't.

Brandon ran to his side, and Jerome looked at him with a blank stare. Brandon's mouth was moving, but Jerome couldn't make out the words. He tried to stand again, but this time, instead of falling back into the seat, he fell hard to the floor.

"Jerome. Jerome. Jerome!" Brandon cried.

Chapter Nineteen

~ *Taylor* ~

Up and dressed for the early Sunday service, Taylor left her prayer chair with a heavy heart. This time it wasn't because of her family or business. Today, Jerome and his wife were the center of concern. It had dawned on Taylor that a continuous relationship between Jerome and their daughter was more than likely contingent upon Renee's approval. Renee was a God-fearing woman, but she had threatened divorce in the past. It was possible that she would give Jerome an ultimatum, and Taylor feared that, given a choice, he would choose Renee over Joi.

Taylor closed her Bible, and before she left the chair, recited the prayer of Jabez. A significant increase in her life had yet to be seen, but Taylor trusted that God would one day turn things around. She just needed to wait patiently. Like Isaiah 40-31 read: *But they that wait upon the LORD shall renew their strength; they shall mount up with wings as eagles; they shall run, and not be weary; and they shall walk, and not faint.* So, although things looked the same, Taylor continued to pray and be patient.

She tipped to the bed, careful not to rip her sheer pantyhose, and lowered her body onto the mattress. Gently, she nudged her snoring husband awake. "I think I should talk to Renee," she said when his eyes opened.

Lance yawned then pulled the covers over his shoulder. "Leave it alone, Taylor. Let Jerome handle this by himself," he said and rolled over, an indication that the conversation was finished.

Although she had more to say, Taylor refrained from speaking. As carefully as she and Lance had planned for this moment, nothing had played out the way they imagined. Neither one of them really understood the magnitude of the situation, making it difficult at times to accept the reality of it all. Jerome would be a part of their lives for a long time. He would no longer be known as the man who sent monthly checks. He'd be around for birthdays, holidays, and special occasions. Lance tried to remain supportive, but Taylor could tell his patience was wearing thin.

"All right," she replied and got off the bed. There was no point in pursuing the matter any further.

Making her way around several objects in the bedroom, Taylor stopped at her dresser. She had ten minutes to spare before she had to leave the house. The last time she'd been to church without her family, her children were toddlers. She needed to go to an early service, in order to attend an open house with Collette Brown, her new realtor, at noon.

Taylor rummaged through her makeup case and pulled out a seldom-used shade of red lipstick. Generally she wasn't a fan of lip colors in the red family but decided to give Revlon's *Mulled Wine* a try. She smoothed on one layer, rubbed her lips together, and gave herself one final check in the full-length mirror behind the closet door. In her navy suit, Taylor felt like she was going on an interview. To give her outfit a splash of color, she searched through a collection of scarves and settled on the only gift she ever received from Gizelle.

She tied the olive and cream scarf loosely around her neck, hiding a small amount of cleavage, and looked in the mirror again. It looked much better.

"All right, babe. I'm leaving," she said as she slid into her year-old Anne Klein heels that looked brand-new. "Make sure the kids are up in time for Sunday School." Taylor grabbed a winter white Coach purse hanging on the doorknob and looked back at her husband. "Did you hear me?"

Lance wiggled his fingers.

"Okay, the open house ends at two, so we should get home around the same time," she said and left the room.

Church let out a half hour earlier than normal, so Taylor took the scenic route downtown to kill time. She cruised around Center City then through Society Hill. None of the stores seemed similar to her secondhand shop. There was definitely a market for her type of business in the neighborhood. As she traveled through the ritzy part of the city, she listened to the sermon her pastor preached on CD. It wasn't often that she purchased CD sermons. She was usually preoccupied with a dozen other things when she was driving. But the message he delivered was powerful, one she wanted to engrave in her spirit.

As she turned onto Second Street, she turned up the volume.

"The Christian life was never promised as an easy way to live," the pastor said. "Instead, Paul constantly reminds us that we must have a purpose and a plan, because times will be difficult and Satan will attack. But we never persevere without the promise of a prize, a promise God will keep."

As Taylor thought about the challenges she was up against, she shouted, "I know that's right!"

The traffic light ahead turned yellow, and Taylor slowed down. Rather than charge through the intersection, she decided to stop and take advantage of the scenery. Other than trips to the fabric district, the only time she was in that neighborhood was to entertain out-of-town guests.

A heap of snow fell from the branch of a tree and landed on the hood of Taylor's car. She looked out the window, checking to see if more snow was soon to follow. Behind the tree was Luxury Inn, a hotel that at one time had been notorious for high-profile parties. Taylor and Sherry used to socialize there often. She had learned, during her affair with Jerome, that Renee was a respected and important part of the Luxury Inn empire. It was possible that their paths had crossed at one of the infamous events. Taylor stared at the front door, wondering if Renee was staying at the hotel or with family.

The light changed, and the white Toyota Rav behind Taylor honked its horn. She put her foot on the gas and circled the corner. Looking at the clock on the dashboard, she had thirty minutes before meeting Collette. As she turned the corner, a car pulled out of a space, and she rushed in the spot. Since the hotel was located in a heavily commercial area of the city, finding a place to park was often near impossible. With the ignition running, she contemplated whether or not she should go inside.

There is a prize at the end, Taylor recalled, believing she needed to take advantage of the moment for the sake of her daughter. She turned off the car, unsure of what was going to happen next. She dropped her hands in her lap and thought about the conversation she had with Lance before she left the house. She knew Lance would be upset about her visit to the hotel, but Taylor believed she was doing what was best for Joi. "Sorry, baby, but I have to do this," she said and got out of the car.

Taylor's feet moved faster than her thoughts. Before she could come up with a plan, she was standing in line at the front desk. Not knowing if Renee was at the hotel, she took a chance and said, "I'm here to see Renee Thomas."

"Sure," the lively clerk said and picked up the house phone receiver. "May I ask your name?"

Taylor remembered Jerome's sister-in-law from a brief encounter when they were dating. "Tell her it's Jocelyn," she said and held her breath as the clerk talked softly into the phone.

She thought for sure her lie had been exposed when the clerk hung up the phone, and she prepared herself for the embarrassment.

"She's in the Mercury Room. Just turn left by the elevator. It's about midway down that hall," the clerk said, and Taylor was relieved.

Taylor followed the instructions given to her, praying for guidance as she neared her final destination. The encounter was not previously planned, so whatever came out of Taylor's mouth would be unrehearsed and unscripted. She had no choice but to flow with the Spirit.

When Taylor finally reached the Mercury Room, she tapped the door lightly and held her breath.

Renee opened the door, and immediately the smile on her face turned sour. "What do *you* want?"

"I'm sorry about using Jocelyn's name," Taylor mumbled, her heart beating fast. "But I-I needed to talk to you."

"I see we need better security around here," Renee said and attempted to shut the door.

Taylor stuck her Anne Klein heel in the door, hurting her big toe. She had come too far to leave. "I know I'm the last person you want to see, but can I please come in?"

Renee looked at Taylor as if she was out of her mind. "Don't you think you've caused enough trouble?"

"Considering what happened yesterday, I thought it might be time for us to talk. If you let me come in—"

"Absolutely not," Renee said strongly. "I have a plane to catch."

Taylor looked through the small crack between the door

and saw two suitcases near the wall. Renee was telling the truth. "I'll only be a minute," she pleaded.

"Then I suggest you get started."

Renee's facial expression reminded Taylor of her fourth grade teacher, a teacher that didn't tolerate foolishness of any kind. At the end of the hall, Taylor heard the house-keeping staff preparing for their morning rounds. She looked back at them, and although they seemed focused on their assignments, Taylor was uncomfortable having them within hearing range. "Are you sure you don't want me to come in?" she asked Renee one last time.

"I'm positive," she replied. "And your time in winding down."

Taylor moved close to the wall and in a whisper said, "I know my apology means nothing to you now, but I am truly sorry. There's no excuse for what I did. But my relationship with Jerome—"

"I wouldn't go around bragging about the affair you had with *my husband*," Renee snapped.

Taylor glanced down the hall. The housekeepers had finished loading their carts and were lined up by the service elevator. "Renee, I know how you must feel."

"Do you?" Renee asked, unenthused. "Are you married, Taylor?"

"Yes."

"Any children?"

"I have four," she answered and noticed a guard coming down the hall. To control her shaking hands, Taylor tightened the grip on her purse.

Renee greeted the powerfully built guard as he passed the door. The phone inside the meeting room rang and she ignored it. "Let me say this," Renee continued, "and then I really do need to go. I spent years building a life for my family, making sacrifice after sacrifice, only to have my husband sleep with another woman when things got tough. Whatever Jerome was going through at that time, instead of facing me and dealing with our problems like a man and husband should, he chose to turn to you."

The phone rang again, and Renee paused briefly. After the second ring it stopped, and she finished her thoughts. "I was helping him become a good husband and father. You were his escape, someone that didn't pressure him about bills, dirty clothes, or kids. I made a promise to Jerome, to be there for him for better or worse. And Lord knows he's tested my commitment. You only know a small portion of Jerome. I have a life with him, children with him. You had a fling."

Hearing her words, Taylor felt demeaned. She hadn't come to the hotel for that. Feeling the need to save face, Taylor was compelled to defend the affair, even though she knew it was wrong. "Renee, we had two years. I was more than some temporary plaything. You can't deny that I—"

Renee cut her off. "And he didn't leave me. What does that tell you?"

Taylor fell silent. The truth hurt. She stood by the door shaking her head in disgust. Disgust with herself and the situation she helped to create.

Just when Taylor thought Renee was done, she said, "But now imagine what I feel after all that I've been through with the man I love; the forgiveness, the trust I had to rebuild . . . here we are again. As a woman, why couldn't you tell me?"

For the first time since she'd been there, Taylor saw the hurt and betrayal in Renee's eyes. "I didn't think it was my place," she said, holding back tears. "I figured that one of the child support letters would include a note . . ." Taylor stopped talking abruptly. From the look on Renee's face, Taylor knew she had said too much. If Jerome never mentioned Joi, he certainly never mentioned the money he sent every month.

Renee's cell phone rang, and she looked at Taylor wearily. She was done talking. "What is it that you want from me?" she asked.

"My daughter is not to blame. She only wants to get to know her father," Taylor explained. "I thought that, as Christians, we could find it in our hearts to make this as painless as possible."

"Don't go there, Taylor," Renee replied. "You were a *Christian* when you slept with my husband one last time. And after all that crying you did on my shoulder."

Renee had punched her in the gut with her words again. She was absolutely right. Taylor had forgotten about that. Many years ago, she and Renee had found themselves standing next to one another at an altar call. Filled with regret, Taylor had cried to Renee and begged for forgiveness. How could she really expect Renee to forgive her now?

The phone in the office rang again simultaneously with Renee's cell phone. The guard from earlier briskly headed down the hall, and before he reached her said, "Mrs. Thomas, you should answer that."

Renee let the door close so that she could answer the phone.

While Renee answered the call, the guard stared at Taylor as if she was the enemy. "You might want to leave. There's been a family emergency," he said.

Looking up at the guard, Taylor buckled. She wanted sympathy, but he had none to give her. Standing in the hallway, her face wet from tears, Taylor thought it best that she leave, but she heard Renee's voice raise, asking for directions to a hospital.

Rushing out the door, one arm in her coat sleeve, Renee glared at Taylor, her eyes piercing through her soul. "I guess I have you to thank for his heart attack, too."

"Jerome's in the hospital?" Taylor asked, trailing Renee

and the guard escorting her down the hall. "He's had a heart attack?"

Renee stopped walking and swung around to face Taylor. "For the love of God," she snapped, her tone mixed with frustration and fear, "why can't you just leave me and my family alone?"

The guard grabbed Renee's arm and stood between the two women. "Mrs. Thomas, your cab is waiting for you," he said. "You really should leave now."

Frazzled, Taylor waited until Renee's cab pulled off. She called Collette to reschedule her appointment then hit the speed dial for her house. "Jerome's had a heart attack!" she yelled.

"What? Where are you?"

Taylor took a deep breath and told her husband that, against his wishes, she had visited Renee at the hotel.

"I told you not to upset that woman," Lance said. "I thought we had an understanding this morning."

"Not now, Lance. Just let Joi know about her father. I'm on my way home."

Lance belted out his frustrations as he replaced a few white lights on their artificial Christmas tree. He handled the lights with such force, Taylor was afraid the tree would fall over. She'd never seen her husband so upset.

"Jerome has only been in town a couple days, and already you've fallen under his spell," Lance said and kicked an empty box aside as he circled the tree, his caramel tone now a deep shade of red. "I pray he'll be all right, but I will not let him turn this family upside down."

Draped in winter coats and accessories, Taylor and Joi stood side by side quietly in the middle of the family room. They were on their way to the hospital before Lance had stopped them.

Finished with the lights, Lance stopped talking long

enough to stand back and marvel at the red and gold dec-
orations on the tree. "I pray he'll make it through okay,
but you have to understand that Renee doesn't feel Joi is
entitled to be with their family. That could change later,
but who knows?" Lance turned to face his wife. "Can you
please listen to me this time?"

"But I am his daughter," Joi stated firmly, her eyes red
from crying. "Why can't I go?"

Lance took a moment to calm down. "Renee just found
out about you. There's a whole lot for her to digest before
she can accept what happened."

"But how will I know that he's okay?" Joi wanted to
know.

"We can call the hospital. But your dad is right, sweetie,"
Taylor responded and took off her coat. It was clear that
she was in for the evening.

"She needs to wait a few days," Lance suggested.

In Joi's defense, Taylor said, "What harm will contacting the hospital do? She doesn't have to call and say she's
his daughter."

"Did it ever occur to you that his children may not
know about Joi either?"

Taylor tossed her coat over her arm. "She has a right to
know how he's doing, Lance."

"Are you sure it's Joi who wants to know about him?"
Lance locked his eyes on his wife.

Taylor couldn't believe the words that came from Lance's
mouth. It didn't matter that they'd been married over fourteen years. Jerome would forever be known as the man
who captured Taylor's heart many years ago, the man that
kept them from being together when they all worked at
SEPTA. It also didn't help that Taylor turned down Lance's
first marriage proposal because she hoped Jerome would
come back into her life. Some wounds never heal.

"I had a feeling in my spirit this morning, and when I

passed the hotel I thought God wanted me to talk to her," Taylor murmured softly. "The sermon said—"

"God didn't tell you to go and upset that woman, Tay. That was all you," Lance said. "The devil laid a trap, and you fell right in. You were supposed to be looking at a new building. Now what if that was the one you were meant to lease?"

"I know what this looks like, Lance, but I needed to say something to her."

"Why can't you see that Jerome needs to talk to Renee first? She is his wife," Lance bellowed, and Taylor jumped. "What is this hold he has on you, Taylor?"

There was no hold; at least none that Taylor could see, other than the connection to their daughter.

"This is all my fault," Joi blurted. "If he hadn't played basketball with me—"

"Don't think like that," Lance said and walked over to Joi. "It takes months, maybe years, for a heart attack to build up in your system."

Teary-eyed, Joi looked into Lance's eyes and asked, "Can you pray for him, Daddy? Now . . . with me?"

Unable to tell Joi no, Lance grabbed her hands.

Taylor knew praying for Jerome was a stretch, but that was the kind of man Lance was. He effortlessly put his own emotions aside for the good of his children. Taylor placed her coat over the rail and joined her husband and daughter, and together they prayed for Jerome.

Chapter Twenty

~ *Jerome* ~

"He's in room 234," the intensive care nurse informed Jerome's children.

Barely reading the numbers on the doors as they raced down the hall, the boys and Zora flew into the hospital room. Two doctors stood over Jerome, exchanging opinions about his condition and writing in their tablets.

"Good morning," Jerome Jr. greeted, interrupting their chatter. "I'm Jerome's son. Can you tell me what happened?"

Unlike his brothers, Joshua paused at the door. The tubes coming from various parts of Jerome's body, and the constant beep of the heart monitor was too much for him to digest at one time.

The boys listened intently as the middle-aged doctor explained the diagnosis.

"But he's in great shape," Jerome Jr. mentioned when the doctors were done.

"The heart can be a tricky organ," the other doctor interjected. "Your father's cholesterol is high, and he has high blood pressure. These things should have been treated a long time ago. He's lucky someone was around him when the attack occurred."

"He needs to continue exercise, but nothing too strenuous, and work on a better diet," the first doctor said.

Reggie poked and touched his father's limbs, checking for any unusual reactions or signs of discomfort. "We'll make sure he does better," he told the doctor.

"We'll be back in a few hours to check on him. He may not be able to talk much when he wakes up, but I assure you he's okay. He'll be himself in a few days," the doctor said.

Still not ready to look at his father, Joshua moved behind his oldest brother when the doctors left the room. "Where's Mom?" he asked.

Reggie looked around. "Good question. Did you call her cell?" he asked Jerome Jr.

Puzzled, Jerome Jr. said, "She was supposed to meet us here. I'll go try her cell again."

"You stay here," Zora said. "I'll go look into it."

Minutes later Zora returned with Renee sluggishly walking behind her. Renee kissed her children one by one then walked over to the hospital bed, her face expressionless and cold. "I was in the waiting room."

"How are you holding up?" Reggie asked.

"I'm fine." Renee crossed her arms and sighed. "I'm leaving tonight."

"Huh?" Jerome Jr. looked at his mother, shocked. "Work can't wait? Do you need me to call Everett and tell him what happened?"

"He knows." Renee rubbed her arms. The room was chilly, even for her. "I need to work, Junior. I'll call the hospital often, and I'm sure you'll keep me abreast of any changes. Your father's strong. He'll live." Renee placed her hand on the metal railing of the bed and gazed at her husband. "Your aunt and uncle are in the cafeteria. They should be back shortly."

"Are you sure you want to leave, Mom?" Jerome asked, still unpleased with her decision.

Renee faced her family. "Don't worry about me. As long as you're here, I'm sure things will be fine."

"But Christmas is in three days," Jerome Jr. added.

"Since you'll be here, maybe I'll go stay with Grace and the kids."

The boys were silent and more confused than they'd ever been. Their parents had been inseparable since the move to Chicago. They knew their mother would never leave Jerome's side at a time like this.

Renee held Joshua's hand. "I promise I'll give each of you a call every day." She looked at Jerome one more time. "Let me know if anything changes."

When Renee left, the boys stared at one another. "You think she's in shock?" Jerome Jr. asked. "Maybe I should follow her."

"Let her go," Zora said and stopped Jerome Jr. from walking out the door. "She's concerned about Pop, but she needs some space right now."

"Space for what?"

"Let it rest, Junior," Zora said. "Let's focus on Pop right now."

Jerome's family sat in the hospital room in silence for hours before he stirred. "This isn't exactly the Christmas present I had in mind," Reggie teased when Jerome's eyes opened.

At the sight of his sons around him, Jerome smiled as best he could.

Finally able to stand the sight of his father up close, Joshua held Jerome's hand. "The doctor said you have high blood pressure and high cholesterol, Pop. You've got to take better care of yourself."

Jerome turned his head from side to side and tried to utter Renee's name.

"She went home . . . home to River Forest," Jerome Jr. replied. "Is there something going on between you two that we should know about?"

"Maybe you shouldn't ask so many questions right now," Joshua said to his brother.

"I'm trying to find out what's going on?"

"Pop's not up for a lot of talking. Can't you ask him later?" Joshua pleaded.

Jerome Jr. looked around the room. "Don't we all want to know what brought on the attack?"

Reggie finally stepped in. "Josh is right, Junior. Pop needs to rest."

"All right, fellas," Zora called from her chair, "take this outside if you have to."

Jerome Jr. backed away. "It doesn't seem odd to everyone that Mom's not here. Or that Aunt Jocelyn didn't come back to the room?"

"My wife is right," Reggie asserted. "You're gonna raise Pop's pressure. Save your interviewing techniques for later."

Jerome Jr. turned to face Zora, as if he'd just uncovered a mystery. "Did Mom say something to you?"

Unaffected by the bass in his tone, Zora continued to edit an article she had written for a DePaul University newspaper. "Mom will talk to you when she gets back."

Brandon, who had been sitting quietly in a corner, finally spoke. "In case you hadn't noticed, your father is crying. Maybe everyone needs to leave for a few minutes just to cool off."

"I'm going to get something to drink," Jerome Jr. said, and, like a spoiled infant, stormed out of the room.

"I'll go with him," Reggie said and looked at Zora quizzically. "We'll talk later."

As Reggie headed out the door, Joshua also turned to leave. "I guess I need to go with them."

Brandon and Zora were the only visitors left in Jerome's hospital room. They looked at one another, their eyes confirming knowledge of the truth. Zora got off her chair and walked to Jerome. She wiped his eyes with her finger. Jerome tried to speak, but she motioned for him to keep quiet. "No matter what you've done, God says that all things work together for the good. You made it through a heart attack, so I have confidence you can make it through this, too."

* * *

"Merry Christmas," Jerome's nurse said as she entered the room. In the last three days, she'd come in twice throughout the night and once in the morning, checking his vitals and drawing blood. The constant interruption and change in his normal routines had started to depress him. He was ready to go home and sleep in his own Sealy Posturepedic®, next to his wife.

"Okay," the nurse said, rolling her mobile station next to his bed. "Let me get a good vein."

Easing his weakened limb from under a blanket, Jerome placed it in the nurse's hand. He turned away, the sight of his own blood making him squeamish.

In the corner of the room, Joshua was sleeping in the recliner. The hospital had been his second home. Head cocked to the side with two thin lightweight blankets covering his long body, Joshua had to be uncomfortable. Jerome hated that his family had to spend Christmas and New Year;s this way.

"The doctor tells me you're leaving in a few days. We're gonna miss you around here," she said as she labeled Jerome's tube of blood. She placed the vial on her cart then reached inside her pocket. "You have a lot of messages from last night." She read off the names slowly. "Reggie, Melanie, Grace, Renee, Joi . . . Joi called a few times. Your phone should be working today. If you need help, buzz me, okay?"

"Merry Christmas," he said and tried to fall back to sleep before visitors arrived.

Reggie entered the room as Jerome strolled out of the bathroom in a new pair of silk pajamas. He wasn't expecting anyone other than family, but just in case, he wanted to look presentable.

"Somebody loves you," Reggie said, lifting a shopping bag full of gifts in the air.

With a little help from Joshua, Jerome got back into bed and opened every gift: a robe, wallet, set of ties, and a golf certificate, all gifts from Reggie and Zora, Jerome Jr. and Grace, the grandchildren. Nothing from Renee. Jerome guessed he should count his blessings that Renee had called at all and left a message.

"I know something big happened between you and Mom," Reggie said as he balled up ripped wrapping paper and stuffed it into the wastebasket. "Zora knows too, but she won't say anything. Whatever it is, I pray God will help you work it out."

Jerome could tell Reggie wanted him to talk, but he wasn't going to say anything until he talked to Renee. "We had an argument," was all Jerome said.

"That must've been a pretty big fight. I mean, you have a heart attack, and Mom doesn't want to be here with you."

Jerome had never been at a loss for words, but he found it hard to speak.

"Your mom and I will be all right. We used to argue all

the time when you were small," Jerome tried to joke. "A little space is all we need."

"This is different," Reggie replied. "We don't need to talk about it. I know married couples don't always see eye to eye. But I hope this won't affect the family."

The phone rang, and Joshua jumped to answer it.

"Well," Reggie said, "I better go. Josh needs to get cleaned up and changed."

"It's Pastor Hampton," Joshua said and handed Jerome the phone.

"We'll see you after dinner," Reggie whispered and tipped out of the room.

Joshua gathered his things and followed his older brother.

"I didn't act fast enough," Jerome told the pastor once his children were gone. "I should've known better."

Jerome told Pastor Hampton the details of his trip to Philadelphia. Talking, he found, was therapeutic. Saying the words aloud helped him see that he had been selfish. He knew Renee and the kids needed a husband and father, and he had been that to the best of his ability. But what about Joi? Jerome had resented his own father for not being around. How could he, in good conscience, let Joi experience the emptiness he felt as a child? As Jerome approached the end of his story, he was ashamed of himself.

Hearing the disappointment in his voice, Pastor Hampton tried to lift his spirits. "As I listen to you speak, I am reminded of Jonah. Do you know his story?"

"Yes," Jerome replied. "He was the prophet swallowed by the fish because he was running from God."

"That's right. God sent a storm Jonah's way when he wouldn't obey Him. Sound familiar?" Pastor Hampton asked. "While Jonah was held up in that fish, he had plenty of time to reflect on things. And look how powerful his life was after the fish spit him out. While you're held up in the hospital, ask God what He wants you to do now. I'll bet He has great plans for your life that will not only bless you, but the kingdom."

By the time Jerome ended the call with Pastor Hampton, it was time for dinner. He removed the protective lid from the plate of food and frowned. Meatloaf wasn't exactly his favorite. Longing for the turkey, ham, macaroni and cheese, greens and stuffing Renee prepared each year, he exhaled. Due to his current condition, Thanksgiving may have been his last soulful meal.

He took a bite of the meatloaf and pretended it was Renee's cooking. This was not the way he wanted to spend Christmas. His heart went out to those who had no family to spend holidays with, and he vowed not to take his for granted. Jerome closed his eyes and thought about his life. He wanted to tell God to have His way, but feared His way wouldn't include Renee. Not wanting to prolong his stay in the "belly of the fish" as the prophet Jonah had done, Jerome put his pride and emotions aside. God was in control, and whatever He had in store for his life, Jerome prayed he'd be able to accept it.

Chapter Twenty-One

~ *Joi* ~

Cuddling an autographed basketball, Joi lay under the Christmas tree listening to a classic Luther Vandross holiday CD. The basketball was a gift from Jerome. He had used his WNBA connections to track down Sheryl Swoopes and have her sign the ball. In Joi's eyes, the only thing that could've topped Jerome's gift would've been Sheryl delivering the ball in person.

With Lance's permission, Joi had called Jerome early in the morning to thank him. It was the first time she'd actually spoken to him since he was admitted into the hospital. Jerome didn't sound like himself, but did his best to appear in great spirits, joking that a rematch on the court was needed.

Leah danced around Joi in her new ballet shoes, holding tight to the souvenir booklet she purchased at a recent Rhianna concert. Besides the new basketball that Joi received, going to the concert was the highlight of Christmas. Joi tucked the basketball under her arm and played a game on her new iPod, a gift from her parents.

This year, Christmas was not the same. In previous

years the holiday season was the one time the house was full of joy and extended family time together. But, so far, there was nothing but tension in the air. Jerome's sudden illness had caused a strain between her parents. They barely talked to one another, and family time activities were often split between the females and the males. Their lack of communication affected everyone in the house. The twins stopped their pranks, and Leah was quieter than she'd ever been, reading a book every spare minute she had.

Taylor and Lance were supposed to go away for a few days, but postponed the trip. Taylor claimed she had a lot to do at work, and Lance wanted to finally finish Gram's house. Joi was disappointed. She had looked forward to staying with her aunt for a few days.

The one thing that had remained the same was Taylor's passion for cooking. She was in the kitchen more than any other part of the house. No one disturbed her, especially not today; not even Lance. He spent the day assembling toys and helping the twins build a Star Wars scene with a bunch of Lego® pieces.

The doorbell rang, and Lance got up from the floor to answer it. They were expecting Gram and Gizelle's family for dinner. Initially the plan was to have dinner at Gram's, but Taylor refused to go. "She can't have Thanksgiving, Christmas, *and* New Year's," Joi heard Taylor say to Lance one night.

Joi put down the iPod and braced herself for her family, praying there wouldn't be any drama. On Thanksgiving, Gizelle and Taylor had cut eyes at one another all evening. Although Taylor and Gizelle never disagreed at the dinner table, Joi had learned that anything was possible.

"Merry Christmas," Kara said as she walked in the house.

Joi smiled. She hadn't expected to see Kara or her husband until after the New Year.

"Harold and I just wanted to stop by and leave a few gifts for the kids," Kara told Lance. "We're on our way to Stephanie's, and since you were on the way." Kara pointed to Harold, his cue to pass out the gifts in his hand.

Taylor came out of the kitchen, the tiny specs of glitter in her black velour dress sparkling under the light. "God's birthday is a special occasion," she'd say whenever someone asked why she was so dressed up, although Taylor didn't need an excuse. She happily embraced every opportunity to put on fancy clothes.

For the next hour, Joi watched her parents talk as if nothing was wrong, like they'd been one happy married couple all week.

Joi's cell phone vibrated against her leg, and she checked the text message. It was from Markus, and he wanted to know what time he should be at the mall. They had planned to meet downtown the day after Christmas and do some shopping together. Taylor didn't have any suspicions about Joi's plans. As far as Taylor knew, Joi was going out with Rayven to spend the many gift certificates she'd received for Christmas.

Joi raced upstairs, the basketball tight under her arm, and closed her bedroom door. She plopped on her bed and placed the ball on her lap. No sooner than she flipped her cell open, someone tapped lightly on her door. The softness of the knock told Joi that it might have been Leah, but she was wrong.

"Hey, lady," Kara said. "I came up to see your room. Taylor said you finally cleaned it."

Joi shook her head. *What else had Mother told her friends?* Stepping aside, Joi invited Kara inside.

Kara browsed the medium-sized room, initiating conversations about school and sports.

Joi could tell there was something on her mind. She actively engaged in the casual dialogue, waiting for the true purpose of the visit to arise. Whenever there was something Taylor couldn't get Joi to confess, she sent in reinforcements. Usually it was her godmother, Sherry. Although Kara and Sherry were her mother's best friends, Joi didn't mind talking to them. They often listened to Joi without judgment and ridicule.

"I hear Jerome is doing better." Kara sat on Joi's bed, her face more serious than before.

"Yeah, I spoke to him this morning," Joi replied and hugged her basketball. "Did you know him?"

"I knew him way before I met your mother. We all worked for SEPTA at one time," Kara answered, her petite frame sitting in a perfect posture. "Learning about Jerome must've been tough. How are you feeling about it?"

"Aunt Kara, I feel like I caused more problems in everybody's life," Joi began. "Jerome wouldn't have had a heart attack if he wasn't here playing ball with me. Then his wife showed up out of nowhere. That was a lot on him."

"You look like your father, but you think and feel the way your mother does," Kara said. "She blames herself for what happened, and you're doing the same thing. You had no control over what took place. The heart attack could've happened anywhere, and Renee would've found out eventually."

"And what about Mother? Her and Daddy are not doing too good either, and I know it's because of me. Why do I keep hurting people? What's wrong with me?"

Kara hugged Joi warmly. "There's not one thing wrong with you, sweetheart. You are a child of the King. That means you're royal. You just don't realize it yet. Your mother and Jerome both have their own battles to fight. You just happen to be the common thread between them."

"But bad things keep happening when I'm around," responded Joi as she placed the basketball next to her.

"It only feels that way. If you stop for a moment, you'd

see that there are tons of great things going on, too." Kara touched Joi's basketball. "You're a gifted player. Do you know how many people wish they had your talent? You have a beautiful sister and fantastic brothers that love you. Not everyone can say that. You're smart and attractive."

Joi smiled, covering the gap between her teeth with her tongue.

"I could go on, but do you know how many people wish they had your life? Instead of focusing on all the bad stuff that's going on, hold on to the good."

There were many things for Joi to be thankful for, but out of everything that came to mind, very little involved her mother. Especially within the last few years, Joi felt like an outsider when it came to Taylor. "Everyone I know seems to be so happy, and their families seem so perfect." Joi traced the lines of her ball with her finger.

"*Seem* is the operative word. You never know what a person is dealing with. Some people do a wonderful job at hiding their problems," Kara said. "Don't judge what you think is going on in someone's life by their appearance. Appearances can be deceiving. And don't base what your life should be like on someone else's. We all have our personal crosses to bear. God tailored a road map specifically for each of us that would make our lives better. That road map is not the same for everyone." Kara lifted Joi's chin with her index finger. "Just do your best, and remember that you are royal, precious."

Gram's hearty laugh echoed from downstairs. Kara and Joi were so busy talking that they hadn't heard anyone come in the house.

"I'd better go," Kara said. "My child is waiting for me, and you have company. We should really do this more often."

Joi agreed and followed Kara to the stairs. "Wait a minute," she said halfway down the steps. "I forgot something." Joi ran back to her bedroom. Quickly she sent a text message to Markus, grabbed her autographed basketball, and ran back to Kara. "Now I'm ready."

Seated at the dinner table, Joi and her family enjoyed the feast Taylor had prepared. She'd outdone herself this year, like she had something to prove. Joi and Taylor didn't agree on much, but Joi had no complaints when it came to her mother's cooking.

Joi looked around the table. Everyone appeared happy. They laughed, reminisced, and shared stories as a family should.

But when the plates were near empty and bellies were getting full, Joi smelled trouble in the air. Gizelle had been quiet for the last five minutes, something no one was used to. Lance often joked that as the youngest of Gram's children, she craved attention; thus the reason she talked so much.

In past years, Gram or Gizelle would wait until the plates were cleared and the guests were out of sight before they'd exchange unpleasant words with Taylor. Joi never heard any of the disagreements, she just knew they occurred, and usually the first woman that flew out of the kitchen was the one who grabbed their family and left the gathering early.

Gizelle buttered one of Taylor's homemade rolls, her lips ready to speak. "So, I hear there's a lot going on in this house."

Everyone seated around the table grew silent, their smiling faces casually subsiding.

"Jerome's in town and in the hospital, huh? Have you heard any news about his condition?"

Joi swallowed a huge amount of cranberry punch. She thought Taylor was going to respond, but her mother sat at the end of the table twirling her fork in a seafood linguini dish. "He's going to be fine," Joi replied.

"We're praying for a speedy recovery," added Lance, cutting a tender slice of roast beef in half with a fork.

"Send him my prayers the next time you talk to him," Gizelle said and scooped another heap of stuffing onto her plate. "Taylor, I hear you're also looking into a second store."

Taylor gave Lance an eerie glare. "I'm considering it, but nothing's been set in stone."

Gizelle frosted her third piece of ham with a special glaze and directed her next question to her niece. "How do you feel about that, Joi? You won't get to see a lot of your mother if she has *two* stores."

Wanting nothing to do with the argument in progress, Joi shrugged her shoulders. She loved her aunt, but was finally on good terms with her mother. "If that's what she wants to do, I guess it's all right."

Taylor stopped chewing the food in her mouth. "My kids and I will be fine. If you have concerns, please address me after dinner."

Under the table, Leah grabbed Joi's hand. This had, by far, been the worst Christmas Joi ever remembered.

"Glad to hear your business is doing well enough for a second location," Gram interjected.

"I'm not sure of the logistics, but I believe it can work," Taylor responded and resumed eating.

"It's a hard enough job being a wife and mother. Can you handle all of that responsibility?"

Gizelle's husband, seated on her left, subtly asked her to be quiet. Last year, Gizelle decided to stay at home, accepting only temporary and short-term projects from her previous job.

"Some women like going to work," Gram said. "When your father died, I had to enter the workforce again after being home for eleven years. I'm glad I did it. It felt good being around grown-ups and having meaningful conversations."

Taylor, her smile masking her anger, looked at Lance. Joi had seen that look many times. "As long as I have my family's support, I should be fine."

"Lance works, too," Gizelle bounced back. "Another store will put more pressure on him. Have you considered—"

Joi felt Gram smack Gizelle's leg. "Taylor will find a way to make it work. She's done a good job this far. Let's just enjoy Christ's day."

"My tournament is in two days," Joi announced to break the tension.

"You sure you want us there?" Gizelle's husband joked.

Lance put a forkful of string beans in his mouth. "We'll be there, Boss. And we'll all be on our best behavior."

The family was able to get through dinner without further incident once the topic of discussion shifted. Gram had done most of the talking. She was excited about her move to Maryland.

Before eating dessert, all prepared by Taylor, it was family tradition to watch a movie and let dinner digest. *This Christmas*, starring Loretta Divine, Idris Elba, and singing sensation, Chris Brown, was the featured selection. While everyone found a comfortable position in the family room, Taylor cleaned up alone, despite Gram's repeated offers to help.

The house was full of excitement and love, just as Joi liked. But as soon as everyone left, things were back to the way they were before the guests had arrived. Lance watched sports highlights in the family room, Taylor went to bed, Leah sat under the Christmas tree reading *Bud Not Buddy*, and the twins played Monopoly in their bedroom. Joi's once vibrant home was again cold and distant.

* * *

It was the day before her tournament, and Joi had not seen Jerome. That bothered her more than she admitted to her mother. Before meeting Markus at the Gallery down-town, she'd decided to make a trip to Delaware County Memorial.

Walking into the hospital, Joi stopped at the front desk for directions then headed to the gift shop. With the money she earned at Second Chance, she bought Jerome a card and single *Get Well* balloon. This was the first time she'd been in a hospital. She walked up two flights of stairs and paused at the nurses' station, in case she needed to sign in. "H-Hi," she said softly and coughed to clear her throat. "I'm here to see Jerome Thomas."

"You must be his daughter. You look just like him," a friendly nurse replied. "C'mon, I'll walk with you. It's time for his checkup." The nurse walked from behind the desk, her long ponytail bouncing with each step. "Your brothers have been here all morning."

A look of concern crossed Joi's face. The possibility that they were going to be there was a thought, but Joi was certain she'd be able to handle meeting them. They should have known about her by now for sure.

"Don't worry, precious," the nurse said. "Your dad is re-covering very well." She took Joi's free hand and led her down the hall.

Jerome's room was full of visitors. Although she'd only met Brandon, Joi felt like she knew the other people in the room from the family pictures Jerome had shown her. She had rehearsed this moment in her head, but now that it was happening, she was more nervous than before.

"I found your daughter roaming the hall, Mr. Thomas," the nurse said, pulling Joi inside the room.

"His daughter?" Joi heard one of them say, and like a motion picture, the activity in the room suspended. All eyes stared at Joi, then at Jerome.

"Pop, do you know this young lady?" Jerome Jr. in-quired.

With a look of shame, Jerome confirmed Joi's identity. "This is what I wanted to talk to you boys about," he said.

Reggie couldn't take his eyes off Joi. She resembled him the most. "Is this why Mom left?"

Joi wanted to leave. Her legs were numb and her mouth dry, but she'd come too far, and the damage had been done.

"Need I remind you that your father just had a heart attack?" a woman Joi recognized as Zora, from the family pictures Jerome had previously shown her, asked then stood next to her. "I think this is something we should discuss later. We are in a hospital."

"Zora, I'm trying to find out what's going on here," Jerome Jr. said and looked at Joi. In a strong and powerful voice, he asked a series of questions. "What's your name? Who is your mother? Where do you live? How old are you?"

Joi flinched after each inquiry. "Her . . . her name is Taylor, and I'm Joi. I live in West Philly."

"Taylor?" Reggie said before Joi could reveal her age. He walked to Jerome's bed and looked his father in the eye. "The same woman from Germantown?"

During all of the questioning, Joi noticed Joshua standing in a corner completely clueless, his head twisting from person to person as they spoke.

"Is she the reason why Mom left?" Jerome Jr. asked.

"I'm sorry," the nurse chimed in, "but I'm going to have to ask you to settle down."

Upset that she had possibly ruined the day for everyone in the room, Joi handed the nurse the card and balloon in her hand and ran out the door.

Not sure where to go, she knew she didn't want to go home. Without thinking, she boarded the 21 bus to Markus's apartment. When she got off at 43rd Street, she walked to

the middle of the block and climbed the steep stairs leading to Markus's house. Joi had held herself together long
enough to travel back to West Philly, but as soon as
Markus opened his door, she burst into tears.

"What happened, Boss?" Markus asked repeatedly, but
Joi couldn't speak from crying so hard. Markus pulled her
inside and led her to his previously-owned suede couch.
"Everything's gonna be okay." He tenderly stroked Joi's
head that was now resting on his shoulder. "Just please
try to calm down."

Joi looked up into his eyes and saw a concerned friend.
Wiping her eyes with her sleeve, she tried to steady herself.

Markus got up and returned with a tall glass of water.

"Thank you," Joi managed to say and drank a quarter of
the water.

"Wanna talk about what's going on?" Markus asked.

Joi shook her head and placed her glass on a cup holder
on the coffee table.

She inched closer to Markus and kissed him. She wanted
him, and it didn't matter that she hadn't started taking
birth control pills. Markus could use a condom. She just
wanted him to make her pain disappear. As she had seen
in the movies, Joi attempted to seduce Markus.

Although he was affected by her touch, Markus grabbed
Joi's hands before things got too far out of control. "We
can't do this today. Not like this, Boss. You're too upset."

Joi pouted, slow tears rolling down her cheek, and
Markus pulled her into his arms, where she stayed until it
was time for her to leave.

Chapter Twenty-Two

~ *Taylor* ~

Taylor left her store early after receiving Jerome's call. After her less-than-friendly, surprise encounter with Renee, Taylor didn't understand why Joi had gone to the hospital. *Like mother like daughter*, she supposed. Maybe there was something they had in common after all.

When Taylor walked into Joi's room, she was lying under the covers and throwing the basketball Jerome had given her for Christmas in the air.

"Jerome called me," she said and sat on the edge of Joi's bed. Rather than scold her for going to the hospital when she should've been shopping, Taylor sympathized with her daughter's pain. "What's going through your mind?"

"They were mean to me," Joi said, her large hands holding the ball in place on her lap. "I don't understand why so many people are mad at me."

"His family isn't really mad at you," Taylor explained. "Me, maybe, but not you. Jerome should've told them, but like me, he was probably afraid. Just give the family some time to sort things out."

"I really wanted to meet him, but if I'd known it would cause so much confusion . . ." Joi started to cry.

"Stop blaming yourself." Taylor reached out to hug her child. Joi's tears ignited the pain Taylor had buried deep inside, and she, too, started to cry. "This is my fault, but God will make it better. Trust me on this," Taylor whimpered, praying that she was right.

Taylor walked back downstairs after leaving Joi's room and entered the kitchen. Lance was seated in his usual spot, watching the news and eating a slice of lemon cake. They hadn't talked about what happened at Christmas dinner, and that bugged Taylor. As she walked by him, she mumbled a hello, and Lance returned her greeting.

The twins had begged for stuffed pork chops for dinner. Taylor took a pack of thawed pork chops out of the refrigerator, seasoned then stuffed them with a spinach and three-cheese mixture. Lance hadn't even looked her way. She'd been standing there for the past fifteen minutes and not a word from him. Something had to change.

Taylor slapped one of the chops onto a sheet of aluminum foil then turned around sharply to face her husband. "We can't go on like this. Don't you think it's time we talked about what's going on between us?"

"Now you want to talk," Lance replied. "You seem to be doing just fine without me."

"Oh, c'mon, Lance. I apologized for going to the hotel. Let it go," Taylor said, frustrated.

"What about getting the second store? You didn't talk to me about that. You didn't talk to me about the increased amount of time Joi spends at the store. And Jerome"—Lance changed the channel—"Where do I begin with him?"

"I didn't know you had so many bottled-up issues," responded Taylor. She continued to stuff the remaining pork chops and then put them into the oven. "But since we're being honest," she said and blocked Lance's television view, "why do you have to tell your mother and sisters *everything* that goes on in our home? You see how they turn things around and blame me for everything. Or maybe that's what you want," she snapped. "And when are you gonna finish our bedroom? I've got bruises a mile long from bumping into things. Meanwhile, Gram is walking around her castle like a queen."

Lance got up from the table and refilled his glass of iced tea.

Taylor wasn't sure if Lance was really listening to her, but she continued to talk, regardless. "And you're blind when it comes to Joi. She's doing better, but she's not the perfect angel you think she is. Joi doesn't share your genes, Lance. She's hardheaded and tough like—"

"Like who?" Lance slammed his glass on the table.

Taylor thought she heard it crack. Immediately, she wanted to apologize. Bringing up Jerome was wrong. "I'm sorry," she said, "but it's just that she needs a stern approach."

"My approach is not good enough for you? Or is it that Jerome has suggested something better?"

Taylor was tired of all the recent accusations concerning her feelings for Jerome. "How many times do I have to tell you that there's nothing between us anymore?"

"Until I believe it," Lance said.

Taylor threw her hands in the air. "You can't seriously be jealous of him, Lance. He's here to get to know Joi better. I thought you were okay with this."

"Is Joi the only person he's getting reacquainted with? You seem to talk to him on the phone more than you do Sherry and Kara."

Jerome was right. Since Jerome and Joi had connected, she had spent a great deal of time conversing with him.

Although they always talked about Joi, Taylor could understand why Lance would be concerned. Taylor and Jerome had a strong history.

"Have you spoken to him today?"

"That's not fair. Jerome's in the hospital. Is it a crime to check in on him? He is Joi's father."

"I know. You've been reminding me of that every day." Lance drank the rest of his ice tea then placed his glass in the sink. "If you need me, I'll be at Gram's," he replied and walked out of the kitchen.

Less than a minute later, Taylor heard the front door close.

At 3:12 A.M., Taylor woke up to find that Lance had not come to bed. That wasn't a good sign. She eased out of bed and walked downstairs, hoping to find him.

Bundled under the twins' old comforter, Lance was sound asleep on the couch.

This was the first time they'd ever slept apart. Rather than wake him, Taylor went back to her room and recited the prayer of Jabez until she fell back to sleep.

Chapter Twenty-Three

~ *Jerome* ~

Jerome looked over the release form and prescriptions the doctor had given him. After eight days in the hospital, he was finally leaving. He wished he was going home to Illinois, but one of his doctors had asked him to hang around for a few weeks. The doctor wanted to see Jerome a few more times before he went back to the Midwest.

Jerome hadn't seen his sons since Joi ran out of the hospital yesterday, so he wasn't sure if they'd come to pick him up. He tried to explain why he never mentioned Joi, but Jerome Jr.'s temper had escalated, and the attending nurse suggested that everyone leave.

He checked his watch and picked up his cell phone. While he waited for someone to show, he wanted to make sure Melanie had everything under control back at the office. *Future Ballers* had come too far for it to fall to pieces. Although Jerome had planned on going back to work full-time in February, he had given his team specific assignments to help move his special program forward.

As Jerome wrapped up his call with Melanie, Reggie

and Joshua walked into the room. Jerome was glad to see them.

"Well," Reggie said, "the doc says you're clear. We just need to wait for the nurse and the wheelchair."

Joshua helped Jerome off the bed and into the recliner.

While Joshua tied Jerome's shoe laces, Reggie made sure all his clothes and toiletries were packed. "This thing with Taylor and Joi could've played out better," he mentioned as he searched the room, "but I pray God will keep you and Mom together."

"They will," Joshua noted. "Have you spoken to Joi, Pop?"

"Yes, and once things calm down, I'll plan an official meeting between her and the family," Jerome responded as Joshua tied his laces. Jerome felt helpless. Renee should've been there taking care of him and making him feel strong. He had called her twice before noon, but she didn't answer. Jerome wondered if she was ignoring his calls on purpose.

As he waited to be escorted out of the hospital, Jerome sat with his sons in silence, positive they were all praying for the same thing—that Renee hadn't left Jerome for good.

Chapter Twenty-Four

~ *Taylor* ~

Taylor and Collette stood in front of an empty downtown building, drinking hot chocolate. It was New Year's Eve, and as Taylor waited for Lance to arrive, she envisioned all the ways God was going to bless her in the New Year.

Collette shared interesting details about the neighborhood, trying to convince her that the property was situated in a prime location. But Taylor didn't need much convincing. This was her third visit, so she was already impressed. She wanted to hear Lance's opinion. They had been at odds too long, and she hoped this could be something that they'd commit to together.

Taylor took a sip of her hot chocolate, and it singed the tip of her tongue. While she waited for her drink to cool off, she was about to call her husband, but spotted him walking down the sidewalk. And he wasn't alone. Gizelle walked closely beside him, her mouth moving nonstop.

Taylor sighed and prayed Gizelle's presence wouldn't ruin the morning. No matter what Gizelle said today, Taylor was determined not to get upset. Lance had taken out time to view a potential property with her, something she usually did alone, and that was a sign that they were headed in the right direction.

Gizelle spoke to Taylor then introduced herself to Collette. "I used to work down here," Gizelle told Taylor, her demeanor mysteriously pleasant. "A lot of people travel down this street."

Lance placed his arm around his wife and whispered in her ear, "Sorry I didn't let you know she was coming. By the time we left Costco, it was too late to take her home first."

"No problem," Taylor replied. "I'm just happy you're here."

"Shall we go in?" Collette used her special code to retrieve the key from the lockbox, then used it to open the front door. "Taylor's been here twice already, but please take all the time you need. I'll be in the Starbucks across the street when you're ready."

The property was huge, leaving room for a number of possibilities. A firm believer in Habakkuk 2:2-3, Taylor had written her vision for a second shop in a small tablet she kept in her purse. She liked to keep it close to remind her that her dream was going to happen in due time. There would need to be some work done to meet all of the criteria on her list, but the space was a near-exact match to her vision.

"So, what do you think?" Taylor asked Lance after she gave him a tour.

Gizelle spoke out of turn, "This is nice, but I thought you were going to wait."

Taylor was too excited to let Gizelle get under her skin. "The selling price isn't too far off what I wanted," she noted. "This place is perfect. There's a secluded spot for a personal shopper service and a small break-room for my employees. I can have a private office, and there are real dressing rooms in the back, not the kind I have at the other store, with a curtain for a door."

Gizelle walked around as if she were a licensed building inspector. "A place in this location and of this size must be expensive."

"What's the selling price?" Lance finally said.

Taylor wasn't sure if she should answer in front of her sister-in-law. She didn't want Gizelle's negativity to cloud his judgment. She moved closer to Lance and in a faint voice said, "Low five hundreds."

"Five hundreds? That's not bad for this area," Gizelle said, her hearing better than Taylor expected. "But can you afford that?"

Taylor's left brow arched. *Who was talking to her?* Gizelle acted as if money was coming directly out of her pocket. Taylor looked inside her purse and pulled out a stick of gum. It was all she could do to keep from telling Gizelle to mind her business.

"I'm sure Tay has thought of all her options," Lance replied and looked at his wife.

"I have, and we'll talk about them at a different time," she assured him to quiet Gizelle, although it wasn't completely true. Taylor had only seriously considered one option: a loan.

"And this is your third time here, correct?" Gizelle asked. "That means you're ready to buy it, huh?"

Taylor ignored her. "Can you get the camera from the car, Lance? I forgot to take pictures the last time I came."

Lance left the building, and no sooner had he closed the door than Gizelle's mood shifted. "Nice place, but are you sure it's the right time to invest in a project this huge?"

"Why wouldn't it be?" Taylor said, desperately holding on to her patience.

"Have you noticed that Joi is getting older and . . ." Gizelle stood by the front door, "more *mature?*"

Of course Taylor had noticed her daughter's sprouting breasts and plump hips. Not long after Joi's attitude changed, her slender physique disappeared. Taylor took a deep breath and silently recited words she shouldn't have. "Just spit out whatever you have to say, Gizelle."

"I hate to bring this up," Gizelle said. "You know I love Joi, but the night she stayed at my house, I overheard her telling Rayven something about birth control pills. She may not be a virgin anymore."

Taylor almost swallowed her gum. "If you don't have proof that she's having . . ." Taylor couldn't bring herself to say the word aloud. "If you can't prove it, then I suggest you not accuse my child of anything," Taylor snapped, trying to hide signs of worry.

"You need to be with her more, especially now that she's into boys," Gizelle offered, but her parenting advice fell on deaf ears.

Taylor looked out one of the smaller windows and tuned Gizelle out. Where was Lance with the camera? As Gizelle rambled on, something Linda said about Joi a while ago crossed Taylor's mind, and she made a mental note to give her a call.

"Look, there's no need to take offense. I'm just concerned about my niece," Gizelle said when she realized Taylor wasn't paying attention.

"You need to be more concerned about your own children," Taylor remarked.

Gizelle placed her hand on her hip and rolled her eyes. "Meaning?"

"Meaning, your boys aren't perfect. Before you throw stones at my house, you need to—"

Lance returned with the camera before Taylor could finish her statement.

Glad to see him, Taylor tried to take the camera from

his hands. "I can take the pictures, Lance. You and Gizelle should probably head back. I'm sure she has plenty to do for her party tonight."

Clearly upset, Gizelle glared at Taylor. Every year after the New Year's Eve service, she hosted a party for family and friends, and every year the attendance grew in number. "She's right," Gizelle told her brother. "I think it's time for me to go."

"I'll only be a few minutes," Lance said. "Besides, you take horrible pictures, baby."

Taylor was too upset to laugh at his corny joke. She leaned against the wall, and Gizelle stared out the large window as Lance played the role of a professional photographer.

When he went into the back of the store, Taylor followed him. She refused to be alone with Gizelle again.

"So what do you think?" Taylor asked.

"It's not bad." Lance took one last picture then put the camera back in its case. "But I hope you aren't getting a loan."

"I'll get money for the down payment," Taylor replied. "I may only need to get a small loan. I should be able to pay it off in two to three years."

Lance sighed. He wasn't in favor of a loan in any amount. "You know how I feel about loans. I know you really want another store, but I can't help you out. I put a lot into Gram's house, and you want me to renovate ours—"

"So you are planning to fix the house," Taylor replied, her tone bordering sarcasm. She wanted Lance to be supportive, not discouraging. "I haven't asked you for any money. God will make a way for this to happen." Annoyed, Taylor buttoned her coat. "Let's just get Collette so we can leave," she said before Lance spout words she didn't want to hear. It would've hurt her heart if he told her to give up on her dream.

Taylor walked back to the front of the store. Gizelle was in the same position, this time with a simple smirk on her face. Taylor turned her back to Gizelle then pulled her cell phone from her purse and called Collette. "We're ready," she told her.

Gizelle walked over to Taylor and pat her shoulder. "Something more affordable will come along."

"I haven't given up on this one yet," she confirmed.

Lance gave Taylor a kiss on the cheek. "I'm going to take Gizelle home then pick up the kids from Gram's. I'll be home after that. We need to be to church at six, right?"

"Five-thirty," Taylor corrected.

As Lance, and Gizelle's paths crossed Collette's, Taylor closed her eyes and prayed. "For the vision is yet for an appointed time. Though it tarry, wait for it, for it will surely come."

Taylor sat in the sanctuary, longing for a word from God. The year had been challenging on many levels, and she was ready for a new season to begin. She closed her eyes as the children's ministry blessed the congregation with their voices. She didn't notice that Leah had stepped to the front of the pulpit.

Seated behind her, Gram tapped Taylor's shoulder. "Is Leah singing a solo?"

Taylor's eyes popped open. She didn't know Leah's voice was strong enough for a solo. "This is news to me," she told Gram and turned to Joi. "Did you know about this?"

"She wanted to surprise everyone," Joi said and smiled.

The choir began singing "Now Behold the Lamb" by Kirk Franklin, and Leah proceeded to the area designed for the praise dancers. Taylor was confused. What was Leah about to do?

As the choir sang, Leah slowly came out of her choir robe and emerged in a beautiful white dress. With grace and elegance, She performed a dance selection without error. Taylor cried. Dance was something she never had a chance to do as a child. Although Leah had been in dance school since she was eight, Taylor thought she was pretending to enjoy it to make her happy. But as she watched Leah minister to the congregation through her movements, Taylor realized her daughter was gifted.

When the performance was over, the church members stood on their feet, many crying tears of joy, others praising God with a dance of their own.

When the energy in the sanctuary settled, the pastor stood in front of the podium and began his sermon. "No matter how old you are, *everyone* has a dream."

The pastor's words excited many of the members. Like Taylor, many of them were waiting for their dreams to manifest. Taylor listened intently as the pastor quoted verses from Genesis, highlighting stages of Joseph's life. "You need to verbalize your dream," the pastor said, "but be careful and beware of dream killers."

Immediately Taylor thought about the Belle women and the negative words they dropped into her spirit. Taylor studied her children and wondered what dreams dwelled inside of them. She prayed she'd never discourage them.

"For many of you," the pastor stated, wrapping up his sermon, "your dream is ready, but you're not ready for your dream. It could be that your attitude's not right, you can't manage money, you don't pray, or you have a poor work ethic. Whatever is holding back your dream, I pray this is the year God gets you ready. This is the year your dream will come to pass!" the pastor shouted.

Taylor jumped to her feet. "This is the year my dream will come to pass!" Taylor repeated, and in her heart she believed it to be true.

*   *   *

On the third day of the New Year, Taylor finally had a chance to reflect on her plans. With the exception of Leah, the kids were back in school, and she had taken a week off from work. She lay across her bed holding the phone. She needed to give Collette an answer about the downtown property soon. Someone else had expressed an interest in it, too.

Taylor stared at her financial statements one last time. No matter how she moved things around, there was no way she could come up with the down payment. She picked up the papers for Joi's college account. The money Jerome had sent through the years had accumulated to a substantial amount. Taylor was tempted to withdraw from that account, convincing herself that she would eventually return the money. But what if something happened and she couldn't? She'd never be able to forgive herself. And how would she explain that to Joi?

Taylor called Collette and relayed the information then got dressed.

Leah, who attended a specialized private school that started and ended a week later than most schools, walked into Taylor's bedroom. "What time are we going to the women's shelter?"

"I'll be ready in ten minutes," Taylor said, stuffing into a pair of black jeans as Leah strut around the room in her mother's Via Spiga heels. "I know you better get out of my good boots before you break my heel." She chuckled. "Do you know how much I paid for those?"

Leah giggled as she took off the boots. "Daddy bought these for you."

"Well, his money is my money, too," Taylor responded as she searched for her brown scarf.

Leah picked up the family picture leaning against the

wall on the floor. Taylor had replaced it with a Georgia O'Keeffe painting. "Why did you take this down?"

"Your father's going to paint soon," Taylor said, although it didn't explain why the other pictures were still hanging on the wall. She pulled out her drawer of scarves and dumped them on the bed. "Have you seen my brown and gold silk scarf? The one with the Coach symbols on them?"

"Joi wore it yesterday," Leah answered.

Taylor didn't normally allow Joi to wear her clothes. She wasn't as particular about clothes as Leah, but Taylor thought sharing some of her clothes would eventually influence Joi to change her style. Taylor walked down the hall and into Joi's room.

Leah ran behind her mother and immediately opened the jewelry box Taylor had given Joi a few years ago. "Don't take anything out of there, Leah. You know how Joi is about the items in that box," Taylor said as she scanned Joi's dresser.

"This is Jerome's family?" Leah asked, referring to pictures inside the box.

Taylor glanced at the photographs and nodded. She walked to Joi's bed and fumbled through the miscellaneous items around the floor, trying not to be invasive. She picked up Joi's backpack, thinking the scarf might be beneath it. As she lifted the bag, she saw a pamphlet on birth control sticking out of the mattress. *Oh God, Gizelle was right.*

Leah yelled, "I found it!" and inspected the scarf carefully. "There aren't any stains, but it smells like French fries."

"Okay, let's go," Taylor said, trying to rush out of the room.

"What's that?" Leah asked, pointing to the pamphlet in Taylor's hand.

"Nothing. Just some of Joi's school stuff," Taylor responded and folded the paper in half. "Let's go."

With Leah standing so close, Taylor couldn't think straight. She knew that girls Joi's age were having sex. That didn't shock her. She had been guilty of that, too. But she couldn't believe Joi was *that* serious about someone. Basketball had always been her primary focus.

After taking the scarf from Leah's hand, Taylor tied it loosely around her neck. It was time for her to have a serious conversation with Joi about boys and sex.

Taylor dropped the clothes off at the women's shelter then took Leah to Gram's. Afterward, she headed to the library to find Joi. She was supposed to be there researching information for an English paper. Taylor turned into the library's garage and parked near the elevator. She jumped out of the car and took the elevator to the second floor.

After Taylor circled the area where Joi should've been, she wondered if Joi had come to the library at all. Before she became angry and assumed her child was up to no good, she rushed into the hallway and discreetly dialed Joi's cell. It went straight to voicemail.

Twisting her lips in varying ways, Taylor sketched out a plan of action in her head. She took the elevator down to the cafeteria and combed each section from front to back. Joi was nowhere to be found.

Before panic set in, she called Joi's cell again. It still went to voicemail, and this time she left a message.

Taylor went back to the main lobby and paced the floor. The library was too big to search, but she felt the need to try. She pulled out an old picture and scoured each floor, asking people if they recognized her daughter.

After many unsuccessful queries, Taylor decided to leave. Back in the main lobby, she stood in the middle, slowly turning in circles. She called Lance, and he advised her to come home. On her way out the door, she was moved to ask one more person.

"By any chance, have you seen this teenage girl?" Taylor asked the guard on duty.

The guard didn't need to stare at the photograph. "She plays ball, right? She wears a varsity jacket sometimes?"

Taylor nodded yes.

"Nice girl. I've seen her, but not today."

Taylor was about to leave.

"You should probably check with her study partner. He was here about an hour ago."

He? "Can you describe him?" Taylor asked. "I want to make sure we're talking about the same boy."

The guard described the mystery boy in great detail then noted the scowl on Taylor's face. "Is she all right?" the guard asked, now concerned.

"Not once I get a hold of her," Taylor exclaimed. "Thanks for your help." Taylor rushed to the parking garage and tried Joi's cell again. Still no answer. She turned on the car and remembered that she hadn't spoken to Linda like she had planned to.

She dialed the store, and when Linda answered, said, "I hate to place you in the middle of my family affairs, but do you know anything about Joi's boyfriend? And please, Linda, be honest with me."

For the next ten minutes, Linda told Taylor everything she knew about Markus.

Taylor was so upset and nervous that she cried into the phone. She pulled herself together when the call ended, and before exiting the garage, she decided to call Joi's best friend. "Hi, Ray. I'm looking for Joi. Is she there?"

Rayven hesitated. "She's at the library."

"I'm at the library, Rayven. Now tell me the truth."

"Oh, she must be on her way here then. We're working on a project together."

"Another project? Then why aren't you with her now?"

"I um . . . had to finish a um . . . history paper and um . . ." Rayven muttered.

"And why isn't she answering her cell?"

"She has to be on her way here, Mrs. B. Reception on the El is bad sometimes and—"

"Don't cover for her, Ray." Taylor practically yelled into the phone. "Where is she?" Taylor demanded.

"She should be here soon," Rayven pleaded.

"Unless you want me to involve your mother, I suggest you tell me where I can find her," Taylor threatened. "And I know about Markus."

Rayven was silent.

"Yes, Ray. I know about her college boyfriend. Is she with him?"

"No, she's on her way here," Rayven insisted.

Taylor knew she was lying, but had to give Rayven credit. She was a good friend. Most teenagers would've squealed by now.

"I'll tell her to call you when she gets here," she said.

"Don't bother. Tell her to hightail it home. I'll be waiting." Taylor pulled out of the garage and asked God to keep her from hurting her child.

Chapter Twenty-Five

~ *Joi* ~

Joi reached for the remote control on Markus's nightstand and turned on the television. She laid her cell phone at the base of the night lamp and flipped to a rerun of *Girlfriends*. She scooted back on the bed until her body touched the headboard then fluffed a pillow and placed it behind her.

Markus appeared in the doorway with a water bottle in each hand. "Comfy?" he asked and tossed one of the bottles to Joi.

Joi caught the water with one hand. "Of course." She grinned and flexed her bare toes. Joi twisted the cap off her water and swallowed a large portion of it. The trailer for a new movie starring Idris Elba aired, and she perked up. The London-born actor was a personal favorite.

Markus gulped down most of his water and leaned against the closet door. "He's too old for you," Markus muttered and finished his drink. His signs of jealousy were cute. He had to know the odds of Joi meeting and/or dating the actor were next to none.

Joi waited for the preview to end before responding. "So are you," she noted.

Markus cut his eyes her way, his full lips protruding.

"Age doesn't matter. Idris is *fine*."

Markus rubbed his newly grown beard. "Not finer than me."

"You're all right," she teased, and took a small sip of water.

Markus ignored her comment and lay on the bed, his head in her lap. Joi chuckled and kissed the back of his head lightly. "You're still my number one man."

"Umm," Markus moaned, but didn't change position.

The house phone rang, and he answered it before voicemail kicked in. "Hey, what's up?" he said. "I had to pick up a friend from Chestnut Hill. Hold on a sec." Markus covered the earpiece and whispered to Joi, "That's my mom. I'll be right back."

He left the room, and Joi made herself comfortable on his bed.

A few minutes later, Markus slid back into the room unnoticed. When he placed his arms around Joi, she held him tight. "You get those pills yet?"

"Definitely next week," she said.

"I hope I can wait that long," he said, and they kissed until the chirp of Joi's cell phone caused them to stop.

Joi leaned over just enough to view the screen. It was Rayven, and she was using the 9-1-1 emergency code. "I better call her back," she said and sat up.

Rayven answered her phone before it could ring two times. "Your mom is going crazy!" she cried almost hysterically into the receiver. "You better leave, Joi. She's on to you."

Markus could hear Rayven through the phone. "Is something wrong?" he queried.

"No," Joi mouthed as she listened to Rayven rant.

"She knows about Markus," Rayven explained. Her voice was filled with fear, and Joi's hand trembled.

"What do you mean, she knows about Markus? You didn't tell her, did you?" she asked.

"Of course not! You know I wouldn't do that," Rayven snapped. "But she knows you're not at the library. I told her you were on your way over here, and she asked why I wasn't with you. Then I stumbled over my words—"

"You stumbled?" Joi exclaimed. "Ray, you know how Mother is."

"And you know I can't think fast under pressure," Rayven retorted. "I told her I had a history paper I needed to finish at home. I don't think she bought it."

Joi knew her mother didn't buy it, but didn't share that with Rayven. It would've only made matters worse. "Everything will be okay," Joi said calmly, desperately thinking of an error-free explanation to tell her mother.

"Well, just so you know, I'm freaking out. She knows about Markus *and* that he's in college."

Joi almost dropped her cell phone. How did her mother know about that? Immediately, Linda came to mind. "Whatever you do, Ray, don't tell her where I am."

"I won't, I won't," she promised, "but I am getting nervous. Be careful. She might be patrolling the streets."

"Just promise me you won't say anything," Joi stressed again.

"I've already been grilled, and it wasn't pretty," replied Rayven. "There's nothing more for me to say."

"Okay, I owe you one," Joi said. She knew how hard it was for her best friend to tell a lie.

"You owe me five! I shed real tears for this one."

As much as she didn't want to, Joi knew it was time to go home. She sat on the edge of Markus's bed, her hands covering her temples while he caressed her back.

"You okay?" he asked.

Joi dropped her hands and rested them in her lap. "I better go," she said. "Mother is on a warpath."

"What else is new?" he answered, disappointed that Joi had to leave.

"I know," Joi grumbled. "But that's Mother."

About ten minutes later, Markus pulled into an open space a few doors down the street from Joi's house. "I'll call you later. I'm going to my mother's for a few hours," Markus said and kissed Joi on the cheek.

"Okay," she said, but remained seated. She was afraid to get out of the car.

Markus tapped the steering wheel. "You might as well get it over with."

"Talk to you later," she said and hopped out of the car.

As she walked to the house, she noticed that the curtains in the front window had moved. Taylor must've been watching.

Joi rehearsed the story she was going to tell her mother as she turned the key. Taylor could usually detect the slightest inconsistent detail.

When Joi opened the door, Taylor was standing in the living room, her arms folded across her chest. "Wanna tell me where you were?"

Joi swallowed hard and took off her coat. The lines she had practiced had escaped her memory. "I was with some friends, studying."

"Umm," Taylor moaned, her lips twisted in disbelief.

"We were at the library for a little while, but we were getting too loud so we decided to leave." Joi was surprised at how easily the lies poured from her mouth. "I know I should've called, but—"

"Stop right there, Joi," Taylor interjected and unfolded

the pamphlet Joi got from the clinic. "I'm going to make this quick because I can't listen to your lies any longer," she blurted in a stern and steady tone. "I found this in your room today."

Taken off guard, Joi's eyes widened. "I'm not having sex; if that's what you think."

"Then why do you need to know about this stuff?"

"I was curious," Joi mumbled.

"I know about Markus," Taylor added. "Is he pressuring you?"

Joi held onto her left elbow and bit her lip. "I'm not doing anything," she stressed, her voice reaching a higher octave.

"Then I don't understand why you'd need to know about taking a pill. Where did you get this information from?"

Joi tapped the floor with her foot and crossed her arms. "Someone from school gave it to me."

Taylor shook her head. She could tell Joi was lying. "What's going on, Joi? We were getting along great, but now I feel like I won't ever be able to trust you." Taylor looked at Joi. "You're running around with a boy too old for you, getting birth control pills, and only God knows how many times you've been to this character's apartment. You were supposed to be at the library studying. I know you think you're grown, but you're not ready for a boy Markus's age. You're still a baby."

Joi bit her lip and picked at a hangnail on her pinky finger. "I'm sorry," she mumbled low.

"I'm not looking for an apology," Taylor stated. "I want to know why you've been lying to me all this time." Taylor fought back tears. "I've tried to be lenient with you. I risked my marriage for you by calling Jerome, nearly jeopardizing his life to make you happy, and you're *still* doing things behind my back. What am I supposed to do now?"

"Mother, I'm not trying to hurt you or anyone. I just—"

"I wish I could trust your words, but I can't." Taylor said with closed eyes.

Those words hurt Joi more than any punishment she'd ever received.

Taylor sat on the sofa and leaned back. "Just go to your room," she told Joi. "Your father will home soon with the kids, and I'm not ready to get into this with him."

Joi headed upstairs and stalled on the landing to stare at her mother. Taylor was sitting on the sofa rubbing a gold cross hanging off a link chain around her neck. It was given to her by her mother before she passed away. Taylor rubbed the cross whenever she wanted to feel close to her mother. Joi could see Taylor's lips moving as she rocked back and forth. She knew Taylor was praying. Joi felt bad, and as she walked into her room, she fell face first on her bed and cried out to God. Why did life have to be so hard?

Chapter Twenty-Six

~ *Jerome* ~

In a hidden corner of a diner on Lancaster Avenue, Jerome struggled to finish eating a weak bowl of oatmeal. Seated across from him, Taylor told Jerome about Joi's recent acts that were causing concern. Jerome was heading back to Illinois after breakfast and wanted to see Joi before leaving town. Had he known Taylor would've spent the entire morning complaining about Joi's behavior, he would've suggested she stay home. He wanted to enjoy the last hours he had to spend with his daughter. He didn't know when he'd see her again.

With her elbow perched on top of the table, Joi's chin rested on the ball of her fist. She'd barely touched her breakfast. Joi stared at her plate, making eye contact only when Taylor demanded an answer to one her many questions.

Although Jerome agreed that Joi was wrong, Taylor shouldn't have discussed her business in an open and public area.

"She has a college boyfriend," Taylor said. "Can you believe that?"

Jerome tried to appear shocked. There was no way he was going to tell her that he knew.

Taylor talked nonstop as they ate, her curly hair occasionally falling over one eye. No matter how many times she pulled the lock of curls behind her ear, it kept returning to the same spot.

Jerome reached for two sugar packets, and Taylor swat at his hand.

"You're not going to have another heart attack on my watch," she said, and Joi dropped her arms on the table.

Jerome leaned back and stared into Taylor's soft eyes. She hadn't changed much over the years. Besides the few soft crow's feet, she was still a buxom beauty with impeccable taste.

"Someone's pretty protective of you. Do you see the way she's looking at me?" Taylor said to Jerome.

And, for the first time all morning, Joi laughed.

Taylor finally changed the subject and talked about delaying her plans to open another store. Apparently Lance didn't want her to take out a loan. From the hint of sarcasm in her voice, Jerome could tell Taylor was not pleased with her husband.

Jerome looked at his watch. It was almost eleven o'clock. Reggie and Jerome Jr. were waiting for him at Brandon's. They had volunteered to drive him back to Illinois. He wasn't looking forward to the long drive back home. Jerome knew his sons were going to bombard him with a string of questions he didn't want to answer, at least not until he had a chance to talk to his wife.

"As much as I hate to leave," Jerome said, "I have to. My boys want to hit the turnpike before two."

Jerome pulled a credit card from his wallet and placed it on the table. While they waited for the bill, he reached inside his coat lying next to him and took out his checkbook. "I might as well give you this now," he said and filled out the check. "Sorry we couldn't hang out more," he told Joi.

Joi's face saddened. "There'll be a next time, right?"

"Definitely," he answered and slid the check across the table to Taylor. "For Joi, and a little something for you. I hope this will ease some of your stress."

Taylor looked at the large number written on the check. It was more than the amount needed as down payment for the retail space she wanted downtown. "I can't take this, Jerome. I'll get the money some other way."

Taylor shoved the check back toward Jerome, and he placed his hand over hers. "Please, let me do this. Consider it a loan if you want, but don't give it back. I blocked your first dream, remember?" Jerome said. "Let me make up for that."

Taylor reluctantly picked up the check when Jerome removed his hand. "Thanks," she said and folded it before putting it inside her purse. "I *will* pay you back as soon as I can."

The waitress approached the table and handed Jerome the bill. "Enjoy your day," she said and rushed off to another table.

"Hey," Jerome said. "How would you feel about spending the summer in Chicago?"

Joi's eyes twinkled, and she looked at Taylor. "That would be fun. Can I go?"

"I don't know," Taylor answered. "Joi's a handful, and you're healing, and Renee . . . well, Renee may not want to entertain our daughter all summer."

"Let me work on that," Jerome responded. "So, if Renee—"

"That's the key," Taylor emphasized. "*If* Renee says yes, I'll consider it."

"What about Lance?" Jerome questioned.

Joi bounced in her seat. "Daddy won't mind."

"Then it's settled," he said and put on his coat. Jerome

didn't know what made him invite Joi to Chicago. Perhaps it was the guilt he felt inside. He wanted Joi to one day call him *Daddy* too. All he had to do was convince Renee.

Reggie opened the passenger door of the rental car. "You've got to get out, Pop."

Although he couldn't wait to be back in the comfort of his own home, Jerome was afraid to go inside. It was one in the morning, but the basement light was on.

Renee had called once during the twelve-hour ride to the Midwest, and talked only for a minute. "I'll be awake when you get here," she had said, then asked if he was feeling okay. Their conversations had been dry and quick since the incident in Philly.

Jerome felt his heart race, and he used one of the breathing techniques he learned from his doctor. It was imperative he remain stress-free, especially within the next six months. He counted backward from twenty slowly then steadied himself. "Okay," he said. "I'm ready."

Renee was sitting in her favorite position on the chaise, her left leg tucked under the right one, when Jerome made it to the basement.

"Thanks for waiting up," Jerome said.

Renee turned the television off. She placed both of her feet on the tiled floor, and Jerome noticed his briefcase sitting open beside the chaise. The checkbooks he'd kept in there specifically for Taylor were strewn across the top of the case. He also noticed that the canceled checks he'd archived in an old shoebox in his home office closet were sitting on Renee's lap.

"You've been sending her money for years," Renee said, her voice mellow and clear. She dropped the shoebox on the floor and kicked it to Jerome, the bottom scratching the tile as it traveled to him.

Renee must've been busy snooping around the house while he was away.

"You told me that was the first time you saw your daughter. But I checked online. You purchased a ticket to Philly before Thanksgiving. I don't understand why you keep lying to me."

Jerome took a deep breath. He could feel his heartbeat elevate. "Everything happened so fast, I forgot. Honest, Renee, that trip slipped my mind. Joi didn't even know I was there. Neither did Taylor."

Renee picked up the few canceled checks that had fallen next to her. "Do you know how much money you spent over the years on her? Is that why you insisted on separate accounts?"

Jerome was busted. After a few years of lame excuses for miscellaneous expenses, he had asked Renee to consider setting up separate accounts. The money Jerome placed into his account was supposed to be used for golf expeditions and electronic devices. Renee's account was used for shopping sprees and regular hair and nail appointments.

"What happens now?" Renee asked and threw the checks at him. "Is there anything else you're keeping from me?"

Believing this was an opportunity to tell Renee about his idea, Jerome cleared his throat and said, "She'd like to spend the summer with us?"

"What?" Renee snapped. "You must've had more than a heart attack. I know you don't think I'm going to—"

"Mom," Joshua called from the stairwell, "why don't you come up to bed? Pop needs to get some rest."

Ignoring her son's orders, Renee finished her statement. "You expect me to welcome the child you had with a mistress into my home?"

"I know this isn't going to be easy," Jerome said. "But she wants to get to know her family."

"You meet the girl for the first time, and now she's family?"

"If you don't want her to come this year, then she doesn't have to," Jerome said, but hoped Renee wouldn't say no. "She is my daughter, Renee, and I have to start acting like her father. Don't you think God would want me to?"

Renee got off the chaise. "She can stay in the hotel."

"I know you're angry, but we can't tuck her away in one of your hotels, Renee."

"Then I guess she won't be coming to Chicago. Gosh, Jerome," Renee screamed, "this is too much to take in all at once."

Joshua walked all the way down the stairs and interrupted his parents again. "Mom, can you and Pop please talk about this in the morning?"

Renee listened to him this time and stormed past Jerome, and up the stairs.

"You all right, Pop?" Joshua asked, concerned.

Out of all his children, Joshua was the most sensitive. "I'm fine, son. Thanks for asking," he said.

Jerome took his time going up to his bedroom, and Joshua patiently walked behind him. The door was closed when he finally made it upstairs, and he tried to open it, but it was locked. From his peripheral vision, Jerome saw his suitcase stationed in front of the guest room. He looked at Joshua. He wanted to cry, but had too much pride.

"She just needs to calm down, Pop," Joshua said. "She won't keep you out forever."

Jerome sighed. Not since the affair did he and Renee sleep apart. "See you in the morning," he said and eased down the hall, praying that Renee hadn't kicked him out of their room for good.

Chapter Twenty-Seven

~ *Jerome* ~

Five Months Later . . .

Jerome woke up reaching for his wife, but instead of her soft, warm body, he touched a cold and lifeless pillow. Renee had gone to work early. For the past month, if she wasn't on a business trip, she was at the office working from dawn to dusk. Although they were speaking, things were not yet back to normal. Jerome missed his wife; the long talks, impromptu dates, spending time with the family . . . the way they made love several times a week. Now he was lucky if they were intimate once a month. And even then, it was as if Renee's mind was in another place.

Easing out of bed, Jerome decided to take the day off. He wanted to spend time with Renee before Joi arrived in two days. Thanks to Pastor Hampton, Renee had agreed to let her stay with them for eight weeks, half of which she'd be traveling across the country for work. Jerome tried to include Renee in the plans for Joi's visit, but something always seemed to come up for work that urgently required her attention.

The boys had prepared for Joi's arrival in varying ways as well. Reggie had remained nonchalant, typical for his character, and volunteered to be her official tour guide. Jerome Jr., who had always sided with his mother since he was a child, got an instant attitude every time Joi's name was mentioned. He'd agreed only to attend Sunday dinners. And Joshua's concern for everyone's happiness was greatly appreciated. He tried his best to help everyone view the situation from different perspectives. He chose to help out when and where he was most needed. It was Jerome's prayer that his children would all come to respect and love one another by the end of the summer.

After he dressed, Jerome called his florist and ordered a large calla lily arrangement. He wanted to show Renee his gratitude for her continued sacrifices.

Jerome pulled his Yukon into the Northbrook hotel parking lot. Not as upscale and elaborate as the main hotel downtown, the Northbrook branch still exuded Renee's touch of class. Jerome entered the building, waving to the employees he knew, including Bianca, who had been promoted along with Renee many years ago in Philadelphia. Like Renee, she had worked her way up the corporate ladder, starting out as Renee's assistant, and was now one of her best managers.

Although Renee's office was on the second floor, Jerome chose to take the elevator. The doctors encouraged him to exercise, but Jerome limited workouts to morning walks and evening strolls around his neighborhood.

The closer he got to Renee's office, the more excited he became. He stood by her door, slightly cracked, and prepared to knock, but heard Renee giggle and stopped. The sound of a man's voice was followed by another girlish chuckle, and Jerome's heart raced. Something didn't feel right. He tried to look through the small open space, but couldn't see anything more than a bookcase. Renee's desk was on the west end of the office.

He prepared to knock again, until he heard Renee say, "Oh, Everett, you're too much." That didn't sound like a phrase someone should use during a meeting with their boss.

Jerome had known Everett for many years. He was instrumental in Renee's career growth within the company and had become a mentor to his wife. Their working relationship had never bothered Jerome, not even when Everett's wife left him for a younger man five years ago, making him a single man again. Jerome never had a reason to worry . . . until now.

Jerome charged inside Renee's office unannounced, and the flowers in his hand dropped to the floor. Everett, dressed like a distinguished mayor or other high-profile official, sat on the edge of Renee's desk, leaning very close to her ear. Despite the surprise, he didn't move a muscle. Poised, he looked at Jerome with a stern glare, not a shred of shock or embarrassment in his eyes.

Renee, on the other hand was surprised.

"What's going on here?" Jerome asked, his heart beating in quick, odd patterns.

"We're in the middle of a meeting. Why didn't you knock?" Renee pushed away from her desk and stood up.

"Didn't think your husband needed to knock. Besides, the door was open." Jerome stared at Everett, wondering why he still hadn't offered to leave the room. "Can I have a minute with my wife?" he finally asked him.

Everett looked to Renee for an answer, and Jerome became infuriated. All the techniques he'd been trying, to maintain a stress-free life, had gone fast out the window. "Have you no respect for me as a man and her husband?"

Everett slid off Renee's desk with a smug look on his

face, and it suddenly dawned on Jerome that Renee might have shared their marital struggles. Soon, images of him and Renee together on business trips came to mind. The thought of his wife sharing her body with another man enraged Jerome even more. Before he could control his impulses, Jerome lunged at Everett.

The two fifty-something men tussled like high school students battling over the girl they loved. It was a sight to see. Renee rushed to close her door while begging them to grow up.

Eventually, Everett backed Jerome into the wall, his finely pressed shirt wrinkled and hanging out of his pants. "I'm not trying to disrespect you, Jerome," he said and let him go.

"Renee is *my* wife," Jerome replied, his clothes just as unraveled.

Everett looked at Jerome with disgust and fixed his tie. "Then you should act like it."

Renee stepped between them, and Jerome waited for her to ask Everett for some privacy. Instead, she turned to Jerome and asked, "What has gotten into you?"

Alarmed, Jerome stepped away from the wall. "You're worried about who may be standing outside that door? Why was he in your face?"

Renee sighed, and Jerome lowered his voice.

"I came here to brighten your day. I wanted to put a smile on your face today, even brought you flowers and chocolate." He pulled out the peanut chews from his pocket.

Renee was speechless.

"I'll be downstairs if you need me," Everett offered.

"No, brother. I think I'm the one that needs to leave," Jerome replied. He looked at the calla lilies on the floor, and then at his wife. "Enjoy the flowers . . . and the peanut chews," he said and walked out the door.

Quickly, Jerome ran out of the hotel, passing Bianca

along the way. By the time he reached his truck, he was gasping for air.

Bianca knew about his medical condition and followed him outside.

Unable to put his key in the lock, Jerome leaned against the Yukon and practiced some of his breathing techniques.

"Oh no," Bianca said when she caught up to him. "I'm going to call the ambulance."

Jerome held up his hand and shook his head. Through puffs of air, he said "No, I'm fine. Just need a minute."

Bianca looked at him and determined that he needed some medical help. She pulled out her Blackberry, and Jerome smacked it with his hand.

"Really," he huffed. "I'll be okay."

"All right," she said, "but if you start turning colors, I'm calling the medics."

"Fair enough," he replied as he tried to wind down. He looked up toward Renee's office window. She was standing there, arms crossed and staring back at him. Jerome wondered if Everett was nearby. Breathing in control, Jerome put his key in the lock. "Thanks, Bianca. I feel much better now."

Jerome couldn't go home. Being alone with his thoughts would only enrage him further. Instead of driving to River Forest, he headed to the United Center and stormed into his office. His chest felt tight, but nothing he figured to be worried about. He sat in his chair, desperately longing to hear God's voice. He had given the situation to God when he was in the hospital, and vowed to follow His lead. But Jerome had no idea what was ahead. *Renee . . . cheating?*

"Are you okay?" Melanie asked as she entered his office. "I thought you were working from home today?"

Without thinking carefully he said, "Renee and I had a small difference of opinion."

Melanie walked to his desk and touched his arm. "Talking helps. Want to grab something to eat?"

Jerome strongly considered the invite, but declined. "Maybe next time. I'm not really hungry," he said and Melanie backed away.

"Just let me know when," she responded, and left Jerome alone with his thoughts.

Jerome couldn't wait to talk to Renee at home. He wanted answers now. He picked up his phone and dialed her office. "How long have you been seeing him?" Jerome asked when Renee picked up her phone.

"This is not the time, Jay. And you really shouldn't be getting all worked up anyway."

"Are you seeing him?" he asked with more authority.

"No," Renee replied coldly.

"Then what's going on? Is our marriage over?"

Renee hesitated briefly then said, "I'm in a meeting. We'll talk when I get home."

"Before midnight?" he asked sarcastically.

"I'll try to be there before seven."

When Jerome hung up the phone, thoughts of a rum and coke filled his mind. He'd been sober for a long time, and although alcohol wasn't the best solution, he rationalized that one drink wouldn't hurt.

Jerome walked into the house after midnight. Instead of going upstairs to bed, he lay on the sofa in the family room. A minute into his sleep, the hall light came on, and he opened one eye.

"You could've called," she said. "I thought something happened to you. The boys are worried. You might want to call them."

Jerome covered his eyes; the bright light bothered them. "All those business trips, Renee. Did Everett go on *all* of them?"

Renee stepped into the room and sniffed his clothes. "Have you been drinking?"

Jerome had nursed two drinks all night. It usually took more than a couple drinks to get him drunk. But his aged body couldn't handle the huge load anymore. He knew to stop after the second one, so he wasn't drunk, just tipsy. "How long have you been with him?"

Too much like old times, Renee knew keeping silent would only aggravate his current stupor. "I don't make a habit of cheating on my husband when I'm mad," she replied.

"Then what's going on?" Jerome attempted to sit up, but failed. "Does he know about our situation?"

"He noticed I was acting different a while ago," she replied. "When you came in, he was trying to cheer me up with a joke."

"What was the joke?" he asked. Jerome hadn't been able to make her laugh that way in months.

"Does it really matter?"

Jerome forced himself up. "Are you attracted to him? Wait a minute, let me answer that." Jerome straightened up on the sofa. "You like men like him. Always have. You wish I was more refined and educated, don't you?"

Renee rolled her eyes. "That's the liquor talking," she said, then snapped. "You have a lot of nerve! *You're* the one that stepped outside of our marriage. *You're* the one with a child I didn't bear. A child, need I remind you, the same age as our son. How do you think that makes me feel, Jerome? You *promised* you would never see her again, but you just *had* to go back for more. And without a condom!"

Jerome couldn't get a word in edgewise. There was really nothing for him to say. "I'm so sorry, baby." He put his arms around Renee, and she cried in his arms. "I messed up."

"What were you thinking? And you're upset because I won't welcome her into the home we built for our children and grandchildren to enjoy, like everything's okay? Everything is not okay, Jerome," she bellowed and pulled away, the stench coming from his pores too much to bear. "I hope you haven't started drinking again," she said and wiped her eyes. "You'll be out of this house for good the next time you come in here drunk."

"It won't happen again. I promise," he uttered and looked at his wife with sad eyes. "Just tell me there's nothing between you and Everett."

"I already did," she responded and walked away. "And you need to get yourself together before Joi gets here. I'm not going to be responsible for her all summer."

Jerome fell back onto the couch, and before he drifted off to sleep, cried out to God. *I will look to the hills from which cometh my help . . .*

Chapter Twenty-Eight

~ *Joi* ~

Joi and Rayven had been in the King of Prussia Mall all afternoon shopping for the perfect pair of jeans. Joi was leaving for Chicago in the morning and needed a new pair that fit the new curves of her body.

"Let's check the Gap," suggested Rayven as they passed the store.

"Okay," Joi grumbled. "But let's make this the last place we try. I'm tired."

The girls headed inside the store, side by side, and without warning, Rayven pulled Joi back out the door.

"What's wrong?" Joi asked, puzzled by her friend's action.

"I changed my mind," Rayven replied. "Let's get out of here."

Rayven started to walk away, but Joi wasn't ready to leave. "Wait a minute. Since we're here I should at least check to see if they have my size."

"I don't think they will," Rayven said and tugged on Joi's arm.

"I'll only be a minute," Joi said and turned so that she

faced the display window. Her knees almost gave out when she discovered Rayven's reason for wanting to leave. Markus was in the store, his arm around a petite and preppy-looking female. Joi froze, glaring into the window like a lost puppy.

Although she and Markus had reduced the amount of time they spent together a great deal, they had not officially broken up. So what was he doing in the mall with another girl?

The girl held up a sheer tank top, and Markus smiled with approval. When she walked around the clothing rack, Joi noticed the blue Burberry hanging from her shoulder. It was an exact match to the one she'd seen in Markus's room on many occasions.

Markus followed the girl, and when he faced the window, looked up and recognized Joi. His demeanor changed, but only slightly, and he continued to talk to his female friend as if Joi wasn't there.

"C'mon, Joi," Rayven said and grabbed Joi's hand. "He's not worth it."

Joi couldn't move. Suddenly all the times she couldn't find Markus had been explained. He wasn't with his mother at all. He was with the girl carrying the Burberry bag.

"Are you waiting for him to come out here?" Rayven queried. "Well, he's not gonna do it. So let's just go."

Like a zombie, Joi followed Rayven then stopped. She backtracked the few steps to the Gap and went inside. "Hey, Markus," Joi said, stopping in front of him.

Markus's friend stared at Joi, her disposition seemingly friendly. She was cute in her own way, Joi reasoned, and older. Markus didn't say anything, causing his friend to become suspicious.

"I guess this is your mother," Joi said sarcastically.

Curious, the girl introduced herself. "My name is Eboni. I'm Markus's girlfriend. And you are?"

Joi couldn't believe her ears. "Eboni from Maryland? Markus told me you two broke up."

"Let's go, Joi. People are looking," Rayven intervened.

Joi wanted to smack, kick, and punch Markus all at the same time, but that wasn't her style. "One day someone will make you feel the way I do right now," she said. "And in that moment you'll remember me. God bless you."

"Remember her, but don't call her," Rayven said and ran behind her friend.

"You are royal," Joi heard her mother's friend, Kara, say in the back of her mind and she thanked God for not providing an opportunity to give her virginity to Markus.

When Joi walked into her room, she immediately dropped the bags of new clothes on her bed. Although she had felt empowered, her feelings were hurt. Her relationship with Markus for all those months had been a fallacy. He never loved her; he couldn't have.

Joi stared at the luggage across the room. Now was the perfect time to leave Philadelphia. She took off her shoes and slid them under her bed. She was hungry. With all the excitement, she and Rayven had decided to leave the mall before they had a chance to eat.

Downstairs, Taylor was frosting a caramel cake, Joi's favorite. "Hey, Joi," Taylor said. "Ready for tomorrow?"

"Almost," Joi said, lacking enthusiasm.

"What's wrong with you?" Taylor asked. "Nervous about the plane ride?"

Joi opened the refrigerator and took out a container of day old spaghetti. "No, just tired and hungry."

"Seems like it's something more than that. Everything okay?"

Joi wanted to share her feelings with her mother, but knew she wouldn't understand. "I guess I'm missing you guys already," she replied.

Taylor stopped frosting the cake and put the knife on the table. "Okay, what's *really* going on?"

"Is it that hard to believe that I'm going to miss you?" Joi said as she dumped a mound of spaghetti onto a plate.

"As eager as you've been to get away from me, yes, I find it a bit strange," Taylor said. "You'll miss Ray before you miss being here with your family."

Joi put her food in the microwave for two minutes then sat next to her mother. "I saw Markus with another girl today." She couldn't hold it in any longer. She had to talk to someone, even if it was her mother.

"Oh," Taylor replied nonchalantly. "What happened?"

For the next five minutes, Joi told Taylor about the incident in the mall as she ate her food. She told her about Eboni and how Markus must've been seeing both of them at the same time. Joi was surprised at how reserved Taylor was, waiting patiently for her turn to speak.

"Well," Taylor said, "I know this doesn't feel good right now, but be grateful God revealed this now. The longer you're with a person, the harder it is to leave them, no matter how bad they treat you."

Joi could tell her mother was speaking from experience. "I really thought he was the one."

"So many girls and women do," Taylor continued. "There will be many boys coming after you, sweetheart. But I pray you'll wait for love. Real love. I don't want you to end up like me."

"Your life isn't so bad."

"No, but it could've been a whole lot easier." Taylor picked up the knife on the table and cut each of them a huge slice of cake. "You do know that I want the best for you, right?"

"Yes," Joi mumbled, suddenly ashamed of the things she'd done to upset her in the past.

"You know," Taylor admitted, "my mother didn't take

the time to make sure I got good grades, or had a decent boyfriend. She wasn't raised that way, so she didn't raise me to aim for anything greater. I was over thirty before my life started to make sense. In many ways, I felt like I wasted my life. I kicked myself over and over thinking about what I could've had in my twenties had things been different." Taylor paused. "I don't want you to have the same kinds of regrets I had. Life is too short, and God has been too good to you. Do you understand where I'm coming from?"

"I think so," Joi said.

"We all do things we're not proud of. I'm proof of that. The goal is not to keep repeating the same bad habits."

This was the first time Taylor had been so open and honest about her life and feelings. As mother and daughter continued to talk over caramel cake, Joi thanked God. She felt closer to her mother than ever before.

Chapter Twenty-Nine

~ *Jerome* ~

"Here's our guest of honor," Jerome said when he walked into his house with Joi. The family sat around the kitchen table, each waiting for the other to speak first.

"Hi," Jerome's grandson said, and everyone laughed. Joshua was the next to break the ice. He even gave Joi a quick hug.

"I'm glad you're here," Grace said then put her teaching skills to use. "Why don't we go around the table and officially introduce ourselves."

One by one, the family shared more than just their names, and Jerome was in heaven.

Renee was the last to speak. She was pleasant enough in her introduction, but made sure she didn't say more than what was needed. "So," she said, "I hope you're hungry."

Without waiting for an answer, Renee walked to the counter and unloaded various containers from a Maggiano's bag.

* * *

Zora did most of the talking over dinner, Reggie chiming in when he could. Jerome Jr. was silent, looking up from his plate only to check on his children. Seated next to Joi, Joshua seemed to be the most excited to have her there.

A fancy cell phone tune boomed over their voices, and everyone grew silent. Joi turned off the phone as quickly as she could and continued to eat.

"Is that your boyfriend?" Grace asked.

"It better not be," answered Jerome.

"You better get used to her having male friends, Pop. Your daughter is a beautiful young lady," Zora noted.

"If they pass my test, Joi can talk to them all she wants," Jerome said proudly.

Renee picked up her plate and emptied the leftovers in the trashcan. "We usually turn off cell phones during dinner."

"I thought it was off," Joi answered. "I'll make sure it won't happen again."

"It's her pet peeve," Joshua added. "If you ever wanna make her mad, you know what to do."

Renee grabbed a glass of water and headed upstairs. "Glad you're here," she said to Joi and walked upstairs.

Jerome tried not to show his disapproval. "Renee has a lot of work to do. She works from home all the time," he said to Joi when Renee left, praying her feelings weren't hurt. "So, who's your favorite NBA team?" he asked and tried to enjoy the rest of his dinner.

At ten o'clock, Jerome could no longer keep his eyes open. With the exception of Jerome Jr. and his family, everyone was still in the kitchen getting to know Joi. As much as Jerome wanted to be a part of the conversations, his body was tired.

Renee was in the bed reading work documents when

he entered their bedroom. He was upset that she had not shown Joi the same hospitality as she would've done any other houseguest, but didn't have the energy to discuss it. "I appreciate you buying dinner," he said as he changed into his nightclothes. "Maybe you'll be able to sit with us through all of dinner tomorrow."

Renee didn't look up from her reading, but said, "I'm not going to make any promises."

"Are you going to church with us tomorrow?"

"I don't know, Jerome. I'm not ready to answer a bunch of questions."

"But how will it look if you don't go?" he asked. "C'mon, Renee. Joi's gonna think you have a problem with her being here."

Renee threw her papers in her lap. "Jerome, tonight was hard, and I can guarantee going to church won't be any better."

Jerome got into bed and leaned over to give Renee a kiss. "Okay," he said. "It's just the first day."

"Just so you know, I'm going to Florida next week," Renee said.

Jerome immediately sat up. "Is Everett going, too?"

Renee placed the papers in her hand on the floor then turned off her nightlight. "Don't even go there with me, Jerome. You knew I'd be traveling this summer," she said and laid down with her back to his.

Now that Joi was in town and Renee on the fence with her emotions, Jerome knew she'd be susceptible to temptation. The thought of Renee and Everett together in Florida bothered him. He wanted to be reassured that his wife would remain faithful. "Is he still telling funny jokes?" he asked.

"Good night," Renee answered and fluffed her pillow.

Jerome lay back down and prayed for his marriage until he drifted off to sleep.

Chapter Thirty

~ *Taylor* ~

Taylor sat at the hair salon, talking to Jerome on her cell as she waited for her niece to finish curling her hair. For a Wednesday afternoon, the shop was bustling with activity. The salon was owned by Janelle, Crystal's eldest daughter. Unlike the other Belle women, Taylor and Janelle got along well.

"Be with you in a minute, Auntie," Janelle called from the back. One of her stylists had given a new client a bad color treatment, and in an effort to avoid a lawsuit, Janelle had stepped in to repair the damage.

Taylor listened to Jerome's update of Joi's visit. It appeared Joi was having a great time. Joi had only been there for two weeks, and already she'd been canoeing, fishing, and rock climbing. She was also acting as an assistant coach to the children's basketball team at Jerome's church. Joi had been so busy, Taylor was lucky if she talked to her twice a week.

Janelle came from the back, the previously enraged client now pleased with the new reddish-brown color in her hair. "Let me wrap her hair and put her under the dryer, Auntie," she said to Taylor. "Then you'll have all my attention."

Taylor nodded. She wasn't concerned about time. "Okay, tell Joi I'll try to catch up with her tonight," she said into the phone.

"Will do," Jerome responded. "Oh . . . I noticed that you still haven't cashed the check I gave you. What's up?"

Someone sat in the empty chair next to Taylor, and she swung her chair around. It was Gizelle, and her hair was in desperate need of a relaxer. Taylor hadn't expected to see her there. Gizelle's regularly scheduled appointments were on Thursday evenings. Taylor waved to her then turned back around.

"I changed my mind. I'll return the check, or if you trust me, I'll rip it up," Taylor said in a whisper.

"No, you can keep it. When you're ready to open another store, think of it as a gift."

"Five thousand dollars is a hefty gift, Jerome. I can't take that from you."

"Hey, people I don't know have blessed my life, and I'm grateful for it. Let me bless you. It's the least I can do."

To make Jerome feel good about his act of kindness, Taylor told him she would accept his gift, but made a note to tear the check up later. It would've been nice to use the money as a down payment on a new building, but she couldn't bring herself to accept that amount of money from an old lover. Taylor said goodbye then placed her cell in her purse.

"That's the new Franco Sarto line, isn't it?" Gizelle asked, referring to Taylor's oblong leather bag. "Where'd you find that one?"

"The T. J. Maxx off of 476," Taylor said blandly. Gizelle loved designer bags almost as much as she did.

"Really? Those bags are expensive. I priced one in Neiman's the other day." Gizelle stood up and took a closer look at her hair in the mirror behind her. "I guess you can afford it, now that you're not getting the second shop."

Taylor rolled her eyes. Gizelle knew nothing about her finances. Had Taylor been thirty years younger, she would've dragged Gizelle around the salon by her hair.

"Talk to Joi today? How does she like Chicago?"

"She loves it," Taylor said and picked up a magazine from Janelle's workstation.

"How about Jerome?" Gizelle asked. "You speak to him?"

This is the day I stand up for myself. Taylor closed the magazine. "What is your problem?"

"No problem. I just wanted to know if you talked to Jerome. I bet you two talk all the time now?"

"That's none of your business," Taylor barked.

"Maybe not. But I want you to know that I'm keeping my eye on you."

Janelle walked over to her aunts and asked them to lower their voices. Clients could hear every word they were saying. Gizelle apologized then reclaimed the seat next to Taylor.

"You need to worry about your own marriage and stay out of mine," Taylor snapped softly then swung her chair around. Although everyone in the family sensed that Gizelle's marriage was in trouble, Gizelle pretended to have the model husband.

Gizelle ignored Taylor's comment and continued to ride Taylor. "My brother is an honest and decent man. He's always been attracted to women that were manipulative and selfish, women that flocked to him after being wronged by some no-good man. I don't trust women like that. Never have, and I feel my only brother deserves better."

"People make mistakes, Gizelle. I'm not going to let you stand here and pretend that your life is a bowl of roses. I know that—"

"You know that I never cheated on my husband or slept with a married man. I'm not perfect. I know that. I just want to make sure my brother isn't getting the raw end of the deal."

"Who are you to judge me?" Taylor bellowed.

Janelle walked over to them again. "Am I gonna have to separate you two?" Janelle joked.

Both women apologized again and turned away from one another.

"Okay," she said. "Let's keep the boxing gloves off. I'll be back in one minute."

The conversation was over, but not before Taylor had the last word. "And you call yourself a Christian."

Gizelle spun her chair around so fast, Taylor thought it had broken. "Don't question my relationship with Christ. Worry about what you're doing behind Lance's back."

"What are you talking about now?"

"I overheard you mention the rather nice gift Jerome gave you. Are you still seeing him?"

Enough was enough. "Don't speak about things before you know *all* the facts," Taylor said and jumped to her feet. "How are you going to say these things to me after all these years? After four children?"

"You didn't answer my question. Are you still seeing him?"

"In case you haven't noticed, I'm married to your brother, not you."

"My brother can be naïve. I'm looking out for him."

Janelle raced back to her aunts before things got any further out of control. "Auntie Gizelle, why don't you go in the back. I'll have my assistant base your scalp."

"She can stay there because I'm leaving. I can come back tomorrow," Taylor said. "Despite what you all think, Lance and I and the kids are very happy. Very," she noted and walked out the front door.

By the time Taylor made it home, Lance had heard about the disagreement between his sister and wife. Janelle had called her mother, who in turn called Gram. Gram had called Lance, pleading for him to straighten out the problem.

"You and Gizelle acted like two teenagers. Janelle could've lost some clients," Lance said. "Now everyone is all upset."

"But what about my feelings?" Taylor asked. "When are you going to tell them to stop hurting me?"

Taylor and Lance sat on opposite ends of the couch in silence. Ten minutes later, Taylor headed upstairs. *Lord, where is my increase?*

Chapter Thirty-One

~ *Joi* ~

"You have a permit yet?" Joshua and Reggie asked in unison.

Joi was sitting in Reggie's backyard enjoying an afternoon lunch. She'd been in Chicago for four weeks, and yet felt like she'd been there all her life. Jerome Jr. and Renee were the only members of the Thomas family missing from the group. Renee was out of town, and Jerome Jr. said he had other plans. Even though he couldn't make it, his wife and children were present.

"No," Joi responded, chomping hard on her second spare rib. "My mother doesn't have the patience to teach me."

That was only partly true. Taylor wouldn't allow Joi to get her permit because she didn't trust teenagers driving on the streets of Philadelphia.

"Maybe I'll give you some lessons before you leave," Reggie said.

"I can show her," Jerome interjected.

"You better stick to teaching her ball, Pop. You're a much better coach than driver," Reggie said, and the family laughed in agreement.

Jerome was a good coach. Since Joi had been there, he had shown her several good plays and helped her strengthen her versatility as a player. There would be no stopping her on the court when she returned for the new school year.

Joi's cell phone vibrated against her leg. It was a text from Markus: *Sorry about what happened. Really miss u.* Joi slammed her cell closed.

"Let me guess. That was Markus," Joshua said, and Joi confirmed his statement. "Later for that clown."

Joi popped her brother's leg. "Don't say that. I was in *love* with him," she joked.

"I better not catch him in a dark alley," Jerome stated. "Nobody messes with my daughter."

As the family finished lunch, Renee walked into the backyard with a handful of gifts. Everyone, especially Jerome, was surprised to see her. She was not due back in Chicago until Tuesday. She kissed her grandchildren then sat on the bench next to Zora and told the family about her latest business trip.

"Ready for your gifts?" she asked when she finished talking, and the kids cheered. Renee passed everyone large bags filled with trinkets.

Joi didn't expect to receive anything and was surprised when Renee handed her a small gift bag. "Thank you," Joi said and eagerly looked inside her bag. She pulled out three T-shirts, one from each of the cities Renee visited in Florida.

Joshua jumped up after looking at his watch. "We better leave, Joi. We're gonna miss our train."

"Where you headed?" Renee asked, clearly upset that Joshua was leaving.

"Joi and I are going downtown. She wants to do some shopping," Joshua replied.

Joi attempted to put a smile back on Renee's face. "I promise to bring him back," she said, but Renee only half-smiled.

Joi and Joshua headed out the yard, and Reggie called after them. "Joi, I'll pick you up after church and teach you how to drive."

Having brothers felt good. "Okay, thanks for lunch."

The last place Joi imagined she would be was in a long line waiting for popcorn. Joshua insisted she taste Chicago's famous Garrett's popcorn. It was ninety-two degrees, and after an hour, the line had grown midway down the block.

After two hours, they finally made it to the counter. Joshua ordered the cheese and caramel mix for both of them. It didn't sound appealing, but once Joi tasted a few kernels, she was hooked. The popcorn was definitely worth the wait.

Joi was down to her last twenty dollars, but Joshua convinced her to walk to Navy Pier. They found a place to sit close to the water and watched the boats as they talked about life. Out of all the brothers, Joi was closest to Joshua.

They remained in the same spot until Joshua's cell chimed. It was Renee, and she wasn't happy. Joi and Joshua were having such a great outing that they hadn't paid attention to the time.

"We have to meet her at the hotel," Joshua said when he disconnected the call. "I don't know why, but she's mad. It's not like I haven't been downtown before."

"It's me," Joi said. "I don't think your mother likes me yet."

"That's not it," replied Joshua. "She's just overprotective."

"Sounds like my mom," Joi said and stood up. She prayed she didn't get him into any trouble.

"Well, we better go." Joshua threw away the soda he was drinking in the trashcan behind him.

Chapter Thirty-Two

~ *Jerome* ~

Jerome watched Renee stuff her swollen feet into a pair of flip-flops.

"She can't just do what she pleases," Renee shouted. "It's almost ten o'clock!"

Jerome looked up from the newspaper he was reading. He didn't understand why Renee was so upset. This wasn't the first time Joshua had gone downtown without an adult. "Are you forgetting that Josh is with her, too? How do you know that he didn't want to stay down there?"

"Oh, so this is how things are going to be?" Renee asked. "You're going to defend her every time she does something wrong? She may be allowed to stay out late in Philly, but I'm not Taylor. She can't do that here."

Jerome put down the paper. "I'm not defending anyone," he said. "The kids are just having fun. I'm glad they're getting along."

Renee mumbled something under her breath and grabbed her purse.

"I'll drive," Jerome said and started to get up.

"That's okay. They're going to meet me at the hotel, and I might stick around for a while," she said and headed to the garage.

Jerome followed her. He knew Renee was still having a hard time dealing with Joi, so he tried to give her some space. But how much longer was he going to tolerate her moods? "Joi isn't going anywhere, Renee. Eventually, you'll have to accept that. Maybe if you just opened up a little more . . ."

Renee opened her car door. "You're trying to make up for the time that you missed, so she can do no wrong in your eyes. You're right," Renee said. "You should've been around her from the beginning. But that's another issue. And your being absent doesn't make coming in here after ten okay."

Renee was about to get into the car, but had more to say. "Why can't you understand why I won't open up to her? I didn't have a daughter for you. You cheated with the same woman. I know God would want me to be forgiving and not hold what you and Taylor did against her, but I'm human. I'm not Jesus. It isn't easy for me to look at her and forget what you did to me and this family." Renee got in the car before she started to cry and rolled down her window.

"Renee, I love you," Jerome said out loud. "We're going to get past this."

"I hope you're right," she said before driving off.

Chapter Thirty-Three

~ *Taylor* ~

The Holiday Inn was packed with women from various parts of the city, all seeking God and desiring to reach for a new level. As a member of the women's retreat committee, Taylor was busy checking that everything ran smoothly. Thus far, the conference had been a success.

Saturday night was the last night of the conference. Before the final sermon was to take place, the women had an opportunity to dress up and attend an awards banquet. At Taylor's request, this year the banquet included a fashion show. When she decided to wait on the second store, Taylor busied herself by creating new clothing designs. The fashion show would be the first time a large number of people viewed them.

In between the presentation of awards, a new collection of clothes was presented to the audience. Taylor was in the back helping the models get ready for the runway. She was applying a new eye shadow on one of the models when she heard someone announce her name. "Taylor, that's you!" several people shouted at once. "You won an award!"

Shocked, Taylor smoothed her hair into place and left the dressing room. As she approached the stage, she was met by a round of applause. Taylor had no idea she had even been nominated. She walked faster when she saw her best friends waiting for her at the podium.

"C'mon, Tay," Sherry said, inviting her up to the podium. She placed a huge bouquet of flowers in her hand.

"Taylor Belle," Kara said, "please accept this award for all of the work you've done with the women in the church and in the community. We don't get to say it often, but we truly appreciate all that you do. Continue to bless the world with your very special gift." Kara handed Taylor a plaque, and before she could speak, Sherry took the mic.

"For those of you who haven't had the opportunity of meeting this wonderful lady, she is the owner of Second Chance in Chestnut Hill. The clothes that you are seeing this evening have all been designed by her hands. Taylor has also donated a wealth of items to various women's shelters in the city, *and* she provides a number of women each year with clothes for interviews, and teenagers their dresses for the senior prom."

Several people stood to their feet when Sherry was finished, and Taylor blushed. This was all unexpected. Taylor kissed her friends and made her way to the forefront. "You have no idea how blessed I feel today. Just when you think God has forgotten about you, something wonderful and special happens." Taylor noticed Gizelle in the crowd and was moved to speak from her heart. "For almost a year, I prayed the same prayer day and night, and for months things in my life seemed to get worse. It's funny that I'm receiving this award. Since my store opened, I've always donated items, but when I couldn't get money to open a second store, I started doing more. As I look out into the crowd, I'm encouraged to keep doing more, because in the end, only what's done for Christ will last. Follow Him and He will reward you. Thank you."

More applause filled the room, and as Taylor made her way back to the dressing room, one of the members tugged at her arm. "I remember the struggle, Sister Belle," the woman said and placed a check in Taylor's hand. "Continue to do God's work. What you're doing for the community means a lot to a number of people."

Taylor had managed to keep from crying, but she could feel tears forming. "Thank you," she said and kissed the lady on the cheek.

As she continued down the aisle, another woman jumped in front of her and placed a hundred-dollar bill in her hand. "I appreciate what you did for my niece," she said and reclaimed her seat.

Taylor was crying now. She walked slower than before, and again she was stopped by a group of women, all stuffing monetary gifts into her hands. She could barely hold everything at once.

As women across the room gathered around Taylor, the choir director played a few verses of Marvin Sapp's "Never Would Have Made It."

Overcome with emotion, Taylor dropped to the floor and cried out to God. Her increase had finally arrived. Life at home was better, and her business was moving in a new direction. All she needed was for her in-laws to accept her for who she was, a child of God.

Chapter Thirty-Four

~ *Jerome* ~

Jerome walked in the house and right away noticed Renee's luggage by the garage door. She hadn't mentioned a business trip, so he was confused. Without exhausting himself, he walked upstairs. Renee was in their bedroom loading a small carry bag with accessories. "What's going on?" he asked.

Without stopping, Renee said, "I don't want to drag this out, so I'll get to the point." She turned around to face Jerome. "I'm leaving."

Jerome fell onto the bed. "What brought this on? I thought things were getting better between us."

"After church yesterday, I got to thinking about Joi's visit. This may be selfish, but at this point in my life, I don't want to rearrange my world to include a child I didn't give birth to. And there's no other explanation I can give you for my feelings. I just don't want to deal with this. I love you, but I need to move on to a new chapter in my life."

"Is Everett the reason you don't want to give this a try?"

"You've got to be kidding me? Trying is all I've been

doing since I found out about her. I've tried to be under-standing. I've tried to accept the fact that you had an af-fair. I've tried to accept that you need time with her. I've tried to cope with her bonding with my kids and my grandbabies. I'm sick and tired of trying

Jerome. Can you please try and understand that?" Renee closed her carry bag and headed out the door.

Jerome jumped up, blocking her way. "Please, you can't leave like this."

"I have to." Renee pushed her way out the door and down the stairs.

Fighting for another chance, Jerome grabbed her waist. "I can't let you leave." He held Renee's face in the palm of his hands and kissed her passionately, hoping Renee would be able to feel the love.

She kissed him back, but when they were done, she looked into his eyes and said, "Goodbye. I'll call you in a few days, and we can talk about this house."

Jerome couldn't believe she was actually ending their marriage. "What about you and Everett? Are you leaving to be with him?"

"Don't turn this around. Everett has nothing to do with my decision. I know I'm supposed to heed the Spirit, but this thing with Joi is taking over my mind."

"Are you seeing him?"

"Everett is a good friend. Always had been."

"Please, Renee. God wouldn't want us to do this."

"I'm not so sure God wants me to spend my golden years unhappy either," she said. "Why did you have to do this to us, Jerome? Why did you have to go back to her? We were finally on the right track."

"I was scared," Jerome admitted. "I was leaving my hometown and friends. I was nervous about not living up to your expectations. I wasn't sure if I'd like the job, but I was willing to do it to please you." Jerome looked at the floor. "I was scared."

"Then you should've talked to me about it. I was your wife!" Renee turned to leave and stopped when Jerome fell to the floor.

Grabbing Renee's free hand, he pleaded, "Renee, please, I'm begging you. I'll do whatever I can to make this better."

Renee pulled away and walked into the garage, loading as many bags as she could in two trips, and Jerome stood by watching as the love of his life slipped away.

Chapter Thirty-Five

~ *Joi* ~

"I'm going to miss you," Jerome told Joi. "I hope you'll come back next year."

Joi zipped her last duffle bag then gave Jerome a hug. She couldn't believe eight weeks had gone by so quickly. "Of course I will. I really enjoyed myself."

"Well, you better go say your goodbyes," Jerome said. "I think Zora and Reggie are here."

Joi reached to lift her bag, but Jerome stopped her. "One of your brothers will get that for you."

Joi walked out of her room, and halfway down the steps she was certain she'd heard Jerome crying. She wanted to cry, too. The summer had gone by too fast. When Joi reached the kitchen, she was surprised to find most of the family there. Everyone except Renee and Jerome Jr. She didn't expect to see Renee, but Jerome Jr.'s absence saddened her. In eight weeks, she had barely spent any time with him.

"Come give us some love before you go," Zora said. "And don't forget you can call me any time."

Joi made her way around the room, kissing and hugging

her new family. When she had given out her last hug, Jerome came downstairs.

"We better go," he said "Your flight leaves in three hours. It's going to take me an hour to get out to O'Hare from here."

Everyone followed Joi to the front door, singing their favorite songs to keep from crying. She opened the door and gasped. Standing in front of Jerome's truck was Jerome Jr. An instant smile crossed her face. Joi wanted to run over to him, but kept her cool.

"This has been hard for me," Jerome Jr. said. "But I'm glad God has given me a sister. You mind if I ride to the airport with you and Pops?"

Joi couldn't speak, but she ran into Jerome Jr.'s arms.

"I guess that's a yes," Joshua said from the driveway.

Joi hopped into the Yukon for the last time this summer and stared out of the window. As she looked at her Chicago family, there was no longer any doubt that she was blessed. God had given her a large family full of people that loved her.

Chapter Thirty-Six

~ *Taylor* ~

Blindfolded, Taylor followed her husband's lead. She had no idea what surprise he had planned. "Slow down, Lance," she said. He was walking too fast, and she could barely keep up in her new leather pumps.

"Hold on," Lance responded. "We're almost there."

The sound of heavy traffic surrounded Taylor as she and Lance headed to their destination. She had no clue where she was or where he was taking her, but after walking a block away from their car and stumbling up one flight of stairs, she was finally going to find out.

"Hold still," Lance told her, and Taylor did as she was instructed.

She felt Lance move away and turned her head, searching for better reception. There were people walking behind her, but from the sound of their voices, Taylor figured that they were not part of Lance's surprise. "Where is he?" Taylor said to herself. She felt like she'd been standing alone for almost five minutes.

Suddenly, she heard a door open, and without warning, an unfamiliar hand grabbed her arm. Hesitant to follow the stranger, Taylor pulled her arm back.

"It's okay, Tay," Lance said and laughed. "I'm standing in front of you. Just follow the sound of my voice."

The stranger reached for her again, and this time Taylor started walking. Lance was singing the lyrics to the song he played when he'd proposed. The suspense was getting the best of Taylor, and she was ready to snatch the blindfold off her face.

"Just one more step," Lance said.

Taylor did as she was told then placed her hands over the blindfold. "Now can I take this thing off?"

"Yes," he said. "But, first, I want you to know that I love you, and as long as we work together, there's nothing we can't do."

With one quick motion, Taylor pulled the dark blindfold from around her eyes. "Oh my God!" she yelped and started to cry.

"Surprise!" Taylor's family and friends yelled at once.

Lance was standing in front of her, holding a huge sheet cake that read: *Congratulations!* Beneath the wording, there was a picture drawn in blue and purple frosting with the letters, *Second Chance 2* in sprinkles across it.

Taylor looked around in amazement. "When did you do all this?"

Lance set the cake on a nearby table. "Well, Collette and I have been working together for a couple months. When I saw this, I knew it would be perfect for you. But enough about that. Walk around and get used to the place."

Someone turned on a radio, and the guests began to mingle. Taylor leaned on her husband and cried. "You're too good to me sometimes," she said.

"You deserve it, Tay. I know about the money Jerome gave you. For you not to use it meant a lot to me. I know how badly you wanted that other building." He wiped her eyes until they were dry. "There's still some work to be done, but I think you can open the store officially, once all the business forms are signed and cleared."

Taylor was speechless. She glanced around the room, waving at all the important people in her life. Although it wasn't the same building, it was just as nice, and located next to the Convention Center. This was a much better position than the property she was originally interested in. God had outdone Himself this time.

Taylor felt a tap on her shoulder, and she turned around. Gram and Crystal wanted to talk.

"I know things haven't been smooth between us, but you're a mother. I'm sure you understand how protective a mother can be when it comes to her childre, especially her only son." Gram's eyes started to water. "I just want to apologize for making you feel unwelcome in this family. I am very proud of you."

Taylor reached out to Gram and gave her a hug. "Thank you," she said and hoped their relationship could grow into something special.

"Same here," Crystal added. "Sisters are protective, too."

Taylor hugged Crystal then realized that Gizelle was missing. "No Gizelle?"

Crystal lowered her head.

"She'll come around. Gizelle is a little more stubborn than we are," Gram said. "But she loves you, too. She has a funny way of showing it, but she does."

When Gram and Crystal walked away, Taylor walked over to where her children were standing. Even if Gizelle never came to love her, she knew without a doubt that she had the love of her children, her husband, close friends and most importantly, God. That's all that mattered.

As blessed as Taylor felt, she could tell something was bothering Joi. While others enjoyed the social event, she and Joi went for a walk.

"Care to tell me what's bugging you?" she asked Joi.

"Not today," Joi replied. "You're having a nice time at your party."

"Yeah, but I can't be happy if I know something's wrong with you."

"I'll be fine, Mother."

"Unless you're about to tell me you're pregnant and on your way to Vegas to get hitched, nothing you can say will ruin my mood," Taylor said. "Now please tell me what's going through that head of yours. You haven't been the same since you came back from Chicago."

"I don't want you to think that I don't like being here, but . . . Jerome started this program for athletes that I think would be good for me and . . ." Joi started to play with her bracelets. "I don't know, Renee might not go for this, but I was wondering if I could stay in Chicago my senior year."

Taylor knew where Joi was going before all the words came out of her mouth. She was glad that Joi and Jerome were getting closer, and happy that Joi had developed a relationship with her half-brothers. But she wasn't ready to send her off to live with Jerome.

"I have information about that program. I really think it's something I should take advantage of," Joi continued.

Taylor didn't want to destroy the excitement in Joi's eyes. She knew becoming a basketball star was her dream, and if it meant she had to sacrifice not having Joi around for a year, then that was a sacrifice she'd have to make. Jerome was in a much better position to prepare Joi for professional basketball.

"Let me pray about it," she said. "Have you mentioned this to Jerome?"

"No, but I have talked to Josh. He thinks it's a good idea, too. He's willing to talk to Renee for me."

"Well, let me talk this over with your dad. In the meantime, put a smile back on your face. There's a party going on in my new place."

Chapter Thirty-Seven

~ Jerome ~

Jerome stood behind a podium at Marshall High School on the West Side of Chicago. He never thought this day would come. Although Renee was not present, he was especially happy to see his family in the crowd.

In front of an eager group of students, teachers, and administrators, Jerome highlighted the key points of *Future Ballers* and reviewed the requirements for participation. By the end of his speech, he had motivated most of the students. There was only room for one hundred participants in the first year, but in the event that some students changed their mind, Jerome's team had collected the names of over eighty students for the waiting list.

"This went better than we thought," an excited Melanie said.

"I appreciate all that you've done to get this off the ground. Thank you," he said and hugged her.

Melanie held tight onto Jerome. "We should really have dinner tonight."

"I can't. You're a nice woman and all, but I'm still married." Jerome said the words, but in reality, he wasn't sure he even had a marriage to save.

Melanie looked at him, her cheeks flushed with embarrassment. "I'm sorry. I just thought you'd like to have dinner. We can all go if you like," she said.

"I'm sorry, Mel. But I'm gonna have to pass." Jerome walked away from Melanie and joined his family seated in the audience. "Anyone up for Lawry's Steakhouse? I'm starving."

* * *

Instead of parking in the garage, Jerome pulled into the driveway. There was a huge basket sitting on the porch. Anxious, he rushed out of his truck to read the note.

Jerome,
  Sorry I missed the opening. I know you did well and I'm praying you'll have a successful year. Don't eat everything all at once.
  Renee

Jerome opened the front door and lifted the basket with both hands. He headed straight for the kitchen and unwrapped his present. A smile crossed his face. Renee had ordered an arrangement of sugar-free cookies in the shapes of various sporting balls: basketballs, footballs, baseballs, hockey pucks, volleyballs, soccer balls, tennis balls . . .

He loved his gift, but longed to share the moment with his wife. He picked up the cordless and dialed her number, but after the third ring hung up. He didn't want to leave a message. Choosing one cookie from the basket, he nibbled on it until it was gone.

The house was quiet. It had been that way since Renee moved out. Not even the boys were around to entertain him. After the *Future Ballers* launch, they had gone on a mini vacation together.

The slam of a car door caught his attention, and he headed to the front of the house. As he approached the door, he realized that it could've been Renee coming home. The boys had been out of town for the past three days. He moved as fast as he could to open the door, not bothering to check for her car through the window. *It has to be Renee*, he convinced himself and swung the door open.

Holding the autographed basketball he'd given her for Christmas, Joi stood on the small porch, smiling wide. Behind her were Reggie, Jerome Jr., and Joshua, standing proudly in front of a U-Haul truck.

"What's going on?" he asked.

"Mother talked to Renee last week," Joi said. "She isn't sure if she's coming back, but she said I was welcome to stay here for my senior year. She thinks I'd be a great candidate for *Future Ballers*." Joi placed the basketball under her right arm. "So, what do you think, Pop? Can I move in?"

Jerome started to cry. He had waited a long time to hear those words come out of Joi's mouth.

As he watched his boys fuss over unpacking the U-Haul, Joi stood beside her brothers, begging them to be careful with her things.

It was going to be a good year indeed. God had brought his daughter into his life. Maybe He'd place it on Renee's heart to come back, too.

The story of Jonah came to mind, and Jerome looked toward heaven. When he was in the hospital, he had asked God to take control of his life. And even if the path he was on didn't include Renee, he was determined to follow God's plan. God had been too good to him to do otherwise.

Study Guide Questions

1. Is there ever a time when a family secret shouldn't be revealed? Did Taylor and Jerome make the right decision by keeping the truth from Joi and Renee? How might their lives have been different if Taylor and Jerome were honest from the very beginning?

2. Describe the relationship Joi had with Lance. Although Lance was Joi's step-father, did he treat her any different than his biological children?

3. How much did Taylor's childhood influence the way she interacted with her children?

4. How do you feel about the way in which Taylor and Lance handled discipline in their home? Was it effective?

5. One of Taylor's friends mentioned that a generational curse was looming over her family. Joi hadn't met her biological father until she was sixteen years old, yet she inherited some of his characteristics. Do you believe children are destined to repeat the habits of their parents, good or bad?

6. Taylor never talked to Joi about sex. How did this affect Joi? When and how should you handle talking to your children about such a delicate subject?

7. Genesis 2:24 notes that when a man marries a woman, he should separate from his parents so that he could be joined to his wife. Did the Belle women interfere too much in Lance and Taylor's marriage? How should Taylor and Lance have handled the Belle women?

8. Why do you think the Belle women treated Taylor the way they did? Were their reasons justified?

9. Was there more than a child that connected Taylor to Jerome? Was there still chemistry between them?

10. Did Lance and Renee feel threatened by Jerome's relationship with Joi?

11. God teaches us to forgive others just as He forgives us for our mistakes. But how should we handle people who continually cause us pain?

12. Both Taylor and Jerome were saved and had a personal relationship with Christ. Discuss situations when Taylor and/or Jerome exercised their faith in God, as well as times when their faith wavered. What were some of the results of their faith in these situations?

13. Did Taylor put her dream before her family at any point?

14. Do you think Renee will file for divorce, or will she try to accept Joi and remain in her marriage to Jerome?

15. Do you think Everett's presence in Renee's life influenced in any way her decision to leave Jerome?

16. Was it a good decision to let Joi spend her senior year in Illinois with Jerome?

17. What are some of the pros and cons of blended families? What are some of the challenges both Taylor and Jerome faced with their families as a result of conceiving a child outside of marriage?

Author Bio

Nicole S. Rouse was born and raised in Philadelphia, Pennsylvania. She developed a passion for writing in grade school. After graduating from Temple University, Nicole became an elementary school teacher, and she took every opportunity to incorporate her appreciation of various forms of writing into the curriculum. As a teacher, she became a member of the Northern Virginia Writing Project, where she promoted and encouraged writing in mathematics. Nicole was a founding member of a literacy team that created plays for students to perform, and developed workshops for parents to help their children excel. Nicole has contributed articles to *South County Chronicle*, a local newsletter for Northern Virginia residents, and *Remah*, a newsletter for the members of New Faith Baptist Church in Matteson, Illinois. After five years in the classroom, Nicole was given the opportunity to pursue a career in publishing and is currently an editor at a major educational publishing company. She is a member of Zeta Phi Beta Sorority, Inc., and resides near Chicago, IL.

Someone to Love Me is her second novel and the sequel to *Happily Ever Now*, released in September 2007.

For more information, please visit *www.nicolerouse.com* or send an email to *nsrouse@yahoo.com*.

To learn about other Urban Christian authors, please visit *www.urbanchristianonline.net*.

Urban Christian His Glory Book Club!

Established January 2007, **UC His Glory Book Club** is another way to introduce to the literary world Urban Book's much-anticipated new imprint, **Urban Christian**, and its authors. We are an online book club supporting Urban Christian authors by purchasing, reading, and providing written reviews of the authors' books that are read. *UC His Glory* welcomes both men and women of the literary world who have a passion for reading Christian-based fiction.

UC His Glory is the brainchild of Joylynn Jossel, Author and Executive Editor of Urban Christian, and Kendra Norman-Bellamy, Copy Editor for Urban Christian. The book club will provide support, positive feedback, encouragement and a forum whereby members can openly discuss and review the literary works of Urban Christian authors. In the future, we anticipate broadening our spectrum of services to include: online author chats, author spotlights, interviews with your favorite Urban Christian author(s), special online groups for *UC His Glory Book Club* members, ability to post reviews on the website and amazon.com, membership ID cards, *UC His Glory* Yahoo Group and much more.

Even though there will be no membership fees attached to becoming a member of *UC His Glory Book Club*, we do expect our members to be active, committed, and to follow the guidelines of the Book Club.

UC His Glory members pledge to:

- Follow the guidelines of *UC His Glory Book Club*.
- Provide input, opinions, and reviews that build up, rather than tear down.
- Commit to purchasing, reading, and discussing featured book(s) of the month.
- Agree not to miss more than three consecutive online monthly meetings.
- Respect the Christian beliefs of *UC His Glory Book Club*.
- Believe that Jesus is the Christ, Son of the Living God.

We look forward to the online fellowship.

Many Blessings to You!

Shelia E. Lipsey
President
UC His Glory Book Club

**Visit the official Urban Christian Book Club website at *www.uchisglorybookclub.net*